# In the Money

## Book 10 in the "By the Numbers" series

### Featuring Carly Turnquist, forensic accountant

By Leeann Betts

(c) 2019

ISBN: 978-1-943688-52-4

Edited by Donna Schlachter
Cover design by Donna Schlachter

Published by PLS Bookworks, Denver, CO

Where Publishing Dreams Become Reality

In the Money

# Acknowledgements

First and foremost, all glory to God because

Without Him, there would be no story.


Thanks to my husband, Patrick. My biggest fan. 'Nuff said.


To my agent, Terrie Wolf, of AKA Literary LLC,

Who believes in me when I don't believe in myself.


To my critique group, Word Crafters.

You know who you are, and how much of you is in this story.

In the Money

**Other Books By Leeann Betts**:
- *Counting the Days:* a 31-day devotional
- *In Search of Christmas Past – a novel*

Available at Amazon.com in print & digital,
& at Smashwords.com in digital

**By the Numbers series featuring Carly Turnquist, forensic accountant**

*No Accounting for Murder*
*There Was a Crooked Man*
*Unbalanced*
*Five and Twenty Blackbirds*
*Broke, Busted, and Disgusted*
*Hidden Assets*
*Petty Cash*
*A Deadly Dissolution*
*Silent Partner*

Available at Amazon.com in print & digital,
& at Smashwords.com in digital

**By Leeann and Donna**:
- *Nuggets of Writing Gold*
- *More Nuggets of Writing Gold*

Available at Amazon.com in print & digital,
& at Smashwords.com in digital

**Follow us:**
**Donna:**
www.HiStoryThruTheAges.wordpress.com
**Leeann**: www.AllBettsAreOff.wordpress.com
We are also active on Facebook and Twitter

Sign up for our free quarterly newsletter and receive a free book:
**Leeann (contemporary)**
www.LeeannBetts.com
**Donna (historical)**
www.HiStoryThruTheAges.com

**Books by Donna Schlachter:**
- *Quiet Moments Alone with God: a devotional*
- *100 Answers to 100 Questions About Loving Your Husband*
- *Second Chances and Second Cups:* A short story collection.
- *The Physics of Love*—where the past, the present, and the future collide
- *The Mystery of Christmas Inn, Colorado*
- *Christmas Under the Stars*
- *Transformation* – a devotional
- *Double Jeopardy* – From Smitten Publishing, releases January 2020

**Mended by God series by Donna Schlachter**

*Broken Dreams, Mended Heart*
*Broken Dreams, Mended Family*
*Broken Dreams, Mended Marriage*

Available at Amazon.com in print & digital,
& at Smashwords.com in digital

**From Barbour Publishing by Donna Schlachter:**
- *Echoes of the Heart* — The Pony Express Romance Collection
- *A Prickly Affair* — Bouquet of Brides Romance Collection
- *Train Ride to Heartbreak* — Mail Order Brides Romance Collection
- *Detours of the Heart* – MISSadventure Brides Romance Collection

In the Money

Bear Cove, Maine is stuck in the 1880's,

right where it belongs


Carly Turnquist is stuck in August 2005,

right where she belongs

In the Money

## Chapter 1

"You what?" Carly Turnquist stared at her elderly neighbor. "How many numbers?"

"Three." James Norwood frowned, his eyebrows bushier than his out-of-control hair. He shook his head, eyes still glued to the television. "Shh!"

Carly, a forensic accountant who loved numbers more than she liked most people, smiled and sat in the easy chair in the older man's living room. Likely just another false alarm in the never-ending lotteries the man bought into. The widower and original owner of his home gripped lottery tickets in his hand and leaned toward the television as the fourth ball dropped into the chute. In the background, theme music rose in volume one moment in a crescendo before fading to near-silence. She glanced at the clock as their Wednesday evening ritual neared its conclusion. Three 'til eight. Right on time. A few more minutes, and she'd head home.

The host held up the next ball. "Twenty-six. Do you have twenty-six?"

James shook his fistful of tickets. "Got that one, too." He closed his eyes, his lips moving as though in prayer. Then he turned to her. "You'll see. I just feel it in my bones. This is my lucky day."

Carly grinned. "I hope so, James, for your sake. You say that every week. I'd like to know somebody who won more than a few dollars in one of these things."

The fifth ball rolled down the chute and came to rest at the end, the television camera trained on it. The host, a suave middle-aged man who probably starred in daytime soap operas—although Carly had no idea who he was—picked up and held the white orb. "Fifty-three. Lucky fifty-three.

Are you getting close?" He dropped the ball next to the twenty-six then faced the camera. "Two more numbers. That's all it takes to win." He snapped his fingers. "No, wait. That's not all it takes to win." The camera panned the live studio audience. "What else does it take?"

In unison, the crowd screamed the well-rehearsed answer. "You gotta buy a ticket!"

"Right." He patted his hair and tugged at his tie. "Let's take a commercial break, shall we?"

Again the crowd went wild. "No-o-o-o-o!"

He tilted his head as though considering their reply.

Carly groaned, earning her another shush from James. They went through this same routine each week, rain or shine, ever since James asked for her help. His failing eyesight meant he regularly mistook sixes for eights, and ones for sevens. After the third false alarm of telling half of Bear Cove he'd won the lottery and facing the resulting ridicule when proved wrong, she offered to join him for the drawings. He'd bought tickets for about five years, certain he was destined to win. Carly once told him he'd be better off giving the money he spent on tickets directly to a charitable foundation that looked after parks and wildlife. He responded saying that would happen when pigs flew.

Oh, well, what was five minutes out of a lifetime?

He won ten dollars about a month ago, the closest he'd come since she began spending Wednesday evenings with him. And despite her eagle-eye oversight, one other time he announced another win. Cataracts blurred his vision so he mistook a sixteen for an eighteen. He excitedly danced her around the living room that night in an awkward Lindy. She barely had the heart to tell him of his mistake.

If he'd thought it was simply the ten-dollar prize, she'd have given it to him herself.

Instead of being disappointed, he took that close call as a sign he'd win sometime. Soon.

The host held his hands out to quiet the audience. "Okay, okay. I'm listening." The music blared then died down again. "Let's go for broke, shall we?"

The audience clapped, shouted, and stomped their feet in approval.

"Then, let's get 'er done."

The final ball dropped from the globe and headed for its landing place. The camera zoomed in. James leaned closer to the point Carly thought he might fall out of his chair. If that happened and he broke a hip, he'd need to win the lottery just to cover his co-pay.

"Forty-two. Four-two. Is the brand new winner you?"

The host's attempt at light-hearted banter wore on Carly's patience. Maybe next week she'd make sure she had something else going on just to give herself a break. Every week the same. James claiming he would win. Saying he had the numbers needed to claim the big prize.

But he never did.

Didn't stop him from trying, though.

She made a mental note of the numbers—now in ascending order—lined up on the display tray at the bottom of the screen. Four. Eleven. Twenty-six. Forty-two. Fifty-three. Maybe she should write them down. She looked around for a piece of paper and a pen, finding both in the drawer of the end table near her elbow. She scribbled the numbers just below an old grocery list: bananas, milk, bread, peanut butter.

The theme music quieted again and the host stepped forward then switched on the globe to his left. "Let's go directly to the final number. The key to whether you've won or not. The prize ball. The big blue one. And here she comes." A second ball-filled globe slowed and a blue ball with white numbers rolled down into place. The host held it for the camera. "Twelve. One-two. Buckle my shoe."

James peered at his tickets, riffling through the pieces of paper then he jumped to his feet. "Twelve. Got that one, too." He twirled around the room like a drunken ballerina. "I won the lottery. I'm rich."

Sure. Likely he did have all six numbers.

On different tickets.

She held up her slip of paper. "Let's go over to the dining table and check your numbers."

He clutched his tickets to his chest. "I'm telling you, I won. The big one. The Big Kahuna. The whole enchilada."

She smiled at his mixed clichés. "You can hold onto them. I'm not going to steal your winnings." Most likely ten dollars. Like last time. "The light is better over here, so I can see the numbers more clearly."

He shuffled over to the table and spread his tickets out in front of him. Same as every week. Three tickets. Bought at three different places. The grocery store. The corner store. The gas station. On different days.

But always he wore his Boston Red Sox hat for a good luck charm.

She scanned the first ticket. "Not that one. No four there."

He scowled at her. "I know that."

She checked the second. It had a four and an eleven, but that's where the similarity ended. "Not this one, either."

He tapped the final ticket. The one he bought at the grocery store. "It's this one. I knew it would be. The girl what sold it to me smiled when I said I'd take her to Hawaii with me if I won." He smiled. "And if I win big, I'll take the guy from the gas station and the woman from the corner store, too."

No doubt he told these people the same thing every week when he bought his tickets. And the clerks likely heard it a hundred times a day from folks longing to win. Hungering to do something nice for somebody.

He pinned the ticket to the table with his index finger. "This is the winner."

She smoothed the paper flat. Four. Eleven. Twenty-six. Forty-two. Fifty-three. Twelve.

She glanced at her piece of paper.

The same.

Maybe for the wrong date?

Nope. Today's date.

Then she must have written a number down wrong.

She checked the television again, but the drawing now over, the numbers were no longer on display. Her mouth went dry. If James won the jackpot of several million dollars, his entire life would change. He wouldn't have to live month to month on his social security benefits. He could afford to get his car repaired—heck, he could afford to buy a new one if he wanted. He could take the cashier to Hawaii as he promised. Along with the other two. And their families.

She picked up a discarded ticket and turned it over, looking for a phone number. She'd call and get the automated system to repeat the numbers to her. Because she must have made a mistake. People like James simply didn't win two million dollars. It was always an office pool of twelve people destined to lose their jobs at the end of the month. Or a single mom with a sick child and no health benefits. Or a young couple just starting their lives with huge student aid debt. Or a widow who gave it all to her church.

Not people like James. So far as Carly knew, alone in the world. Comfortable but not wealthy. No children. His wife gone. She'd never heard him mention even a religious institution or an alma mater that would tickle his fancy to give some additional funding.

Just a cashier at the local Saving Way who never expected an old man to remember her if he did win. And a clerk at a corner store. And the guy who swiped windshields at the gas station up on the highway.

And none of them really expected him to fulfill his word.

She located then dialed the toll-free number, putting a little check mark beneath each number as the girl-next-door robotic voice read them off.

She disconnected the phone and sat back, her ears ringing.

She hadn't made a mistake.

James possessed all five white numbers.

He had the blue number.

He'd won. . . the whole enchilada.

$ $ $

Mike sighed as he crossed his lawn and headed to James' house. Carly must surely be up to something. Again. Her cryptic call of a few minutes before said little other than she needed him at their neighbor's. Now. No, not an emergency, in response to his question. Yes, important that he show up.

By the time he climbed the three steps to the door, the tiny twitch at the curtains morphed into his wife at the door, smiling and gesturing him in. He studied her features. All of the circumstances he'd conjured as he made the short journey now seemed pointless. No masked intruder forcing her to call him. He sniffed the air. No fire in the kitchen needed his attention. She led him into the living room. No James on the floor from a heart attack or something equally horrible.

In fact, the older man sat at a dining table, an angelic grin on his face, eyes closed, as he hummed along with music only he could hear.

Mike paused. "So what's up?" He kept his voice low so as not to startle their neighbor. "And why did I need to come over now? I'm in the middle of a television program."

She waved off his words. "You can catch it in reruns." She tipped her head toward James. "He won the lottery."

"You called me over here for that? He's won dozens of times before."

"No, he won the Big One."

Mike glanced at James who still seemed to revel in his own world. "You mean—"

Carly nodded. "The big prize. In the Blue Ball Lottery. Two million dollars."

He leaned closer to his wife. "So why do you need me? Are we going to kill the old guy and steal his ticket?" He waggled his eyebrows to show her he was only kidding. "Or will he adopt us so we can inherit?"

She slapped his arm. "Don't be ridiculous. No, we're going to talk him into doing the sensible thing."

"And that is?"

"Wait until the media furor dies down then claim his winnings, invest them in a secure way, and live off the interest."

Mike nodded. "Makes sense." He paused. "There's a big but coming, isn't there?"

"Yes." She steered him toward the kitchen. "He doesn't trust banks. So he wants to keep the money here, in his house. He doesn't care about interest, he says. He has nobody to leave it to. So he wants to enjoy it while he has some time left."

"Is he sick?"

"I don't think so. He didn't say anything to me. But he is old."

Mike grinned. Seemed the older he got, the younger everybody else seemed. Including those senior to him in years. "Okay. How about you get us some coffee, and I'll see what his plans are."

She agreed and left him alone with James. Mike walked over and sat across the table from his neighbor. Funny how they'd lived next door now for several years and he'd never entered this house. The mirror image of his own bungalow, it seemed obvious there'd been a woman's touch many years before, but not recently. A pair of faded lace fans dripping with dust bookended a mirror that topped a low hutch on one wall of the dining room. Dark paneled walls everywhere. Green shag carpet underfoot, traffic patterns matting down the pile.

In the living room, faded and worn furniture—likely new when James and his wife moved in—now simply looked tired. Not a bright color in sight, as though the years had drained the hues like grains of sand through an hourglass.

Mike scratched his ear. Would Tom and Denise, his own adult children, visit him in about ten years and think the same of him?

Perhaps he should give Carly a redecorating budget.

He cleared his throat softly and James opened his eyes, blinked a couple of times, then grinned at him. "I won the lottery."

"Yes, Carly told me."

James looked around. "Did she go home?"

"She's making coffee."

James pursed his lips. "Sounds good. Maybe she'll find that package of ladyfingers I bought this week."

Mike smiled. "If there are cookies to be found, she will. Especially if chocolate is involved." He leaned across the table. "One time I hid three chocolate-covered doughnuts in the kitchen in a brown paper bag. She walked in the door, sniffed, and asked where they were. She's like a hound dog, tracked them down before I had the chance to tell her."

His neighbor nodded. "My wife did the same with oranges. Couldn't hide them from her. During the war—WW2, you know—they were hard to find. And if you did, usually they were dried up. But one Christmas, I had a friend coming home from California on leave, and he brought me a bag. I hid them around the house like an Easter egg hunt. When Sadie got up that morning, she smelled oranges. But because they were everywhere, she couldn't find them."

Mike chuckled. "Did she eventually?"

"All ten of them. They were her gift that year." Tears wet his eyes. "She always said it was the best Christmas ever."

"You never had children?"

James shook his head. "No. The good Lord never saw fit to bless us that way. But we had each other. And once we accepted it, we were enough for each other." He looked over Mike's shoulder at a faraway spot. "I did all the right things. Got a job. Stuck with it."

"What kind of work did you do?"

"Engineer on the railroad. Moved here just over thirty years ago. Planned to retire but Sadie got sick, so I kept working to pay her doctor bills." He dropped his chin to his chest. "Didn't matter. She's been gone almost twenty years now. She'd have loved to see this money. Although it was never important to her."

Seeing an opportunity to broach the subject, Mike did. "But this money is important to you now."

"It is. Two million dollars will change my life."

"You won't get the whole amount, you know."

James nodded. "Government has to get their bit. I know."

"Plus, lottery winnings are designed to be paid out over thirty years."

James frowned. "I don't have thirty years."

Mike smiled. "You're still a young man."

"Seventy-eight my last birthday."

"You still have a lot of years left in you." Maybe if he could convince the man to look to the future instead of the past, he'd be more interested in safeguarding his winnings. "And whatever you don't manage to spend, you could leave to family or a charity."

A quick shake of the head indicated the older man's rejection of his suggestion. "Got no family. And my will takes care of everything else. Although maybe I need to make a new one now. Make sure this money goes to the right place, too."

"If you take it in one lump sum, you lose about forty percent off the top."

"Why?"

"Well, there's an accounting concept known as present cash value that says money is worth more the longer it takes to receive it."

"Sounds like skullduggery to me."

"Yeah, I never completely understood it either. Accounting wasn't my field."

"Mine neither." The older man blinked several times. "And they still take taxes?"

"Yep."

"Well, that means I'll have less to worry me."

What did the old man mean? "Worry you?"

James pulled his gaze back and met Mike's, his pale gray eyes set in a long, narrow face marked by time. "Don't trust banks."

"So Carly said. But this is a lot of money." Mike did a quick calculation in his head. "About eight hundred thousand. What about if we spread it around several banks? They're all federally insured now, you know, so if somebody robs one, or if one goes bankrupt, you'll still get your money."

His neighbor shook his head adamantly. "That's what they told my father during the Depression. He had money in savings. And a mortgage. And when the banks closed, they wouldn't let him move the money into his current account. He didn't want the cash. Just wanted to make sure his bills got paid. But they said no. And he lost his house because they foreclosed on his mortgage."

Mike had heard similar stories of disreputable financial institutions taking advantage of the letter of the law that said funds on deposit had to remain in their original accounts until the government straightened out the mess.

Which usually didn't happen until too late.

He tried again. "Well, at least wait a few days until the story isn't on the news anymore. The lottery commission likes publicity. It encourages more people to buy tickets. When a winner comes forward right away, they like to take advantage of that. There will be reporters and cameras around the office for a few weeks." Mike leaned across the table. "You might even get your face on the news."

James grunted. "Don't want that."

"Then wait a bit. No point in letting everybody know you won a bunch of money. You'll have friends and family and business offers and charities showing up on your doorstep."

James peered at him. "I can take care of myself, you know. Might be old, but I'm not stupid. Been around the block a few times."

Trying to lighten the mood, Mike chuckled. "I know you have. We just want what's best for you."

Carly returned with the coffees and, sure enough, a package of chocolate covered cookies. "Here we are. Hope you don't mind that I opened this?"

Mike scooted a chair out for her. "I just told him the story of the doughnuts." He sipped his coffee. "I think I figured out how to hide them without you finding them."

"Oh, what's that?" Carly pushed James' cup toward him. "Some high-falutin' plastic container?"

"No. I'll buy them by the dozen, and leave them all around the house." He winked at James. "That way, you won't be able to find them because the whole house will smell like a bakery."

Carly bit into a cookie. "That's cruel."

James dunked a delicate finger-shaped cookie into his cup. "But it might work."

The three sat in companionable silence for a few minutes until the cookies were eaten and their cups almost empty. James folded his ticket and tucked it into his shirt pocket.

*Time to press on.* "Do you have a safe place in the house to keep the money?"

A quick nod.

"Fireproof?"

"Don't plan on burning the old shack down."

Carly squirmed in her chair, and when Mike cast her a glance, she settled down again. He clasped his hands together in his lap. "We never plan on a catastrophe, James, but they happen."

He peered at him. "Don't I know. Won't use a bank."

Carly pushed her cup aside. "Will you at least wait a couple of days? And if you want, Mike or I could go to the lottery commission with you to claim your check."

James blinked a couple of times. "Check?"

Mike sat back. "They'll give you a check, which you can then deposit. If you want to cash it, you'll need to alert the bank in advance so they have enough stock on hand."

"Didn't think on that." Another quick nod. "I'll look after it."

"But will you let me or Mike go with you?"

"I'll think on that, too."

"We just want what's best for you."

"Ayah, that's what the bank told my father."

Carly looked to Mike, her brow furrowed.

He patted her arm. "I'll explain later." He turned to James. "Let us know how we can help."

"If I need help, I'll let you know."

Somehow, Mike was fairly certain James would never call.

The old man—as stubborn as a mule—would do this on his own.

$ $ $

Back at home, Carly sank onto the sofa and flicked on the television. Time for some old-fashioned mind-numbing news. The pert brunette and her too-handsome-to-be-real co-host bantered back and forth about the latest political scandal, referencing a satirical cartoon in today's *New York Times* that Carly hadn't seen and didn't really care about. Something about a candidate for senator who misquoted a well-known Mark Twain-ism.

Mike dropped into place beside her. "Well, that was an interesting hour or so."

"Interesting is one word for it." She snuggled against his arm. "Do you think he'll listen to us?"

"Don't know." Mike drew her closer. "I'm worried he might think we're after his money or something."

"He never gave me that impression before when he thought he won."

Mike peered at her. "Remember the time a while back when you pointed out he hadn't won, and he suggested you were trying to steal his jackpot?"

"He soon came around, though, when we called the jackpot toll-free number and he heard it for himself."

Her husband sighed. "I wonder if he's struggling with a little dementia. Or something worse."

"I hope not." Using the remote control, she raised the volume a couple of notches. "Oh, let's listen to this. It's right up our alley."

Mike chuckled. "Our alley. You mean your alley."

"Ssh!"

The female co-anchor led out the story. "If you wondered why health insurance costs are going through the roof, our next story might give one explanation. A healthcare system on the east coast recently announced they've discovered that dozens, perhaps hundreds, of double and triple billings for the same services and products have been issued to health care insurers."

Her associate took over at this point. "Why, Brandy, what does that mean to patients and customers of these insurers?"

Without batting an eye, Brandy performed true to character in her lead role. "Gavin, it means that either the billing departments in the hospitals in this particular network are inept, or the processing system in the insurance company leaves something to be desired. After all, how could so many invoices be issued for the same thing and nobody see that?"

Mike sighed. "They're always quick to blame the potential source or end of the chain. What they don't talk much about is the cause."

Carly muted the rest of the story and turned on subtitles. "What other reason could there be?"

He lifted one shoulder and let it drop. "Simple. Hackers."

Carly stared at her husband. "You mean somebody is purposely stealing?" Her eyebrows lifted. What an exciting way to end the day. "How would they do that?"

"Break into the billing system, produce new invoices with a different name and mailing address, set up a dummy company and post office box to handle the payments, and laugh all the way to the bank."

She mock-punched his arm. "I declare, you'd make a good thief."

"Not as difficult as it sounds. Saw something like that earlier on the program I watched before I got yanked out of my comfy chair by a call from a damsel in distress."

"Moi?" Using her thumb, she did her best Miss Piggy impersonation that never failed to bring a laugh from her husband. He didn't fail her now, either. "Really?"

"Yes, you." He glanced at the television. "Oh, turn that up again. I know this man. He's an expert in computer forensics."

She did as he asked, and the nasally tones of a New Yorker replaced Brandy's non-accent. ". . . so what we have here is another example of a cyber-security breach."

Brandy, the consummate actress, tipped her head in question. "Dr. Goldman, we're five years past Y2K, touted as the biggest computer catastrophe in history. And here we are faced with this new threat. How can we avoid it?"

Carly snorted. The news host talked about the problem like it was the common cold. Wash your hands. Replace handshakes with fist bumps. Drink plenty of water. She muted the television then changed her mind when Mike tossed her a glare. Fine. They could talk about it later.

Dr. Goldman continued. ". . . not like the flu, Brandy."

Carly smiled. Birds of a feather and all that.

"The problem is actually more widespread than we realize. Most of the time, this kind of activity is accomplished from within an organization. Often, when discovered, the company chooses not to prosecute because of the small scale of the problem. An employee sees an opportunity to make a few extra bucks on the side. Nobody gets hurt, or so they think. And when the amount is only a few thousand dollars, the cost to provide records and witnesses for a court case could easily cost much more, so the company fires the thief, often sending them on their way with a good reference, unfortunately."

Gavin chimed in with his two cents' worth. "But sometimes it's a lot more money, isn't it?"

Dr. Goldman nodded, his dark glasses magnifying his eyes to unnatural proportions. "The most common victims are organizations that are bureaucratic-heavy, such as government, hospitals, and insurance companies. As you can imagine, with multiple layers of middle management coupled with a senior management that rarely knows the processes of the entity, it's very easy to slip a second or even a third invoice through for the same service."

Brandy nodded, her usually perky smile now replaced with a more somber expression to match the tone of the story. "I recall a news story that broke last year about a military project which exceeded its original budget by some one billion dollars. The supplier and the department head in charge tried to defend the cost by saying there were unforeseen changes and additions. However, an audit of the project revealed that those costs were only about twenty-five percent of the overage. Several key components of the project were billed three times."

Gavin shuffled some papers. "Do you think that's what happened here, Dr. Goldman?"

"I suspect an audit will reveal that multiple billings have been purposely generated with the intention of defrauding both the hospital and the insurance company. Because there is no single person impacted by this crime, perpetrators often argue that it's victimless. Nobody gets hurt."

Brandy smiled into the camera. "And is that true?"

A quick shake of the head. "No. Insurers pass on higher costs to all participants in the health care system. Prices increase because of additional security and audit costs. Less money for hospitals means rationed health care is now a real possibility. A loss of trust in the integrity of the hospital's computer security creates a loss of trust by the consumer. Which means these particular hospitals could experience a decrease in patients and thus revenue. It's a spiral-down effect. Fewer patients means loss of staff. People might die if they have to travel further for health care."

Mike nodded. "So people could get hurt."

This time when Carly muted the television, he didn't complain. She set the remote on the coffee table. "This crime is just as bad as a burglary."

"Worse, really. More like murder. Or assault, at least."

"How so?"

"Hundreds, maybe thousands of people can be harmed." He stood and headed for the kitchen, pausing in the doorway. "All this talk of criminal activity made me hungry. Want some toast and cheese?"

"Or peanut butter. With regular butter. Surprise me."

She flipped through several channels, but they all carried much the same stories, albeit with different experts. When Mike returned with her snack, she bit into the toast soggy with both butter and peanut butter, eying the cheese sandwich on his plate, wondering if she wanted both.

She closed her eyes as the flavors exploded in her mouth. "Oh, this is so perfect." A mouthful of milk washed down the deliciousness, leaving her ready for another bite. "But there is one good thing that comes from this kind of criminal activity."

He eyed her over his own glass. "Oh, what's that?"

"We'll never be out of work."

He laughed. "Don't let law enforcement hear you say that. They might think you're behind this."

"Why?"

He held up a hand and checked off each point on a finger. "Means. Ability. Knowledge. And motive."

Her brow drew down. What was he talking about? "Motive?"

"Sure. You want to keep up with the Joneses. Or should I say the Jameses? He just won two million bucks, remember."

She chuckled. "Right. That's me." She gestured around the living room. "Are you implying I don't already have everything I want?"

"I thought so. But if he starts redecorating his house, you might want to follow suit."

She waved off his words. "No worries. I'll just kill the old guy and take his money."

A chill ran up and down her arms.

Had a goose just walked over her grave?

Chapter 2

The next day, Carly rose earlier than usual. She had a lot on her plate today. An upcoming court case to prepare. A report to mail. Filing. Bills to pay. She sighed. Just thinking about the work made her tired.

A glance out the window into the morning sunshine revived her, and she pulled on her normal office attire of baggy jeans and a t-shirt. Mike went for a walk, so she decided on her own version of a stroll—over to see James. Sure, she didn't go in for the three-mile treks her husband preferred, but then again, she didn't have to break a sweat to accomplish her own version of exercise.

Plus, slippers were appropriate footwear for a neighborly visit.

She exited through the back door and clambered over the adjoining fence, admiring James' late summer garden. Over there, beneath a plum tree, purple and yellow anemones mingled with goldthread. And up against the house, in a neatly tended bed, sundew and cup plants basked in the sun.

She envied them. Spending a day in the garden tempted her. Not bent over, weeding, or digging in the dirt. But doing just as those plants did. Relaxing. Enjoying the morning breeze coming in off the ocean, seasoned with salt water and a tinge of seaweed.

Not today. She sighed. And not likely tomorrow, either. Work called.

She tapped on the window in the back door, enjoying the soft song of a house sparrow in a crabapple tree while she waited. After a minute or so, however, when James didn't answer, she knocked on the wood and the door swung in.

"James?"

Heart in her throat, she stepped over the threshold, half expecting to see him sprawled on the kitchen floor. After all, he *was* an old man who just experienced a major life change—albeit a pleasant one. She peeked around the corner. Not there. She exhaled.

A low murmur from the living room met her ears, and she crept through the tidy kitchen, dishes stacked neatly in the rack, and paused in the doorway.

He sat at the far end of the dining table, the telephone receiver pressed to his ear. When she cleared her throat softly—no point in scaring the man to death—he glanced at her then shifted in his seat.

*He doesn't want me to hear what he's saying.*

She shrugged mentally. His private conversations were—well, private. She caught his eye and gestured back to the kitchen, tossing him a smile when he peered at her beneath bushy eyebrows that reminded her of Mike's out-of-control drunken caterpillars. A giggle escaped.

He turned his back to her and lowered his voice, nodding several times.

Curious before, that particular combination triggered something in her, igniting the sleuthing instinct Mike always accused her of possessing.

As if that was a bad thing.

She cocked an ear in James' direction. Maybe her husband was right—the mystery gene cursed her. Always thinking circumstances weren't that they appeared. After all, she walked in on his phone call. The least she could do was be polite.

Still, that whole thing of making it obvious he didn't want her hearing his conversation. She glanced toward the living room. Funny how folks thought if they lowered their voice and turned their backs that others wouldn't eavesdrop. If anything, that kind of behavior made her ears perk up all the more.

Still—as her mother said, eavesdropping wasn't polite. She headed back to sit in the kitchen, hoping she'd conveyed she was in no rush and for him to take his time. She sat at the scarred wooden table and allowed her eyes to roam the room, taking in exactly the same things she noticed the previous evening: how the edge of the wallpaper up near the ceiling in the far corner curled, as though the glue was dried out. A cobweb dotting a plastic fern on the plate shelf that went around the room. How there weren't any plates on that same shelf. Too many memories? Or perhaps his wife wasn't into collecting plates.

What would folks notice about her house? The pale yellow paint in the kitchen? Would they think of butter when they saw her choice of color? And her office? She shuddered.

Not going there.

James appeared in the doorway, his usually rumpled outfit appearing a little more-so this morning. As if he slept in his clothes. Again. "G'morning."

"Hi, James. How're you doing?"

"'Bout the same as last night. Not much has changed in—" He glanced at the clock on the stove. "Twelve hours."

"Telemarketer?"

"Huh?"

She quirked her chin toward the cordless phone in his hand. "They seem to get started earlier and earlier in the morning, don't they?"

"Ayuh." His two-syllable response, typical of the quintessential Down-easter, signaled his reluctance to divulge information. "Want coffee?"

*Interesting. Abrupt change of subject. A typical avoidance technique.*

She shook her head. "No, thanks. Just wanted to pop over and make sure you're all right."

"Thanks." He stood. "Better get my day going."

She took the hint and pushed her chair back. "Give more thought to what Mike and you talked about last night?" When he didn't answer, she continued. "About waiting a few days before claiming your winnings?"

"Don't worry about me. Called the bank and ordered up my money. Can't figure why I need to wait until tomorrow, but that's what they said." He peered at her, his pale gray eyes piercing beneath his salt-and-pepper eyebrows. "Like you said." He stood. "Anything else?"

She could take a hint. "Nope. Just wanted to make sure you're all right." She quirked her head toward the telephone. "Was that the bank?"

"Nope. Financial counselor. Said he'll look after me. Won't let me do anything stupid, he said."

"Sounds good." Still, something niggled at the back of her mind. Interesting how he connected so quickly with somebody since last night. He sure hadn't mentioned knowing anybody like that. Not to her. Not to Mike. "If this guy is any good, maybe Mike and I should hire him to help with our finances."

"Maybe." James shoved his hands into his pockets. "Anything else?"

"Could you give me his number?"

"Nope."

"Oh, come on, James. It's not like we're going to steal him away. He'll still have time to help you."

"Don't have his number."

Well, that was strange. "So he called you?"

"Yep."

Alarm bells went off in Carly's head. Somebody learned James won the lottery. It didn't come from either Mike or herself, of that she was certain.

Which meant James told somebody else. Either last night or early this morning. But who would he call?

She stood and headed for the back door to retrace her steps home, her mind swinging wildly first one way then another. She paused before stepping out. "James, don't do anything rash. Check out this person before you commit to working with them. Mike and I never trust somebody who calls us and offers their services until we get the names of several people we know who worked with them in the past."

"Don't worry about me, Carly. I got it all under control. I might have been born at night, but it wasn't last night." He tapped his temple with a forefinger. "I'm old, not stupid."

The old James stood before her now. Not the stubborn man from last night. Not the suspicious senior from a few minutes ago. Just like that, a ray of sunshine changed the darkness to light.

She hadn't noticed abrupt mood changes in him like this before.

Was something else going on she didn't know about?

Or was she—as Mike said—looking for a mystery where none existed?

$ $ $

Deciding to check for the morning paper, Carly cut through James' garden and came out at the front of his house, which was every bit as attractive as the back yard. Well-manicured grass, trees pruned back, and a large oval-shaped bed of wildflowers enhanced with cute garden gnomes created a storybook feel.

Made her sad little patch look even more pathetic.

She sighed. Nothing she would tackle today.

And likely not tomorrow, either.

The *beep-beep* of a large truck backing up caught her attention, and she slowed as she crossed her property line. A moving truck eased its way to a standstill in the driveway of the house across the street that used to belong to Mrs. Winters. The older woman moved to Rockport a few months ago, and the house stood vacant ever since. Not exactly a real estate hub, Bear Cove residents found it often took up to six months to sell their home. Or years, like the MacQuarrie estate outside town that created such a hubbub a few years back.

Carly missed her friend. They sometimes met for coffee, and even though the woman was as nosey as a long-nosed anteater, Carly enjoyed the fact the woman had her ear to the town grapevine. Nothing happened in Bear Cove that didn't have the older woman's approval.

A four-door sedan stopped on the street in front of the house, and a man emerged, giving directions in the old-fashioned Italian way: with his hands. The moving truck driver nodded then spoke to the two guys sitting beside him. All three stepped down and disappeared around the end of the truck, where sounds of locks popping and tailgate lifts screeching into place drifted across the street.

Carly continued to her front step, keeping an eye on the activity less than fifty feet away. The driver of the car, dressed in pleated khakis, tasseled loafers, and a windbreaker, strode across the lawn, unlocked the front door, then plucked the SOLD sign from its place in a flowerbed before turning to nod at her. She lifted a hand in response. Seemed friendly enough.

She bent low to look through the windows into the car. Nobody else. Maybe his wife was coming in a separate vehicle? Or perhaps he's single. She straightened. Time to introduce herself before he wondered if she was some crazy, nosey woman.

Well, he'd get two out of three on that one, at least.

She plastered on her friendliest smile and crossed the street. "Hi. I'm Carly. My husband and I live in that house." She turned and pointed. "Welcome to the neighborhood."

"Thanks." He offered his hand, which she shook. "Bob Powell."

"Glad to meet you." She glanced up and down the street. "It's a nice place to live. Quiet. Nothing exciting ever happens."

"Just what I'm looking for. Peace and quiet."

Her curious gene kicked in. "Move here from the city?"

"Yep."

Well, that wasn't exactly helpful. She tried again. "New York or Boston?"

"Nope." He turned to the moving crew. "Be careful with that. It's an antique."

The men pushed a roll top desk up the sidewalk, and the driver-lead grunted. "Sure thing."

Bob winced when they bounced the piece up the two steps and in through the doorway, his cheeks flushing. "It's hard to train a gorilla to drink from a china cup."

She nodded, understanding what he meant, even if she didn't agree with his assessment of the moving crew. Trusting his worldly possessions—some of which he obviously cared about—to folks he distrusted and demeaned didn't seem wise. "Well, I'd better get to work."

He eyed her up and down, and she winced at his unspoken thoughts written across his face as clear as a neon sign. "Casual day?"

"No. I work from home. And you?"

He paused an extra heartbeat, his jaw muscles working and a vein in his temple throbbing. Then he exhaled and took half a step closer, leaning in as though to share a confidence. "Like the famous line in the movie, 'if I tell you, I'll have to kill you'."

She stepped back, putting some space between them. This guy was way too serious about himself. She'd do well to stay away.

Because somewhere, down deep, she suspected his words were only half in jest.

## Chapter 3

The next morning, Carly woke to the sound of a car engine revving nearby. Pulling her robe around her shoulders, she twitched the bedroom curtains and peered through the crack.

James.

Threading her arms through the sleeves, she hurried downstairs. A glance at the clock confirmed her thoughts: just after seven. Out through the front door, she headed across the lawn as her neighbor put the car into reverse and weaved his way down the driveway.

Strange.

Where was he hurrying off to this early?

She raised a hand in greeting, but he kept his eyes fixed straight ahead.

Not on his rearview mirror, where a miniature Pink Panther stuffed toy dangled—a gag gift from Sadie, he once told her—to watch for oncoming vehicles.

Not on his side view mirrors, keeping an eye out for pesky trash cans or the mailbox at the end of his driveway.

Almost as if he didn't want to acknowledge she stood there.

She sighed. Exercise wasn't on her list today—or any day, for that matter—but she gathered the bottom of her tea-length bathrobe in one hand and trotted toward him, waving with the other hand and calling out his name.

The hood of the car slid past as she reached the edge of his concrete drive.

But this time, when she called his name a final time, his glance flicked over her. His brow furrowed. And he turned to look over his shoulder.

Ignoring her yet again.

Very strange.

He paused, put the car in drive, and headed down the street toward the main drag. Out of town? Or for breakfast at the Dew Drop Inn? Maybe she should get dressed and follow him. Although, if he was simply going for pancakes and sausage here in town, she'd feel pretty silly.

She shrugged. No point in worrying. He was a sensible man who could make his own decisions.

All eight hundred thousand of them.

He'd survived long before she came on the scene. She wasn't his mother. She wasn't his wife. And judging by the way he ignored her this morning, not even a good friend.

But by the time she reached her front door, that worry gene had kicked into high gear. And although she wasn't his mother or his wife, she already imagined him dead in an alley, or crashed into a ditch, or wandering the streets of a big city in the midst of a full-blown case of amnesia from a blow on the head.

Thankfully, Mike was up and puttering about in the kitchen.

She'd take her concerns to him. He had a sensible head on his shoulders, too.

And he'd agree she was right to be worried, and when he suggested they get in the car and track the silly old man down before he made a huge mistake, she'd praise him for being so wise.

$ $ $

"You think we should what?"

Mike shook his head at his wife's ridiculous suggestion and resumed making a fresh pot of coffee to go along with the scrambled eggs and hash browns staying warm in the oven.

Sometimes that woman could come up with the craziest notions.

"I just said maybe we should follow him. Make sure he doesn't get into trouble."

Mike paused, a tablespoon of ground coffee in midair. "Unless we catch him doing something criminal, we have no authority in his life to stop him from making a bad choice."

"But Mike—"

What would he do with her? Always getting herself mixed up in other peoples' lives. He held up a hand to stop her. "No 'but Mike'. You know I'm right."

She glanced toward the front of the house. "We might catch him—"

"And what?" He shook his head. Again. "We can't stop him."

"Could we ask the police to keep an eye out for him?" She wrapped her arms around herself and shivered. "I just feel like something bad is going to happen."

He dumped the coffee into the filter and set the spoon down, then pulled her against his chest. "No. You just hope something bad will happen so you'll be right and you'll be able to infiltrate yourself into his life." He held her at arms' length. "I love you. And I love how you have such a tender spot for the old coot. But we have to leave him be."

"But you didn't see him this morning." She waved her hands in time with her words. "He looked everywhere but at me. And he knew I was there. He avoided me."

"Just like you tried to avoid that nosey neighbor who used to live across the street? The one who wanted to come for coffee every morning at ten? You finally had to tell her to stop because she was interrupting your work."

Carly's hands dropped to her side. "Do you think he thinks of me that way? I mean, I *was* there on Wednesday night. And I popped over yesterday morning for a few minutes."

"And there you were this morning dancing in the driveway." He tossed her a grin then pressed the button for the coffee to brew. "Some people would call that stalking."

Her eyes widened and her mouth formed an 'O'. He chuckled at the sight. It wasn't often he—or anybody for that matter—rendered his wife speechless.

"I hadn't thought of it that way."

"You rarely do. Remember the trouble you got into in Arizona?"

"That was different. That was the mob. James isn't involved in anything like that."

"Really?" He folded his arms across his chest as the coffeemaker burbled behind him. "That's not the impression you gave yesterday."

She mock-punched his arm. "I never said—"

Mike closed his eyes. "I seem to recall you came home and said he hid something from you. That whoever he spoke with on the phone seemed shady. And you thought it strange James didn't want our help." He opened his eyes. "Not the mob, granted. But something sinister. And crooked. Your words. Not mine."

"Well, what should we do?"

He turned when the coffeemaker went quiet then he poured two cups before heading for the table. "First, we should sit and have breakfast. Second, we should leave James alone. If he wants our advice—any more of it—he'll ask. We've told him we're willing to help." Mike sat and gestured to her chair. "If we pester him again, he might think we're the ones trying to get his money."

Her brow raised this time while she fetched the hot items and set them on the table. "Oh, surely he couldn't. He wouldn't." She sat and sipped her coffee. "Still, he was so friendly before, and now he just seems. . . I don't know."

"Suspicious?"

She sighed. "I guess so. But we were friends long before he won the money."

"And we'll be there to help him pick up the pieces if he makes a huge mistake with it. But it won't kill him. He'll survive. He'll still have his pension and his house. Car. Savings." He pushed the plate of toast toward her. "And he'll still have us as friends."

"I guess."

He peered over his cup at her. "You guess we'll still be his friends?"

"No. I mean I guess he'll survive." She tossed him a smile. "You're right. Absolutely right."

He blinked a couple of times. This easy acquiescence wasn't like her. What was she up to?

She ate a forkful of scrambled eggs. "So, what's on your schedule for today?"

Ah, the old change-the-subject-so-fast-a-body-got-whiplash tactic. Well, he wouldn't be lulled into a false sense of security by that move. "Not much. Kind of between projects right now. At least, until next week. Then I start on the aeronautical engineering program."

"The one that figures out how little fuel to put in the tank and still get the plane where it's going?"

"Well, that's a simplified layman's summary, but yes, that'll do. How about you?"

"Same old, same old. Prep for a court case next month. Filing. Pay bills. Keep an eye on James. Decide if I want to take on the investigation into the embezzlement charges for a defendant in another case. I told defense counsel I'd let her know next week."

He laughed. Nothing was ever same old, same old with his wife. "Don't think I missed the part about James. What do I always tell you?"

She rolled her eyes. "Don't look for a mystery where none exists."

"So?"

She stuck out her bottom lip. "What if I don't know if there is a mystery or not? Can't I look just to see if there is?"

"Carly, Carly."

She smiled, warming his heart and brightening his world. "I know. I'm a full-time job."

Yes, she was.

But he wasn't looking for an early retirement from that particular occupation any time soon.

$ $ $

James adjusted the sun visor to block the morning rays, then reached across the bench seat of his older four-door gas-guzzler and snapped the passenger visor against the window. Driving north in the early morning was almost as blinding as driving west at sunset.

Especially with the sun reflecting off the ocean to his right, lighting up the water so it looked like it was on fire.

Sure, he could have waited another couple of hours until the sun was well risen, but he would be the first person the folks at the lottery commission saw when they came into work today. The commercials for the lottery on television made it seem as if they were really glad to give away money. He wanted to see for himself if that was true, or just an act they put on to get folks to buy more tickets.

He chuckled to himself. Sadie would be so proud of him. If she was here. Once they accepted the fact they'd never have children, they'd scrimped and saved, did without all their working lives so they could enjoy their retirement. Plans to travel. Visit places they only ever saw on television. Maybe learn a foreign language.

But then that dreaded disease came and sucked the life out of her. Tears welled, blurring his vision. He checked his side view mirror then let off the accelerator and eased into the slow lane until his eyes cleared.

He gritted his teeth then carried on a conversation with his car like he always did on a road trip. Made the time—and his life—less lonely somehow. "I know, old girl. You could take on any of those tin cans on the road with four of your eight cylinders tied behind your back. Three-fifty-seven horsepower is something these guys can only dream of." A compact sped past, taillights taunting him and his classic ride. "But this old man's eyesight isn't as good as it once was, so we'll let those whippersnappers go on by. Let's see where they are in about thirty years, hey? Most of 'em won't even outlast the loan."

He cast his thoughts ahead to his goals for today: get his check. Get his cash. Then what? Beyond that, he had no plans. Maybe eat dinner out? Nah, too lonely sitting in a restaurant by himself. Maybe fill his freezer with steak and lobster? Probably not. One meal, maybe two, but then he had to watch out for his gout.

He sighed. Getting old really stunk.

He settled back into the seat, feeling the spring that threatened to poke through ever since he bought the car. But it never had. He entered a fog bank and flipped on his headlights. No point having an accident this close to the happiest day of his life.

No, not quite the happiest. But it ranked up in the top ten. Meeting Sadie. Wedding her. Retirement. Winning the lottery just two days ago. And now this.

He gripped the steering wheel and started singing to himself. "We're in the money. We're in the money." He didn't know the next bit, so he hummed along before chiming in with what he did remember. "The skies are sunny. We're in the money."

Yes, siree. The best day of the rest of his life.

$ $ $

Mike glanced over at Carly, whose focus was fixed on her computer screen and her finger poised on her mouse. Doc, the cat, curled up on her inbox, looked so peaceful it made him sleepy just to watch him. What would go good right now was a cup of coffee.

Almost as though reading his mind, Carly stood. "I'm going for a tea. Want one?"

"Coffee, please. And a couple of those peanut butter cookies on the side."

"Coming right up."

As she headed down the hallway, the landline rang. Mike answered. "Hi, this is Mike."

"Hi, this is John Paul Matins. I'm the director of the Bear Cove

Community Hospital. We're part of the Downeast Regional Healthcare System, which has fourteen clinics and smaller hospitals under its banner. I hear tell you're a programmer and your wife is a forensic accountant."

Mike straightened. He was accustomed to receiving calls from potential clients in his own area of expertise, but this was the first time Carly's work was also referenced. Maybe this was an opportunity for them to work together on a project. "That's true. We are."

"Great. I was wondering if you'd both be available to meet in the next day or so? We have a situation here at the hospital. Honestly, we don't feel we have time to look around and check prices, so consider yourself onboard. Tomorrow will be a briefing on the project with Ted Wilson, hospital director."

Mike glanced at the oversized white board that occupied half of their office wall. Their joint calendar. Or at least, it was supposed to be. Neither of them was particularly detailed when it came to getting appointments and such on the board. "Let me check." He covered the mouthpiece as Carly returned, balancing two plates with cookies on top of two mugs. "Carly, can we meet here in town tomorrow?"

She set her load down and checked the calendar. "Nothing on for tomorrow."

He sighed. "At least, nothing we wrote on there." He lifted his hand. "How about ten?"

"That would be great."

"Can you tell me a little more about the project?"

Some papers rustled at the other end of the call. "I don't want to say too much over the phone. Suffice it to say it appears somebody has hacked into Downeast's system and issued multiple billings for the same services."

"So why do you need us?"

"I need your wife to determine the extent of the damage, and I need you to design a foolproof firewall. We thought we had one, but apparently not."

Mike chuckled. "Just when we come up with something foolproof, somebody comes up with a better fool."

Seemed John Paul wasn't amused because a long silence ensued before the director cleared his throat. "Right. Well. This is serious to us. The government is one of the victims of this scam. If we lose our

Medicare accreditation, we'll be in serious trouble financially. And I don't need to tell you that we're trying to keep a low profile here and fix this before the media—and ultimately the public—find out about it. The last thing we need is patients worrying about confidential health information being leaked or misused."

Mike understood. A recent national news story about a theft, which included a laptop belonging to a hospital employee out west, ran for weeks until the media moved on to another juicy tidbit. People lost their jobs, and numerous lawsuits emerged in various districts across the country as patients sought damages. To make matters worse, with nobody charged to date, and officials not certain how much information made its way onto the black market for false identification, passports, and social security numbers, many folks were antsy.

John Paul Matins had every right to be solemn about this situation.

"Right you are. Carly and I will see you at ten tomorrow. Will you be there also?"

"Nope. I'm just making the arrangements and okaying the expenditure."

"Great. Who do we report to?"

"Wilson."

After receiving—and writing down—the meeting room number, Mike hung up and reached for his coffee and cookies. "Sounds like we have an interesting assignment coming up. One we don't have to bid on."

She munched a cookie before answering. "That's unusual."

"Unusual situation. The hospital's data security was breached. They need you to find out how much and hopefully who, although he didn't specifically say the who part. And they need me to make it so nobody gets in again."

"Sounds like both jobs are right up our alley. But didn't you have a project coming up next week?"

He groaned. He'd forgotten about that. Probably because it wasn't on the calendar. "I'll call the client. I'm pretty sure I can push their project out to the next week."

Carly stood in front of the whiteboard with two dry eraser markers in her hand. "I'll mark us both out all next week, and put the other client on the next week." She wrote BEAR COVE COMMUNITY HOSPITAL in blue for Mike and in green for her. "What's that other client's name?"

"Johnson." He sent off a quick email to that client, and almost immediately received a response. "They say that works better for them. It will take me about three days. So Wednesday to Friday of the next week."

Carly marked that off. "Whew. We have a busy month ahead of us."

"Nice, though. Income we weren't expecting."

She smiled. "How does that old song go? We're in the money." She hummed a few bars. "That's all I know."

He attacked some papers that needed filing. Best to get his desk cleared—in more ways than one—before beginning a new project. "Me, too. But that's a good thing to know."

While money wasn't the most important thing in the world to him, it ranked in the top ten.

In the Money

## Chapter 4

Thursday night passed slowly for Carly as she huddled on the sofa, wrapped in an afghan, while Mike snored comfortably in their bed down the hall. She couldn't see him, but she certainly could hear him.

The latest mystery novel lay in her lap, virtually unread, as her lids drooped. But when a car's headlights hit her living room window, she sprang wide awake, peering through a crack between the curtains, hoping against hope that James had returned.

Because if it wasn't him, where was he?

She tried to rationalize his absence. Perhaps he decided to stay in Portland and enjoy his winnings. A check online confirmed more than a hundred hotels and motels in the Greater Portland area. Far too many for her to call. Plus he had every right to spend his money on himself.

But the vehicle continued down the road, turning at the next stop sign.

Not James.

She glanced up and down her street. At ten past one in the morning, the only lights shone from front porches or over a garage. Everybody tucked into their beds.

Everyone but her, that was.

And her elderly neighbor.

Where was he?

She stretched and yawned. At this rate, she'd look like she'd been pulled through a knothole in the morning. Not a good face to present to the hospital director looking to hire her and Mike. Without a gallon of coffee, she wouldn't be able to string four words together into a coherent sentence, let alone make a rational decision about the job.

Maybe a short walk would quiet her mind enough to be able to sleep.

Not that she really wanted to snooze away the night. Knowing James was safe and snug in his home was her preference. Or safe and snug somewhere.

Pulling her sweater around her shoulders, she headed out into the night. Just a little trek next door. Maybe James returned when she dozed off.

But three minutes later confirmed she hadn't missed his return. No lights—which wasn't completely unexpected. Standing on tippy-toes and cupping her hands around her eyes, she peered through dingy little panes into his garage. No car. And James always parked his vehicle inside. Never on the street. And certainly never around the corner.

If his old sedan wasn't here, neither was he.

She sighed and returned home, pacing the floor rather than sitting. If she was James, what would she do? Where would she be?

One thing was certain: she wouldn't be worrying her neighbor.

She paused then chuckled. The man she knew wouldn't purposely worry anybody. How was he to know she was wearing a path in the carpet at—a glance at the clock on the mantel and she groaned—two o'clock in the morning. He'd assume she was like most normal people in Bear Cove, tucked into her bed, sound asleep.

Which is exactly where she should be.

So why couldn't she shut off her mind, still her thoughts, and rest her eyes just for a few minutes?

Because the knot in her stomach the size of a grapefruit kept her awake.

So what could she do?

She sat on the sofa, the telephone near her elbow, staring at it, willing it to ring. But despite her best intentions, her lids drooped, along with her resolve to stay away until her friend returned.

Several hours later, at the sound of footsteps in the hallway, she looked up.

Mike.

What time was it? She groaned. Six thirty.

She rose and met him halfway, slipping her arms around his waist and burying her face against his chest, all warm and sleepy-smelling. "How come you're wandering the halls this late at night?"

He pulled her closer. "Don't you mean this early?" He laid his chin on her head. "What're you doing?"

She sighed. He wasn't going to like this answer. Maybe she could sugarcoat the truth a little. "Just checking the neighborhood."

Mike chuckled.

*Rats. He'd seen right through her.*

"If by checking the neighborhood you mean checking on a certain neighbor, then I believe you."

She smiled up at him, the sight of his cleft chin and dark eyes warming her from the inside out like melted chocolate. "You know me too well."

"That, plus I heard you going through the front door a few hours back." He exhaled. "No sign of him?"

She gripped his hand and led him to the sofa where they both sat. After she arranged the coverlet over their legs, she snuggled close. "I'm getting worried."

"So what do you want to do?"

"You do know me too well."

"I know the mama bear in you wants to search every motel and hotel between here and Portland."

She smiled. "Yes. But that would be silly, wouldn't it?"

"Not silly. But time consuming." His brow pulled down. "You have no legal standing in James' life, you know."

"I know. But he's all alone."

"He is. But so are millions of others who live safe, productive lives. And he's already made it plenty clear he doesn't need—or want—our help."

"You're right. I should just leave it be."

He stood and held out a hand. "Coming?" He quirked his chin toward the kitchen. "I can put a fresh pot of coffee on. And I'm pretty sure I saw some bagels in the fridge next to a tub of cream cheese."

She moaned. At the mention of food, her tummy reminded her *suppa*—as a true Down-easter would pronounce it—was hours ago.

"You spoke the magic words, Mister." Once in the kitchen, she sat while Mike served up their impromptu breakfast. As she bit into the chewy goodness lathered with cream cheese and sliced banana, she eyed the phone on the counter. "Maybe I'll call the chief. See what he thinks."

"You know what he's going to say."

She sighed and washed down her mouthful of food with her coffee. "I know. But I have to do something." She stretched across the space between the table and the counter and snagged the receiver the dialed the non-emergency number and asked to be connected to Chief Donovan.

He answered within a few seconds. "Good morning, Carly. What can I do for you today?"

"I'm worried about my neighbor, James."

"What's'up?"

She glanced at Mike, whose brow pulled down in warning. Right. Best not to mention the lottery thing. "I saw him drive out yesterday but he didn't come back last night."

The chief chuckled and settled into his chair, which squeaked and rustled in her ear. "He's an adult, Carly. He doesn't have to answer to you."

"I know that." She rolled her eyes. Men. They just didn't get it. "But he's also elderly. And he doesn't usually stay out all night."

"Maybe he found a woman."

That was a picture she could have lived the rest of her life without seeing. "I think he would have said something to me. I was over there the night before. And I saw him earlier in the day yesterday."

"How did he seem then?"

Good question. Irritated at her meddling. Resistant to her suggestions. Evasive as to his plans.

But if she told the chief that, he'd never do anything.

Perhaps now was an acceptable moment for a little fib.

"Fine. His usual self."

The chief laughed. "Right. Sorry, Carly. An elderly man goes away for a few days. I can't use town resources to track him down. And I sure can't ask the state patrol to get involved."

"Could you put out a be-on-the-look-out-for?"

"You're not family. He hasn't been gone long enough to qualify for a BOLO. Technically, he isn't missing yet. Even family has to wait forty-eight hours. Unless he's a vulnerable elder, which he isn't."

"What would constitute vulnerability?"

"If he has dementia or Alzheimer's. A known mental health condition. Prior evidence of harming himself or others." The chair squeaked again. "Anything like that?"

"Not that I know of." The chief was right. She was sticking her nose in where it didn't belong. No wonder James was avoiding her. She sighed. "Okay, Chief, thanks."

She disconnected the call and faced Mike. "You men are in a conspiracy to undermine me."

Mike gathered their dirty dishes and set them in the sink. "I cooked. You clean."

She snorted. "I don't think brewing coffee and toasting two bagels constitutes cooking."

He raised his hands and backed out of the kitchen. "Just sayin'. I did my part. Gotta get to work."

His footsteps echoed down the hallway toward their shared home office. She turned to the sink, plopped the stopper into place, then added hot water and dish suds. After clearing away their breakfast dishes, she'd go check with the neighbors to see if anybody knew more than she did.

Which she sincerely doubted.

Maybe she was nosey.

$ $ $

An hour later, and she was no closer to knowing where James was than when she started. Most of the neighbors were home, being of the retired type, but nobody had new information to share. And she tried, that was for sure. So far she'd drank four cups of coffee, a delicate china cup of tea, and ate more banana bread than was healthy. But still no additional tidbits she could use to either track the man down or convince the police to look into the matter.

The final house—the one she avoided so far—was Bob's. Surely the man was at work. Wherever that was. Then again, perhaps he was independently wealthy and came to hide in Bear Cove. He hadn't told her anything about himself apart from his name.

She drew a deep breath for courage then crossed the street. She'd leave no stone unturned. She chuckled to herself. Why her mind would correlate Bob and creepy things living under rocks she wasn't certain. After all, she'd met him just the one time. Hardly enough time to form an opinion about him one way or the other.

Up the walkway to his front entry, and she rang the doorbell. Chimes akin to Westminster Cathedral sounded behind the solid slab door. She waited, glancing around at the corners of the overhanging roof. No spider webs. No wasp nest. Not even a mud warbler nest. Apparently the real estate company did a good job cleaning the place up. After all, it had lain empty for a long time.

She rang the bell again and waited, shifting from one foot to the other as she did. Carefully tended flower beds lined the area below the front window, and pots of geraniums stood at attention on the three steps up to the doorstep, handfuls of buds waiting to burst forth in the cooler days of fall.

She sighed then pressed her ear to the door. Voices. No, wait, the television. A popular game show that pitted families against each other in an attempt to identify the most popular answers to inane questions.

He must be home. Surely nobody left the TV on when they left the house.

She knocked on the door, a polite rat-a-tat-tat, waited, then repeated the summons. No response. Maybe he was in trouble. Her pulse pounded in her ears. Was it possible to have two neighbors in difficult circumstances at the same time? Jessica Fletcher often did, and she lived in a town no bigger than Bear Cove.

She should have brought her cell phone. Then she could call the police and—and what? Tell him her new neighbor—who she'd met just the once—was in trouble and they needed to come busting down the man's door? The chief would certify her as a genuine loony.

More likely, Bob was avoiding her.

Just like James seemed to be doing.

Was it rudeness on their part? Bad manners?

Or something much more sinister?

She wheeled about and headed home.

She had work to do, and worrying about one neighbor at a time was enough for her.

Today, she'd focus on James.

When she arrived home, Mike was talking on the phone.

"Sure thing. Thanks for the invitation. See you at seven."

She entered their office and sat at her desk. "Who was that? And where are you going?"

"That was Bob. Our new neighbor."

She flipped on her computer. Whatever he wanted was of no concern to her. "What did he want?"

"To invite us to his housewarming tonight."

She swiveled in her chair. "What?"

"Yeah. He was going to invite you when you dropped by this morning." Mike brow pulled down. "Why did you go there?"

She shrugged. "Just canvassing the neighborhood. I knocked and rang and—"

"He said as much."

"He was home and he ignored me? How rude."

"Actually, he was unpacking boxes in the basement and didn't hear you until you pounded really hard. And by the time he got up the stairs, after tripping in a box and almost spraining his ankle, you were gone. So he called."

"Well, if that sob story is supposed to make me feel bad for calling on a neighbor, it isn't working." Still, the image of the man sprawled on the basement floor, unable to get to the phone, did bring a lump to her throat. Maybe she was being too harsh on her new neighbor. "Wait a minute. How did he get our phone number? And why didn't he call out to me? I would have gone back and talked to him."

"Maybe he didn't have an hour to spend right now."

She lifted one corner of her mouth in her best Elvis-style smile-sneer. "More likely he didn't want to talk to me at all." She turned back to her computer and typed in her password. "Still, I guess I can talk to him tonight."

"Now, Carly."

She tossed her husband a smile. "Don't 'now Carly' me. He invited both of us, right?"

"Yes."

"Then I'll have a chance to talk to him. Not to chat would be rude. And I've had enough of rude neighbors to last a lifetime."

Yes, siree. She'd get some answers tonight.

$ $ $

Bob Powell surveyed the group gathered in his living room and dining room. Neighbors from the street, business owners from town, a couple of friends from Portland who drove down for the evening. All chatting, a glass of something in hand. The hubbub of conversation soothed him like Muzak in an elevator, designed to calm the nerves and cover those awkward silences where folks tended to debate whether to make eye contact or not.

This was a good idea. Normally social, he missed his busy New York schedule. Still, coming to this small town was expedient. At least, for the time being. Nobody would think to look for him here. Not that he was actually hiding out.

No, more of a forced sabbatical.

Keep a low profile, make some new connections, recover from the last project.

He smiled at the elderly woman dressed to the nines in a Chanel suit from the mid-eighties, her ears adorned with diamond studs the size of blueberries—three carats each, at least. A hundred thousand bucks, if they were a dollar. He glanced at her hands. Gnarled, knuckled, every finger bedecked with a ring. But not a wedding band in sight.

Maybe he should get to know her better.

He crossed the room, his eyes fixed on his quarry, a smile pasted on his face. Be charming. Be gracious. Be complimentary. Sweep the old biddy off her feet. Convince her of his sincerity. He chuckled. The only thing truly sincere about him was his ability to spend a few hours alone with her and walk away with a couple of these trinkets. She'd never miss them. And if she reported him, he'd remind her that she gave him these gifts and how it would look to her family if he told her about them.

They'd lock her up in a loony bin.

The scheme worked before with others, and it would work this time with her.

These lonely, old women were all alike. Dying for attention. Clamoring for affection. Grasping for the fountain of youth.

And he'd give them what they wanted.

As he passed the entryway, the door opened, and he slowed to greet his new guest. The woman could wait. He had all the time in the world.

Or at least, as much as he needed. The old biddy wasn't going anywhere soon.

But at the sight of the new arrivals, his heart slipped a notch. Mike, the guy from across the street, and his nosey wife. Oh, yes, he knew all about her. Like a bulldog, one neighbor described her. Gets herself into scrapes with the law all the time, another said. And the police chief and he shared a private laugh earlier today over coffee. Seems Casey?—Carrie?— no, Carly—got herself all worked up because her neighbor stayed out last night.

If he'd known a den mother lived across the street, he'd have bought elsewhere. The last thing he needed was somebody keeping an eye on his movements.

Still, she was no match for him.

He replastered his smile in place and stepped toward Mike, his hand outstretched. "Welcome. So glad you could make it."

Not really, but this little white lie might cause her to let her guard down.

And in his experience, when people didn't suspect him, he was home free.

$ $ $

Carly sighed as she glanced at the clock on the range in Bob's kitchen. Almost eleven. She'd been here more than four hours, and she'd not had the chance to corner her host even once. Seemed the man had a Carly-alert radar going. Every time she saw him alone and headed his way, he latched onto another guest or slipped into another conversation knot.

Almost as though he was avoiding her.

But why would he? From the first time they met, her mystery gene alerted her. There was something slippery about him she couldn't quite put her finger on. But really, wasn't the purpose of a housewarming to get to know everybody? Wasn't she an everybody?

Who was he afraid of? Or what? That she'd see through his smarmy smile and fake smile?

Well, too late.

Already happened.

And what was his preoccupation with Sarah Noble? The elderly widow was never more than a few feet from him all evening. And she old enough to be his mother. Maybe his grandmother. Then again, the attentions of a handsome younger man turned some women's heads. At least, that's what she'd heard.

Although why a woman of Sarah's years couldn't see right through him was strange. Maybe she spent too much time alone. Perhaps Carly could should visit her once in a while. Invite her over for dinner. Go shopping with her.

Carly sighed. Then again, maybe not. Although she knew Sarah, she didn't really run in her ultra-rich circle of friends. Carly was more the bury-her-nose-in-a-book type, while Sarah was art galleries and theatre opening night material.

Their host entered the kitchen, several empty wine bottles in his arms. He slowed ever so little when he caught sight of her.

Any suspicions of his avoiding her were now confirmed.

She leaned against the counter and crossed her arms. "Nice party."

He nodded as he dropped the empties into the trashcan. "Just getting more wine."

Not exactly the appropriate response to her comment. And it wasn't like she'd asked him what he was doing. Was he socially inept?

Or hiding something?

She suspected the latter, since he had no trouble talking with strangers in his living room.

He didn't even recycle. Another point on the why-I-don't-like-him side of the tally sheet. Bottles were so easy to dispose of responsibly.

She nodded toward the oven. "Those little quiches are amazing. Another batch baking up now?"

"Yep."

"Want me to serve them when they're ready?"

Without turning from his task of opening another case of wine, he shook his head. "No need. You're the guest, and I'm the host."

Nice avoidance technique. She'd have to keep that one in mind.

If she ever needed to be rude to somebody.

She crossed the kitchen to the fridge. "How about I check the cream and stuff for the coffee and tea? Wouldn't want to run out." She yanked open the door before he could respond and peeked in. Almost empty. Which seemed strange for a man hosting a party. "I can't remember the last time I saw the shelves in my fridge."

He stepped close and pushed on the door, forcing her to step back or chance being squished. "Want a glass of wine?"

"No, thanks. Coffee would be great."

He turned to the counter and poured her a cup. "Cream?"

She glanced back at the fridge. "Where were you hiding cream in there? All I saw was one egg, half an onion, and a sliver of cheese that I'm pretty sure wasn't supposed to have those green spots growing on it."

He opened a cupboard over the coffeemaker. "Shelf stable or powdered?"

Ah, the man kept little in his fridge. Not food. Not wine. Not cream.

"Shelf stable, please."

He set three small cuplets on the table, perfectly aligned with a spoon, and gestured for her to sit. And waited until she did. She peeled back the covers and dumped the cream into her coffee then stirred. He seemed to be waiting for her to taste it, so she did. Then his shoulders relaxed and he sat across from her, his original reason for being in here with her apparently forgotten.

Or postponed.

Or contrived.

She studied him over the rim of her cup, trying to figure out what made him tick.

He tossed her a smile. "So what would I see if I looked in your Kenmore? Ten cans of cat food of various flavors?"

She froze, her breath trapped in her throat. "How do you know I have a Kenmore? Or a cat?"

He shrugged. "You told me."

She shook her head. "You and I haven't talked more than to introduce ourselves."

"Must have been your husband, then."

"I doubt Mike would have told you the brand of our refrigerator. That sort of thing rarely comes up in housewarming party conversation. Unless you're in the market for a new fridge." She turned in her chair to look at the brand new model in his kitchen, the energy use label still displayed on the front door. "Nope, guess not. And I know we aren't thinking of replacing ours until it breaks." She leaned across the table. "So how do you know that?"

He lifted one shoulder and let it fall. "Lucky guess."

"No, I think there's more to it than that."

He glared at her, any false joviality or good humor now gone. Faded into black like a dying match in the night. "Think what you like." He stood. "I've wasted enough time trying to be nice to you. I have other guests to see to."

"Is that what this has been? A waste of time?" Seemed strange words to use by a host at his own party. "What were you hoping to accomplish?"

"None. Of. Your. Business." He leaned close, his brow pulled into a straight line. "And if you try to make something of it, you'll regret it."

She sat back, stunned. Very strange behavior.

She didn't like the man, but she sure hadn't expected him to threaten her.

## Chapter 5

First thing the next morning, before she and Mike headed out for their meeting with the hospital director, Carly ducked next door. This time, however, she was clad in more than her slippers and jammies under her robe. Her usual business attire—black jeans, t-shirt, and sneakers—were her choice today.

However, despite her wardrobe upgrade, James was still not home. No car in the garage or driveway. Mail from yesterday—and likely the day before—now filled his mailbox near the front door almost to capacity, with several pieces sticking up. A good wind might snatch them. She reached for the bundle of envelopes then paused. Was taking her neighbor's mail for safekeeping considered theft of federal property? Maybe that only applied if she was stealing it, which she wasn't. Then again, if somebody else saw her take it, they could think the worse.

She jammed her hand into her pants pocket to avoid the temptation of even checking the dozen or more envelopes of varying sizes and colors, along with a couple of magazines, some obvious solicitations, and this week's edition of the *Bear Cove Gazette*. Full of all the news she'd already heard through the town grapevine.

All except where James might be.

A chill wind swept in off the water, belying the fact that it was the height of summer and should be warmer. She envisioned James wandering alone in the woods. Or his car stuck in a ditch. Nights had been cooler recently, with a storm projected within a few days. She didn't like the idea of him out in the open. He might be fit and spry, as Mike reminded her, but he was still older.

A final peek into the garage—everything looked the same as yesterday. No car. No James. Shelves lined with boxes marked as to their contents: PHOTO ALBUMS, COOKBOOKS, CAMPING GEAR. Well, that was interesting. Camping. She scanned the remainder of the single-vehicle unit. Fishing poles and one of those nets on a long pole stacked in a corner. A set of hip waders and a fish basket at the ready beside them.

Satisfied she'd left no stone unturned, metaphorically speaking, she returned home. Mike's off-key singing indicated he was in the shower. She had time to make a quick call. She slipped into the kitchen and turned on the coffee maker, then dialed the police chief's number and waited to be connected.

"I'm guessing you aren't letting me know James arrived home safe and sound last night, and you're calling to apologize for taking up valuable police time with your groundless worrying?" The man's deep baritone held a scratch of not enough sleep. "But I don't think that's right, because last I heard, the bad place is still scorching hot."

"Ha, ha." Not funny. His offhanded remark to hell freezing over wasn't lost on her. "No, James didn't come home last night."

He sighed. "What do you want me to do?"

Good question. "I don't know. Go out and look for him."

"Carly, like I told you yesterday, James is—"

"I know." She sat back in the chair, the wood pressing into her shoulder blades. She shifted to a more comfortable position. "James is an adult. He can look after himself." She lowered her voice. "But what if he can't? What if he's dead in a ditch?"

The chief chuckled. "Now you sound like my mother. She always thought the worst when we kids were even ten minutes late getting home."

Carly didn't know the man's matriarch, but she sounded like her kind of people. "I don't know the law, Chief. What can you do?"

"It's still too soon to file a missing person's report. And because he hasn't done anything wrong, a BOLO would be going overboard. Wouldn't want an ambitious young trooper to see it, not read the details, and think James is wanted for bank robbery or something."

"No, we wouldn't want that." Mike's singing stopped and the water shut off. She didn't have much time. Cupping the receiver between her shoulder and her ear, she stood and popped a couple of English muffins into the toaster then dug through the fridge for two slices of cheese. "I can't think where he might be."

"Probably taking a few days away to enjoy himself. No family, you said?"

"Right. And as far as I know, no romantic connections either." Not that she knew much about her neighbor. Nothing more than came up on a lottery draw night. Should she mention the money? If James wasn't in trouble, he'd hate it that she told about it. For now, she'd keep quiet. "There should be some kind of alert like you use for missing children."

"Right. Amber Alert. It's helped a lot of kids get home again. I've heard talk about one like it for the elderly, especially for dementia and Alzheimer's."

"Which so far as I know, James doesn't have."

"Maybe he's gone fishing."

"Don't think so. Saw his pole and tackle through the garage window."

"You have been poking around, haven't you?"

"Not poking, as you put it. Concerned about my neighbor."

"Uh-huh." His chair squeaked. "I could notify the other chiefs up and down the coast to keep an eye out for him. He'll turn up in a few days and we'll laugh about this."

Carly wasn't convinced. She was, however, fairly certain that even if James returned home safely, she wouldn't be laughing.

His disappearance wasn't in the least bit funny.

And despite how hilarious the chief seemed to find it, neither was her concern about his well-being.

$ $ $

Ted Wilson, hospital director, sat behind his desk much as a king occupies his throne—with authority, confidence, and a hint of disdain for those he considered beneath him. Which, from Mike's viewpoint of standing in the doorway, appeared to be everybody.

Flashing back to grade school and the numerous times he'd been summoned to the principal's office, Mike swallowed hard and pressed his hand into the small of Carly's back. She glanced up at him and offered a smile that trembled at the corners of her mouth.

She knew exactly how he felt.

He straightened his shoulders and exhaled. He could do this. He was a professional. Much sought-after for his ability to see through a complicated issue and come out the other side with a credible solution.

So why did his knees tremble?

Ted waited until they stood within inches of his desk before standing and offering his hand. "Mr. Turnquist." He turned slightly to Carly. "Mrs. Turnquist."

Carly waved off his words. "Please, call me Carly. Mrs. Turnquist is Mike's mother."

Who'd been dead several years at this point, and who had insisted people address her by her married title unless they were members of family or the privileged few.

Ted dipped his head once. "Carly."

Mike shook the man's hand. "And please, call me Mike."

"Glad we got that out of the way." He sat again and shuffled several folders and sheets of paper, aligning them perfectly with the edge of his desk. Then he tented his hands and stared at each of them in turn. "You're probably wondering why I called you here today."

Carly opened her mouth to reply, but Mike squeezed her hand. One of their signals to remain quiet. For the time being. He leaned forward. "Mr. Matins said you had a problem with some invoicing and you think somebody may have hacked into your computer system."

"Right." Wilson leaned back and clasped his hands behind his head, the image of the successful professional. "At least, that's what our IT guys say. And they've convinced JP, as well. Me, not so sure."

Mike nodded. "So why don't you have them look into it and fix the problem?"

"I'm concerned it's more deep-seated than a simple, single breach."

Carly snorted. "That's an oxymoron if ever I heard one. A simple breach."

Wilson swiveled in his chair to address her. "Do you have special training in this area?" He glared at her, and she sat back. Silent. Withered, Mike would call it. "As I said, our highly trained IT group is at loose ends when it comes to identifying both the source and the extent."

Then Carly recovered her tongue. "Actually, I do. In cybersecurity. Electronic fraud. And in implementing systems to limit fraudulent activity in the future." Another snort, this one softer. "Of course, at this point, it's like closing the barn door after the horse is out."

Mike winced. This guy could be put off by Carly's attitude—even though, the man deserved it. Keeping them waiting for almost twenty minutes. Lording it over them. Now calling their credentials and capabilities into question.

Then again, he wasn't convinced Wilson's attitude would make for a good working relationship.

If the man tossed them out on their ears, at least they'd still have their heads.

Wilson straightened and leaned on his desk. "So you think you can help us?"

Interesting how when he needed help, he used the collective 'us', but when it came to personal thoughts or beliefs, they were his own.

Another one of those psychological tools the director has no doubt learned at—Mike scanned the walls, studying the framed certificates—then gulped. Yale, of all places. A double master's in Business Administration and Health Care Management. At the same time.

Mike crossed his ankle over his knee. "I'd need to look at the computer system. Carly would check the specific physical entries as well as how they were booked in accounting. And I'd spend time wandering around the programming protocols for the billing module."

Concern etched the man's forehead. "How long will that take?"

"Several hours today just to get an idea of what's going on. After that, we can give you a written estimate of the amount of time to correct the problem and build a stronger firewall."

"Sounds expensive."

"You get what you pay for." Mike stood and reached for Carly's hand, hoping she'd take the hint and follow him. "And Mr. Matins said we were already onboard because of the urgency of the matter, and that cost wasn't an issue. But if you're the real decision-maker, it sounds like you aren't ready to make a decision today. You—or rather, Mr. Matins—indicated the hospital needs our help. We're here and ready to work."

Wilson pushed away a millimeter or two from his desk. "I'll need to check your references."

Mike headed toward the door, thankful that Carly shadowed him. "Mr. Matins has already done that, or we wouldn't be here."

"Please, wait."

Mike turned. "Look, my wife and I know what we're doing. This isn't our first time at the races. So show me your computer system, or we're going home."

"But—"

"Now."

In the Money

Wilson locked eyes with him. Mike sighed. So this was how it would be. He held his ground. If he capitulated now, he'd have to bite and scrape for every penny later on.

They didn't need the work that badly.

A long minute stretched into two. Despite this young man's top-notch education and his apparent competence in his role as director of a health care group, he didn't have more than thirty years' experience under his belt as Mike did. He stifled a chuckle. Ted Wilson was likely still in short pants when Mike graduated college.

No, he could afford to wait.

A decision that paid off not ten seconds later when Wilson gave a single, curt nod. "Fine. I'll take you down to IT." He nodded toward Carly. "And you to Accounting. We have a skeleton staff on today because it's the weekend, but we should be able to find you both a workspace."

*Where you won't get in anybody's hair.*

Mike smiled at the unspoken implications of Wilson's statement. Should he rise to the occasion? Or let it slide?

He chose the latter. Let the man feel he won at least one battle—no matter how small—today.

Mike squeezed Carly's hand, a lot more relaxed at this point. "Good. The clock starts ticking as of now."

Wilson joined them at the door. "Clock?"

"On our billable hours."

$ $ $

Two hours and—Carly glanced up at the clock on the wall—twenty-four minutes later, and she was no closer to the beginning of the rabbit trail than when she started. She snapped a file folder shut and shoved it toward the corner of the cubicle assigned as her working space.

*How can people work in these things day after day?*

She stared at the fabric-covered wall less than two feet from her nose. Pale-grey, stained with splashes of coffee. Paper clips partially straightened and shoved through the material to hold up a calendar, a curling photo of three kids, and a yellow sticky note dated more than two years ago.

Was the cubby vacant because the worker relegated to this less-than-inspiring pod failed to address that single task?

Or had they, just perhaps, died of boredom?

She pushed back from her desk and grabbed her coffee cup. Time for a walk and a fresh mocha. Mid-afternoon—maybe somebody thought to take pity on their co-workers and deposited a box of doughnuts in the break room.

The clickety-clack of a keyboard greeted her as she neared the door, and she exited right to enter the IT room where Mike worked. He was ensconced at a cubicle similar to the one she occupied, this one lined with shelves of very technical-looking books and binders.

She shuddered. Although her own workspace was aesthetic and uninspiring, she much preferred her space to his.

Then again, he looked happy as a clam. Never one to ask questions about his surroundings or poke into other people's business—unless part of his current work assignment—he often accused her of being too nosey for her own good.

She stood behind him and did a one-handed massage at the back of his neck, and his fingers paused as he pressed against her, leaning his head forward until his chin touched his chest.

"Oh, that's good."

She drove her thumb into the muscle at the base of his skull, earning another moan of pleasure. "Want a coffee? Tea? Doughnut?"

"Herbal tea would be great. Had enough caffeine for the rest of the week. And no doughnut." He opened one eye and peered up at her. "How's it going in your neck of the woods?" He chuckled. "No pun intended."

She eyed the surrounding workspace. Woods, no. Even a dense forest had more open space than this place. "Feels a bit of a rabbit warren, don't you think? I wondered if I should leave a trail of breadcrumbs to find our way out."

Mike chuckled then turned back to the computer screen. "I'm glad they put me near the door. Less likely I'll get lost."

"If we hang around until quitting time, we can follow the mass exodus."

He groaned. "I don't know if I want to be here to see that. Besides, it's the weekend. Didn't you hear Ted? Skeleton crew."

"More likely because they died here and nobody noticed."

He chuckled. "Didn't you offer to fetch me tea?"

She quirked her chin toward his terminal. "Making any headway?"

He shook his head. "I know somebody breached their system, but I can't figure out how. The firewall is strong and intact, although I tweaked it a little to improve it. Double blinds, dead ends, triple encryption—"

She laid a hand gently across his mouth to stifle his words. "Don't confuse me with your brilliance."

His warm lips against her palm sent a tingle all the way up her arm, reminding her why she loved this man so much. Honest, hard-working, loyal.

And romantic.

Until a muffled raspberry blew hot air between her fingers, and she snatched her hand away.

Right. Romantic, indeed.

She tilted her head to one side. "And what was that for?"

"To see the look on your face."

"Satisfied?"

"Absolutely. You had such a sweet expression, like you were a hundred miles away in dreamland."

"And you couldn't let me linger there just another minute?"

"Not with your hand over my mouth."

She swiped her palm against her thigh. "Sorry."

He tilted his chin back toward the Accounting office. "How are you doing?"

"I've looked at the records in the accounting system. Studied the original documents. They don't agree."

"You mean you can't find evidence of multiple billings for the same services?"

"Oh, they're in the accounting system, which is how the payment was triggered. They simply aren't in the paper files."

He leaned back in his chair and clasped his hands behind his head. "So somebody with access to the computer system entered records without paper to back them up?"

"Looks like it. Unless they filed them somewhere else." She glanced around. "Since we don't know who our suspects are, how about we take a walk down the hall while we talk about it?"

He pushed his chair back and stood. "Good idea." He stretched his arms over his head. "I need a break anyway."

She linked her free arm through his and together they left the workroom and turned left out the doorway. This wasn't the way to the break room, and she reminded him of that fact.

He nodded. "I know. The offices on this floor run on all four sides, so the hall is like a track. I thought a longer walk would be better."

How the man thought more walking could possibly be better was beyond her. A loyal subscriber to the limited-number-of-heartbeats theory, she never looked for ways to increase her heart rate, burn calories, or exercise.

Still, this one time shouldn't hurt.

So long as she didn't make it a bad habit.

Mike already thought she had enough of those.

Besides, she got plenty of exercise, according to him. Jumping the gun. Passing the buck. Ducking the blame. Stretching the truth. Leaping to conclusions. Once or twice he'd even accused her of running her mouth.

They rounded the first corner and Mike slowed then peeked around the corner before nodding and continuing. "Good. Nobody behind us."

She mock-punched his arm. "Now you're starting to sound like me. Thinking people are following us." She pointed to a security camera in the corner. "Next you'll be saying they're spying on us."

He exhaled. "We know somebody compromised the hospital accounting computer. And we don't know the extent of that breach yet."

"True. But I bet that happens all the time. We hear in the news every week about a government employee taking an office laptop home and leaving it in their car and surprise! It goes missing. With tens of thousands of social security numbers and bank accounts and passwords. But nobody seems to take it seriously. And we never hear anything else about it."

"Just because it happens with some surprising regularity doesn't mean it's not serious. And how about when we do hear that somebody in Russia is using stolen identities to create passports or set up charge accounts? That was just a few weeks ago, too."

She sobered. He was right. Sometimes the backlash came months or even years later. "Here's the break room."

They turned into the bedroom-sized area and headed for the coffee and tea station. Several other employees occupied chairs at tables around the area. Carly nodded to a woman sitting near the microwave. But instead of greeting her, the stranger sniffed and turned away.

Strange reaction. Carly looked down at her clothing. Had she spilled coffee on her shirt? Nope. And the two were dressed similarly, apart from the designer shoes the employee wore. Oh, well. They hadn't been hired to make friends or win congeniality contests.

She rinsed her mug and poured herself another cup—decaf this time. She wanted to sleep tonight. Mike's fingers walked their way through the basket containing individually wrapped tea choices until finding one he wanted. He tore the package open and dropped the bag into his cup, topping it off with hot water.

Then he held out his free hand to her. "Let's finish our walk."

She nodded and led the way out of the room. He tossed her a look—drawn-down brow and squinty eyes—indicating she should wait to talk. Sometimes the man was paranoid. She tossed him a single nod, proud of herself for catching his signal.

When they rounded the next corner, he repeated his actions of before, but this time, his shoulders didn't relax. "That woman is following us."

When Carly leaned forward to see whom he meant, he pulled her back and pinned her to the wall, then pressed in close. "Good thing you're my wife, or we might get thrown out of here."

What was the man on about? Had he lost his mind? She planted her free hand on his chest. "Mike Turnquist. Step away. What will people think?"

The woman who seemed so rude in the break room came around the corner, cutting them a wide swath when she noted them.

Mike chuckled and stepped away. "Caught me trying to steal a kiss from my wife. I figure if we're too busy to kiss, we're too busy." He planted a wet smooch on Carly's cheek. "Right, honey?"

"Uh, right." Carly offered a lopsided smile to the woman, whose cheeks burned red. "Men. No sense of decorum."

Instead of replying, however, the woman gave the same response as before: she stuck her nose in the air and sniffed, then did an about-face and disappeared from sight.

Mike waited a couple of seconds then peeked around the corner again. "Good. This time she's gone."

"Do you really think she was following us?"

"She came out of the room right behind us. Stepping softly. And when we caught her out, she went back the way she came. Seems suspicious to me."

Carly laughed. "Honestly, I never thought I'd hear those words coming from your mouth."

He squinted at her. "You must be rubbing off on me." He offered his arm. "Now, shall we continue our clandestine discussion about our mutual project, or will we stay here kissing until somebody else finds us?"

She looped her arm through his. "Walk, by all means."

He smiled down at her. "A day for new beginnings, perhaps."

"How so?"

"Never thought I'd hear you say walk, either."

She snugged his arm against her side. Even if they didn't accomplish anything else today, they had a good laugh while doing it.

In the Money

## Chapter 6

By the end of the day, Carly narrowed down the timeframe of the fraud to within the last six months. Not only a cybersecurity breach occurred—according to Mike's part of the investigation, and he was rarely wrong—but also a breach from inside the operating division of the health care system. Whether in this actual office or another, she wasn't certain.

But she would be before this job ended.

After a quick chat with Mike, she called Ted Wilson to alert him as to their findings. "The first instance of a double billing of a service was in late March, and I've identified more than seventy-five additional instances since then."

"Can we simply contact the suppliers and tell them we want the money back?"

She sighed. "There are no suppliers. That's why this is fraud. The invoices didn't originate from outside the company. They came from somebody working for the network."

"No, that can't be."

"I know it's not what you wanted to hear. Mike also confirms your system was hacked on multiple occasions. He's managed to insert a couple of temporary fixes and will work on building better firewalls for you next week. For now, your system is secure."

"Are you saying one of our employees has been stealing from us?"

"Most likely at least one employee in one of the network offices. Of course, they might have had help from outside sources. We'll be able to narrow that down in the coming days."

"So what do you need from me?"

She appreciated he was willing to help without inserting himself into their scope of work. "Most likely this kind of thing is covered by fraud insurance. And even if it's not, you'll need to alert your insurance company of what we found."

Papers rustled. "I hoped to avoid that."

"Why?"

"Premiums are already high enough. Even a hint of impropriety will likely cause an increase."

"Ted, we could be talking hundreds of thousands of dollars here." She sat back in her chair and shrugged aching shoulders. "If you don't alert them, even if you don't make a claim through your policy, they'll wonder if you're hiding something even bigger from them, and your premiums will go even higher."

He exhaled. "I guess you're right."

"I am, Ted. I've been through this kind of thing before."

"Okay. I'll call the company and ask for an investigator. What else?"

"I'll call the FBI and—"

"What?"

She yanked the handset from her ear at his outcry. "Ted, I'll call the FBI. They have a special unit that handles this kind of crime with even more expertise than I have. And they have a darned sight more authority for getting subpoenas and arresting folks than I do. Not to mention shiny badges and guns on their hips."

"I don't want this getting out. If the cops are involved, the media will soon get hold of it."

"Sorry to burst your bubble, Ted, but we saw a news story on television last evening about this very thing. And if they weren't talking about your hospital network, somebody else has been hit. Recently. This isn't just a one-time thing now. It's an epidemic."

"Oh, my."

The telephone line scritched and scratched like he'd put his hand over the mouthpiece, but she still caught a word here and there. . . . . fraud. . . boss. . . no promotion. . . bonus. . .

While waiting for him to make up his mind about what he would do, she stacked the files she no longer needed in preparation for filing. In an attempt to keep her investigation low key, she'd done her own retrieval, planning to return the files where she found them. No point in alerting the guilty employee that she was on to him. Or her.

Because honestly, at this point, she had no clue who was involved. Or if they even worked for this office. She could be smiling at the thief at the water cooler. Or it could be the woman who followed them from the break room. Heck, it could be Ted Wilson himself. Which would explain why he was so hesitant to involve law enforcement.

"Carly? Are you still there?"

"Yes, Ted." She set her notes inside a blank file folder to protect them from prying eyes. "Come to terms with the scope of this project?"

"I never had a problem with the scope. I simply didn't understand the impact. But yes, go ahead and call the FBI. See if they can have somebody here today. I don't want to wait another minute to get on top of this."

She disconnected the line and made her call. The closest office was in Portland, but, after a ten-minute wait on hold, she learned there was a cybersecurity expert on his way back to the city from a conference. He was less than thirty minutes from Bear Cove, and could divert there to look into the situation. She advised Ted, who told her the insurance investigator would arrive at about the same time, so they set up a meeting for six o'clock in the conference room.

Sad she wouldn't get home in time to see her favorite game show over the dinner hour, she strolled down the hall to Mike, even though she doubted he'd commiserate with her. He thought the game show boring and repetitive, while she insisted the benefits included better spelling skills, which naturally led to better reading skills, as well as exercise from laughing.

She wrapped her arms around his neck and rested her chin on his head as he sat at his desk while she filled him in on the upcoming meeting. "I think we have time to run down to the hospital cafeteria for a quick bite."

"You go ahead." He peeked up at her. "I need to finish this one last thing and then—"

She chuckled. Her husband was nothing if not predictable. "I know. Send one more email." His electronic communications were legendary in their family. One more email could take thirty minutes or more. "Then maybe instead I'll wait and you can take me out to dinner."

He turned back to his computer. "Sure. Eat in or take out?"

"How about delivery?"

"I don't know. The fries will be—"

"Soggy. I know. Just the way I like them." Just thinking about the malt vinegar-soaked potatoes made her mouth water. "You've got a date."

She left the room and headed for the director's office. Once she learned the location of the conference room, she'd wander the hallways for a few minutes before picking Mike up. Stretching her legs would help clear her mind. Make her sharp for the meeting with the FBI agent and the insurance investigator.

And maybe—just maybe—along the way she'd see the woman who followed them earlier.

And maybe—just maybe—she could get answers from her to questions.

Such as why she thought it necessary to ignore her in the break room then shadow her in the hallway.

$ $ $

Mike settled into a high-backed chair in the conference room and clasped his hands behind his neck as he eyed the other occupants of the room. Ted Wilson, the hospital director, sat in the chair at the head of the table.

*Typical power position. Wonder why he's claiming the lead spot?*

Perhaps he didn't want to be outdone by the federal agent who just entered the room.

Not that the man flashed his badge or anything as gauche as that. No, the military-style haircut, reflective sunglasses, dark suit, and oversized briefcase that he thunked on the table screamed FBI.

Or some other agency accustomed to subterfuge.

Mike found it ironic that an organization that prided itself on getting at the truth often relied on half-truths and innuendoes to get people to open up to them.

Mike gave a curt nod in the agent's direction. The agent's gaze, still hidden by his sun specs, slid over him and landed on the man in the seat of authority. Mike didn't move another muscle, interested in the power dance playing out before him. If he were a betting man, Mike would place his money on the Fed.

But then Wilson surprised him. "I am a punctual man, Agent. I expect others to be punctual."

Wilson glanced at the clock at the far end of the room. The clock which only he could see without turning around. Mike noticed that oddity as soon as he entered the room. Usually clocks were placed so those contributing to the meeting kept an eye on how much time remained in their presentation to a supervisor or higher-up.

Apparently Wilson applied a different branch of management

psychology.

Without moving, Mike slyed his eyes over to the agent, expecting a gruff response that would put Wilson in his place. After all, the man was asking for help in a criminal investigation involving his hospital and his employees. Any sane person would adopt a modicum of humility.

But not Wilson.

However, the agent dipped his head. Submission? Deference? Or simply to lull the director into a false sense of security? "Thank you, sir, for the reminder. I received notice of this meeting—" He thrust out his right hand then drew his fist toward his chest, exposing his wristwatch. "Exactly forty-nine minutes ago. I was sixty-three miles out."

"Thank you, Agent, for your acknowledgement. It seems that the one furthest away managed to arrive sooner than those who were closer." Wilson eyed Mike, who shrugged. "Do you know where your wife is?"

Time to remind the man who needed whom. "I don't know where my *wife* is, Ted. But I believe *your* forensic accountant is arriving now."

Carly paused in the doorway, and he waved her in, then sat forward and patted the chair beside him. She scooted around the table big enough to seat a couple dozen people and slid into the chair. "Sorry I'm late. I got lost."

Wilson grunted, and the Fed sat.

She leaned closer to him, her hair tickling his cheek. "What's going on?"

"I'll tell you later."

"Everybody here?"

"Not quite. The insurance investigator must be coming from Anchorage."

She peered at him, her brow drawn down in confusion. "Huh?"

"Later."

Movement in the doorway caught his attention, and he turned in that direction.

Bob Powell, their across-the-street neighbor, entered. He hesitated as he took in the agent and the director, and when his gaze lit on Mike, Mike stood and reached across the table to shake his hand. After all, they'd spent a pleasant evening at his home recently.

But the man didn't acknowledge the gesture, and when he moved on to Carly, Mike was certain electricity passed between them. Not the friendly recognition kind of shock, either.

No, siree. Bob's reaction was pure a billion-watt lightning strike kind of electricity.

Which might explain Carly's reaction at the party. Mike hadn't pried, but Carly definitely couldn't wait to get out of there. Which was unlike her. She usually liked people.

Except when she didn't.

And in this case, Bob Powell's half-sneer reverberated with open animosity.

Mike sighed. What had Carly done this time?

Truly, he couldn't let her out of his sight. Not even for five minutes at a housewarming party.

Then again, if Powell had an issue with Carly, he surely didn't have one with him. So why an iceberg-sized rebuff instead of just a cold shoulder? Perhaps he should give the man the benefit of the doubt. Surely he'd met a number of people in recent days. First in the neighborhood, then at his place of employment, and now here at the hospital. Called in on what should have been his day off. Maybe Wilson intimated he and Carly called this meeting on a Saturday evening.

That could explain it.

Or perhaps he had short-term memory problems. Difficulties recalling names and faces. Wasn't there a name for a syndrome like that? Prosopagnosia or something like that? They'd watched a documentary about that a few weeks ago.

Mike stifled a chuckle. Was there a name for the inability to recall names of television shows? If so, he should nominate himself for poster child.

Powell sat next to the agent, leaving a vacant chair between them. Another bit of psychology? Aligning himself with the Fed's authority and credibility while not joining himself completely? Perhaps in the next meeting, Powell would leave two chairs' worth of space between them.

Or maybe, if they really hit it off, he'd sit in his lap.

Unable to smother the laugh this image created, he covered it as best he could with a cough.

Carly leaned in again. "Need some water?"

He shook his head, his hand covering his mouth. Otherwise, she'd see his smirk and wonder what he was on about. He regained his composure and sat back in his chair. "Sorry. I'm fine."

Wilson exhaled. "Well, now that we are all *finally* here—" He glanced around at each in turn. "We can get this meeting going. Some of us—" A pointed look at Mike and Carly this time. "Have families to go home to."

The agent leaned back in his chair and propped one booted foot on the corner of the table. "Not me. Staying in a ho-tel down the road."

The man moved up another notch in Mike's estimation.

Wilson snorted. "Be that as it may, it's been a long day, and I'm sure there are other places we'd rather be."

Mike leaned forward and clasped his hands on the table. "I'd just like to say I appreciate the FBI taking this situation seriously and sending you here so promptly."

The agent removed his sunglasses and set them on the table. "And you are?"

"Sorry. Mike Turnquist. I'm the programmer hired to look into the cybersecurity breach."

"And hopefully to correct it." Wilson peered at him. "You can correct it, right?"

Mike tossed him his most disarming smile. At least, Carly said it was disarming. "That's the plan."

Carly leaned forward. "I'm the forensic accountant hired to look into how the fraud was conducted, and its extent. Carly Turnquist."

The agent nodded. "John Backman. Sounds like you two are my kind of people."

Powell shifted in his seat. "Bob Powell, insurance investigator."

Carly tossed a smile at him. "Your company didn't waste any time putting you to work."

"I don't officially start until tomorrow."

Her smile slipped away. "Well, I for one won't have any trouble pretending you aren't here." She batted her eyes at him. "Would that work for you?"

Mike groaned to himself. Powell was likely looking for a reason to drown them with bureaucratic resistance, and the hospital director wouldn't be pleased at all if he did.

The door opened, and a woman dressed in a fishing vest, hoodie, rumpled khakis, and loafers, filled the space. At least six feet tall, her broad shoulders almost touched each side of the opening, and the numerous fishing lures stuck into the olive-green vest attested to the fact her vest was no fashion statement.

This woman was a serious fisherfolk.

She glanced around the table, nodded to Ted Wilson, then sat on the side nearest the door, two chairs separating her from Powell.

Had his reputation preceded him?

Or was she simply shy?

"Sorry I'm late. Called back early from vacation." She nodded to each in turn. "Martha Winn. IT director for the Down East Health Group. Stationed in Portland, but I happened to be down this way for a week with my family."

Carly reached across the table and the two shook hands. "Carly Turnquist. Forensic Accountant. Where were you staying?"

"At a lodge near Penobscot. Best fishing in the state."

Wilson cleared his throat. "If we can get started. You can share knitting patterns and recipes on your own time."

Martha cast a hard glance at Wilson. "This is my own time. Which I— and my family—are graciously gifting you. So put away the hard-nose attitude, Ted. We're all here for the same reason. To catch the bad guys. Or gals."

Backman rapped the table with his knuckles. "Okay. Now that we've got the pi—spitting contest out of the way, can we get started?"

$ $ $

By the time seven o'clock rolled around, Carly was more than ready to be done for the day, too. Actually, truth be told, she'd have been happy to call it quits—not in the literal sense, of course—before the meeting even got underway.

She closed the file in front of her and tucked it into her attaché case, along with her pages of notes and a list of contacts, which included the regional FBI Cybersecurity Office, gleaned from an internet search. The other participants of the meeting also exchanged business cards, and she tucked them into the pocket of her pocket.

Beside her, Mike folded his single sheet of paper and stuck it into his shirt pocket. Martha and that nice Agent Backman stood and left the room, while Bob Powell chatted across the table with Ted.

Seemed her new neighbor could be polite when he wanted to.

Just not to her.

Or, by extension, to Mike.

Who stood and reached for her hand. "Still want to order in?"

She groaned. "You've changed your mind."

"No. But you know what ordering in means. You have but one café in town that delivers but one of two items."

She gripped his hand and led the way to the elevator. "We had pizza a few days ago, so fish and chips it is."

"Deluxe, though."

The doors swished open and they stepped in. Carly leaned against the back wall. "Of course. Peas, dressing, and gravy." Her mouth watered again at the thought of soggy fries with lots of malt vinegar. And flaky Atlantic cod, likely caught fresh that day. And gravy, thick and lumpy. Just the way she liked it. "Think we could talk Victoria into including a couple sides of wings?"

"Maybe. If you're nice to her and also order a couple slices of pie."

"We'll buy whatever is left, since it's so late."

"You'll be her best friend forever if you do that."

"Yeah. Unfortunately, it'll probably be apple. Not my favorite."

He waggled his eyebrows at her as the lift came to a halt at the main floor and the doors opened. "But we have butter pecan ice cream to go on top."

She moaned. "And sharp cheddar. So it's all healthy."

He laughed. "Right, so long as you ignore the gazillion calories."

She mock-punched him. "Don't take all the fun out it."

The humidity struck her in the face when they stepped out the doors into the driveway of the hospital, and Carly wished they'd driven instead of walked. Still, it was just two blocks or so to the joint promise of home, and dinner, and relaxation. Even if that was mostly uphill.

She shrugged back her shoulders, hefted her attaché case in one hand, and clasped Mike's hand in hers, then stepped boldly forward. "Why do you think Bob Powell doesn't like me?"

"He seemed nice enough before the party." He slowed and peered at her, eyebrows drawn tight, resembling a drunken caterpillar. "What did you say? Or do?"

"Nothing. I went to the kitchen, and he came in. We chatted."

Mike stopped, forcing her to do the same. "You didn't accuse him of anything, did you?"

"I don't know him well enough to think he might have done something wrong." She sighed. "There was something strange, though."

Mike groaned and began walking again. "I knew it."

"I looked in his fridge for cream for my coffee."

"Not everybody appreciates people poking into their stuff."

"I wasn't poking." Well, maybe that wasn't quite a hundred percent true, but it was a small intrusion. "After all, he was hosting a party. It wasn't like I breezed into his house and said I wanted to do a fridge inspection."

"Okay. Granted you looking in his refrigerator wasn't strange, what was?"

"He made a comment about my Kenmore fridge and ten kinds of cat food."

"So?"

"How did he know I have a Kenmore? Or a cat? Or that I spoil him?"

"A guess?"

"Maybe one of those three details. Not all three, though. I mean, what are the odds of guessing three different facts about a person he'd only talked to one time before?"

"Maybe you mentioned it then."

This time Carly drew them to a halt. "Maybe the cat. Maybe that I spoil him by offering him a choice of food. But not the fridge." She frowned. "Besides, I know we didn't talk about anything like that."

"So maybe he's psychic. Or talked to James. Or one of the other neighbors who knows us."

"Maybe." She continued walking, putting a little more effort into it since they were now at the bottom of the hill leading up to their street. The exertion made talking sketchy if she wanted to keep up with Mike's longer legs. "I think it's mysterious."

Mike sighed. "Not another mystery. We have to work with this guy."

"Fine. I'll keep my meerschaum pipe and deerstalker cap out of sight."

But that didn't mean she couldn't investigate their neighbor.

After all, if none of Mike's suggestions panned out, how did Bob Powell know those details of her life?

And what else did he know?

But more importantly, why would he feel the need to ferret out this information?

Chapter 7

First think Monday morning, Carly called Chief Donovan from her kitchen. "Hi, Chief. Wondering if you heard anything about James?"

"Nothing yet. I'll let you know if I do."

"His car hasn't been sighted either? It's pretty unique."

A sigh carried over the line. "Do you know how many old blue cars there are on the roads in this part of the country?"

"Not many. Either the salt in the air from the ocean or the salt in the chemicals on the highways in winter eats them from the inside out. You should know that, Chief."

"Not much need for chemicals in Florida."

Right. She'd forgotten that. "Well, you know what I mean. How many are there? Ballpark?"

"A thousand in Maine alone, give or take. And he could be anywhere." Another sigh, this one long and drawn out like a whisper in a graveyard. "Face it, Carly. He doesn't want to be found."

She gritted her teeth. "I'll agree that somebody doesn't want him found, but I don't think it's James. We've lived next door to him for many years, and he's never just gone off without telling one of his neighbors when he expected to return."

"Which means—"

"Which means he didn't intend to be gone overnight."

"Because—"

"Because otherwise he'd have said something. I was there, in his house, the day before he left. He never said anything about going away for a few days. All he said was—"

She paused. Should she mention the lottery winning? If this was just James taking time for himself, and he learned she told anybody about the money, he'd be angry. And rightly so.

As the chief said at one point, James had every right to take a vacation.

Still, if he was hurt or sick, he needed finding quick.

She made her decision. James' safety was more important than being best buddies. She'd risk his ire.

"Chief, there's something I neglected to tell you last time."

The squeak of the officer's chair hung heavy in her ear. "There usually is, Carly." Fingers drummed on a desk. "Why do people think it's okay to withhold information from the police, but as soon as they think we're keeping something back from them, they claim their constitutional rights or some other claptrap?"

Carly rolled her eyes. He was right, of course—a fact she'd never admit to his face. But all this melodrama was not going to find James. "I learned this in confidence. I wasn't sure—and I still don't know for a fact—that this has anything to do with his disappearance."

"He hasn't disappeared. He isn't missing. He's an elderly man who has been gone from home for a few days without telling every Nosey Nellie in the neighborhood first."

"Do you want to hear what I'm going to share? Or not. Because I can keep it to myself."

"Go ahead. Probably has no bearing on where he is."

"James won the lottery on Wednesday night."

"Right. So did I. Ten bucks. What's that got to do with him being gone?"

Men could be so obtuse. "No, he won The Lottery." She waited a couple of heartbeats. "You know, the two million dollars?"

The chief whistled a single drawn-out note. "Wow. Imagine that. Bear Cove sold a winning ticket. I mean, what are the chances?" A pen tapped the desk this time. "Let me write this down." Shuffling through pages. "Go ahead. Tell me again."

"He won the lottery. I was with him. I double-checked and triple-checked the numbers. Then Mike talked to him about waiting a few days until the media hubbub died down, but James was adamant. Said he wanted his money. Didn't trust the lottery commission or the banks. Was going to take it in cash."

"Doesn't sound good. Did he tell anybody else?"

Carly leaned against the kitchen counter. This might be a longer call than she originally thought. Maybe she'd get a cup of coffee to go with the leftover cinnamon buns from yesterday. "I don't know." She sidled over to the coffee maker, but the phone cord wouldn't reach the fridge where she stored the sweet treat. She'd have to get an extension to rectify that problem. "The last time I saw him—make that the last time I talked to him—he'd just gotten off the phone with somebody he called a financial advisor."

"Get a name?"

"He wouldn't tell me. Seemed cagey about the whole thing. I asked for the guy's contact information so Mike and I could talk to him about our finances. Said he didn't have the number because the guy called him. Which I thought was sketchy. When I brought up his discussion with Mike, James said he would think about it. That was late Thursday. Friday morning he drove out early. Wouldn't even make eye contact with me."

"Maybe he got himself scammed and is too embarrassed to come back home."

"If he did, he has nothing except his house, his car, and his retirement. He'd need somewhere to live. Friends around him."

The chair squeaked again, and in the background, a telephone rang. "Let me check into this and I'll get back to you. With no known family and all that money, James is now an at-risk senior." A long pause ensued, and Carly thought she might have gotten disconnected. Then the chief cleared his throat. "And if he picked up even part of his winnings, he's also at risk for mugging or robbery."

"He insisted he wanted cash. We guesstimated that present value minus taxes would net him more than seven hundred thousand dollars."

Another long whistle. "A lot of money. I'll get back to you."

Carly eyed the refrigerator. The cinnamon buns called to her. "I'll be here at home waiting for your call."

She hung up the phone and headed for the fridge when Mike paused in the doorway.

He quirked his chin toward the telephone. "Who was that?"

She filled him in on her discussion with the chief as she retrieved breakfast and popped the container into the microwave. "Light breakfast today. Early dinner and snacking for supper. Sound okay?"

He sniffed the air, a smile lifting the corners of his mouth. "Is that you smelling so sweet?"

She pulled the plate from the microwave and set it on the table. "You silver-tongued devil, you."

They sat and sipped coffee and devoured cinnamon rolls while waiting for the chief to call. Which he did, just as they finished their second cups. Carly answered the call and held the handset between her and Mike so he could hear the conversation as well.

"Carly, I called the lottery commission. They confirm he picked up his check. And I called the bank, even though it's not open yet. Explained the situation, and the bank manager said James came in Friday morning with the check and wanted it cashed. Said he called in and ordered it the previous day, but it wasn't in yet. Expecting the shipment at noon. The manager said James sat in the lobby, drinking their coffee and eating their cookies, until the cash arrived."

"Then what?"

"James insisted he wanted the cash in tens and twenties, which they produced. He put it into an old-fashioned suitcase that looked like it came from a museum, then left. Last they saw, his car headed up the street and out of town."

"Did he say anything about his plans for the money?"

"The manager let me talk to the teller, who said he was kind of quiet. When she asked if he was planning on taking a vacation, he said he was. To Hawaii. With three friends. But I checked the Bangor and Portland airports, and no James Norwood booked a flight anywhere. Also checked Boston and NYC. Nada."

Sounded like James. He remembered the clerks at the stores just like he said he would.

The chief interrupted her thoughts. "The bank manager also talked to him. Advised him no credible financial advisor would ask for cash. They would accept an official check or a wire transfer. But he said he didn't trust banks and wanted his money in his own hands."

"Which is kind of ironic. What did he think the advisor would do with the money? Likely deposit it."

"True. But he hinted to the manager that he had a line on a ground-floor investment that was a sure thing."

Carly groaned. "Oh, I never like the sound of that."

The chief chuckled. "I hear you. But just think of the money you could have made if you bought into one of those computer giants when they first started up? Shares have like quadrupled."

"True. I'm still not convinced, though."

"Understood. Now that we know about the money, I'll get on that BOLO. Likely it's something as simple as that old clunker of his broke down somewhere along the highway, and he's holed up waiting for repairs."

"I hope so, Chief."

Carly hung up then turned to face Mike. "What do you think?"

"I agree with you."

"About what? And wait." She dug in the junk drawer and pulled out a pencil then crossed the kitchen to the calendar on the wall. "Let me write this down."

"Don't be silly. We agree lots of time about stuff and you don't make a big deal about it."

"But this time involves a mystery. One that you said just a few days ago didn't even exist."

"I'm not agreeing there is a mystery. I am saying we were right to worry about James."

"We?" She scribbled on the space for the day. "So it's okay if I look around?"

He sighed. "You were going to do that whether I agreed or not."

"True. But at least this way, when I find out something, you won't be so aggravated."

He shook his head. "Carly, you are a—"

She stopped him from finishing his sentence by planting a kiss on his lips, then she stepped back and smiled up at him. "I know. A full time job."

$ $ $

While Mike worked in his office, Carly figured a quick trip to the grocery store would be in order. She needed a few things, including bananas and milk, and there was the clerk James promised the vacation to. Maybe she could kill two birds with one stone.

She shivered and rubbed her bare arms. Images of James and killing shouldn't be in the same thought.

After calling down the hallway she was headed out on a grocery run, she backed out of the driveway and navigated the short drive to the local store up on the highway. Not technically inside the town limits, a lot of discussion preceded the issuance of a permit to build. Many townsfolk were concerned about loss of business in the downtown section proper. After much negotiation and many town meetings, those in power concluded the store wouldn't impact existing shops very much, because there weren't many to begin with. Apart from the local pharmacy—and who would trust anybody except Mr. Olson to prepare a prescription, or Mrs. Olson to recommend a shade of lipstick or hair color?—and the bakery—and everybody agreed nobody in their right mind preferred store-bought cookies over handmade—the town granted the permit to build and operate.

Carly pulled through a parking space and eased her car to a halt, then grabbed a cart from the nearby corral before heading inside. Secretly, she loved all the eye candy—likely because she loved food. Aisles so tall she couldn't see over, filled with dozens of choices of everything she wanted to buy, and more beside. Fresh produce, some bins containing food she'd never even heard of. Exotics brought in from places she'd never visit. Maybe in addition to bananas, she should get something different today.

She strolled the vegetable section and chose a salad mix containing kale and shredded beet, then ventured over to the fruit bins where she retrieved her bananas, several yellow apples that weren't Golden Delicious, and, of course, her favorite—Granny Smith. Blueberries for muffins tomorrow, and perhaps something called a tangelo—a cross between a tangerine and a minneola? She wasn't certain, but it sounded good, and looked kind of funky with its orange skin and cone head design. She set the net bag into her car.

Along the way, she nodded to several other customers who she recognized but didn't know personally, until she almost ran into Mavis, the postmistress. If anybody knew what was going on in Bear Cove, it was her.

Not to mention the fact the older woman lived in the house on the other side of James.

Carly eased her cart back from the older woman's ankles. "Sorry. Not watching where I was going."

Mavis smiled, the wrinkles at the corners of her eyes and mouth now canyons. "No worries, dear. Today I'm just an old woman tottering about, looking for a bargain."

In the Money

Carly held up her bag of tangelos. "I'm trying something new this week. It's so easy to get stuck in a rut."

Mavis nodded, her double chin wagging in time with her words. "The only difference between a grave and a rut is the dirt in your face."

Another mention of death. Another shiver.

Carly pasted on a smile. "Nice weather."

*How lame.*

"Yes. Summer is short, so I like to enjoy every minute."

"Do you have the day off?"

"Cutting back my hours, I am. Half-time now." Mavis made a sliding movement with one hand, her bright pink nail polish flashing. "Easing into retirement."

Something in her downcast look and slumped shoulders communicated loud and clear she wasn't quite ready—or happy—with the plan.

Time to change the subject and maybe cheer up the old dear at the same time.

Killing two birds—no, no more thinking about death.

"Your garden looks lovely this year. I wish I could get my peonies to grow like yours." Carly nudged her next-to-next-door with an elbow. "Maybe I could hire you next year as my personal gardener." She leaned closer. "This could be a new career for you."

Mavis waved off her words. "Pshaw. Nobody would pay me to grow a weed like a peony."

"I bet you know lots about growing flowers. I have a black thumb. Kill almost everything I plant."

"Yes, I've heard that." When Carly raised her eyebrows in question, the woman hurried on. "Not that I listen to gossip, mind you. But folks sometimes comment on your straggly coneflowers. Or your run-amuck capflowers." She tempered her words with a half-smile. "There are some very particular gardeners in our neighborhood."

Yes, Carly recalled that from discussions about whether pansies or petunias were better suited for the civic garden boxes along Main Street. Deciding to use equal numbers of both barely averted World War III. The pro-pansy and pro-petunia factions made certain every year that there truly was equal numbers, even going so far as to toss out an extra two or three plants of the opposing choice.

Carly sighed.

*Some people and their children.*

And now for another neck-snapping change of topic.

"James has some lovely anemones in his yard. Is he the gardener?"

Mavis shook her head. "Yes. So sad about his wife. He really misses her."

"They were married a long time." Carly eased her cart out of the way of a harried mother with three toddlers in the cart and followed closely by two more. "And they never had children."

"No." Mavis stared after the small family as it turned a corner, their jabbering and crying diminishing considerably. "And he just rattles around in that house by himself."

"Do you see him often?"

"Oh, we usually have coffee a couple of times a week. Sometimes I'll bring over a movie and we'll watch it together." She peered at Carly. "Just friends, you know."

"Oh, of course. I never thought different."

Another squint then a huff. "Well, I don't know why you mightn't. Aging isn't the same as getting old, you know. You young ones think you have the patent on love and romance."

Carly gulped. "That wasn't what I meant."

A sniff. "Well, we have coffee every Tuesday and Thursday morning. Saw him Tuesday, but he said he was busy on Thursday. Which seemed strange. We've met every week since before his wife died. We three loved our chat, and we ended up scheduling things around that time." Mavis blinked a couple of times. "Maybe it's more important to me than to him."

"You're a good friend, Mavis. I'm sure your commitment is a comfort to him."

"Maybe. Maybe not."

"I talked to him on Thursday morning, and he said he had an appointment. Practically ran me over when he backed that land yacht of his out the drive."

Mavis chuckled, almost erasing the crinkled skin on her face, but doing nothing to diminish her second chin. "Sure sign he's got something on his mind. I wouldn't take it personally."

"So, have you seen him or talked to him since?"

"No." The postmistress's brow pulled down, and she chewed on a fingernail. "Now that you mention it, his car hasn't been there since Thursday. Which is strange."

"Why?"

"When I talked to him on Tuesday, he didn't mention plans to go anywhere."

Should she mention the lottery? Better not. It was one thing for the police to know, quite another for a nosey neighbor to broadcast it all over town.

Carly gripped the handle of her shopping cart. "Well, if you hear from him, let him know I was asking after him."

"I will. And if you see him first, let him know I've been taking in his newspaper." Another frown. "Also strange. He always lets me know if he won't be around to pick it up. Even if he goes out early, I'll get it for him. He didn't ask me to, but when I saw them piling up, I thought I'd better. No point in telegraphing there's nobody home."

"What about his mail? I noticed it was accumulating."

"He always has me hold that at the post office. I'd forgotten about that. Strange, as I said."

"Agreed. Nice chatting with you. And think about that job offer for next year."

Mavis snorted and pushed her cart in the opposite direction, heading for the rear of the store, while Carly opted to cut her shopping trip short as soon as she picked up milk. Mike would soon wonder where she'd gotten to, and she did have work she needed to complete.

But before she returned to locating information on the breach at the hospital, she had another mystery to solve: had anybody else heard from James since last Thursday?

In the Money

## Chapter 8

Mike glanced at the clock after the third ring of the phone.

*Where was Carly? Strange she's not answering.*

*Did she go out?*

Thinking maybe it was her, he snatched up the handset. "Hello?"

"Mike, it's Ted from the hospital. We just had another patient contact us about some strange charges on their credit card. Apparently it's a new one they opened specifically to pay for a recent hospital stay. Something about no interest or payments for a year."

"Oh, this is good. Now we can narrow down when the information was stolen." Mike jotted the information on a slip of paper. "Great. I'll let Carly know, too. She's been working furiously on the project." Never mind she wasn't at her desk right now. Plus he had no clue as to where she might be. "I plan to come over this afternoon."

"Good. I think our guys in IT are a little nervous about the hacker. They keep looking at each other like they're not sure but it might be one of them."

"That happens. Pretty common, actually."

"You've seen it before in cases like this?"

Mike chuckled. "All the time. Folks think they know the people they work with, but they really don't."

"Do you think it could be somebody on the inside?"

"Pretty sure it is. The breach wasn't closed in the computer system, and if it's still going on, it's important to keep it on the hush. I don't think it's in IT. I suspect it's either in Finance or somebody higher up. Middle management, most likely."

"Any idea who I should look for?"

"Leave that to me." Mike pictured Ted going off half-cocked like the Lone Ranger or something. "We'll ferret them out. They're bound to make a mistake at some point. Get too greedy. Call for a payment."

"Should I alert the patient insurers?"

"Only the ones you know you can trust. Tell them not to pay any more invoices without talking to you first."

"Will do. Thanks. You've set my mind at ease. See you later today."

Mike ended the call but sat for several minutes until the steady drone reminded him to hang up. Still no Carly. He sighed. If she didn't return soon, he'd have another missing person on his hands.

The question was: how long to wait?

He shook his head. Maybe a better question was: how long did it take her to get into trouble?

Knowing Carly, she already had too much of a lead on him in that department.

He turned back to his desk. He had a lot of work to do, and not much time. If she didn't show up by dinner, he'd go looking for her.

Until then. . .

But as much as he determined to work, his mind kept wandering to his wife. And what she was involved in. Strange how she wasn't content unless she had at least two mysteries going on at the same time.

Well, she certainly had her hands full now. First James, and now the breach at the hospital.

She should be ecstatic.

Him? Not so much.

The turning of the lock in the front door caught his attention, and he bounded out of his chair and trotted down the hallway as Carly entered and tossed her purse on the sofa then set a couple of grocery sacks on the floor.

"Oh, Mike. Glad you're here. Have I got something to tell you."

Obviously she hadn't worried one minute about him.

He crossed his arms over his chest. "It better be good."

She didn't even have the good grace to blush. "Oh, it is. You'll never believe—"

"Coming from you, I probably will." He rolled his eyes. "Who have you been pestering now?"

She stopped in her tracks. "Pestering? Me?"

He gathered her into his arms. "Yes, you." She melted against him, like she belonged there. He rested his chin on the top of her head. "I was worried about you."

She leaned back and stared up at him. "I was never in any danger."

"Did you tell me you were going out?"

"I called to you as I headed out the door."

"Did I answer?"

"I thought so. A grunt, or something."

He kissed her forehead. "A grunt or something."

She stepped out of his embrace and mock-punched him. "C'mon, Mike. You're not a kid. I don't have to do the two-fingers-look-me-in-the-eyes thing, do I?"

"No. But something more than a grunt would be good." He picked up the groceries and peered into the bags as he led her into the kitchen. "Sit and we'll have a snack while you tell me all about your adventures."

"Not adventures." She sat and toyed with the salt and pepper shakers while he set the coffee maker to brew. "No more cinnamon buns. Sorry."

"Since you went shopping, you could have picked up more." He shrugged and set the bags on the counter. "Nothing interesting here."

She chuckled. "You wouldn't say that if you wanted cereal. Milk and bananas both. Must-haves for cold cereal. A salad for dinner. Fruit."

"True." He stepped to from the fridge. "I'll put the milk away." After pouring their coffee, he sat. "So, spill the beans, Bean Counter."

She winced over her cup at him. "You know I hate that."

"I know. But you had me worrying about you."

"Not much. You don't look like you've got one more wrinkle or worry line than when I left."

"Talk."

She leaned forward and set her coffee down. "So I went to the grocery store and talked to Shannon, the clerk who sold James his ticket."

"And?"

"And, I'm amazed at how many people live in this town that I don't know."

Would she never get to the point? "Bear Cove might be small, but it's like a river. People always flowing in and out. Carry on."

Another sip. "Well, Shannon is doing a gap year."

"A what?"

"She graduated high school last year, and now she's trying to save money so she can go to college."

"What does this have to do with James?"

She batted her eyes several times before setting her cup down. "Well, I wouldn't have known all this if I hadn't gone looking for information about him."

"As interesting as all this might seem to you, I have work to do." He glanced at the clock on the stove. "And so do you."

"Okay. Synopsis. But you'll might miss the best parts. She wants to do veterinary sciences at the community college in Riverdale next year. And she has her first boyfriend. And do you know what she told me?"

"No doubt after you pestered her with questions."

More bats of the eyes. "I did not. But I saw a ring on her right hand, and I asked about it. She said she and her boyfriend both took a vow of chastity. And they're really struggling, but they're holding true to their promise to each other." One corner of her mouth lifted. "Isn't that sweet?"

"A tough decision to make, given today's culture." He sighed. "We weren't so great with that, were we?"

She reached across the table and covered his hand with hers, stroking his thumb with her own. "No, we weren't. But we knew we were getting married. These kids don't know that for sure yet."

"Even so, I'm glad the kids never asked us about that."

"Me, too. You know how it is. Kids think their parents don't do that kind of thing. Unless they're trying to have a baby."

Tears gathered at the corners of her eyes, and her voice hitched on that last word. Mike's heart dropped to his toes. If he had one regret, not having a baby with Carly was it. But it wasn't for lack of trying. Apart from that one time about three years ago, however, she didn't mention it. And then Bradley came along—a surrogate son, nephew, and grandson rolled into one.

Time to change the subject. "So where else have you been this morning?"

"Oh, I didn't finish my story about Shannon."

She'd recovered her composure nicely. "Continue."

She released his hand and leaned back, triumph written all over her face in the form of a grin and one eyebrow quirked almost to her hairline.

"She hasn't seen James or heard from him since she sold him the ticket on the Monday before the drawing."

"Did you tell her he won?"

"No. That's his news to share."

"Okay. So what did you do next?"

"How do you know there's more?"

He smiled. Did she think he was an idiot? Strike that question—or at least, he was smart enough to never ask it out loud. "Because he had three tickets. Which he always buys at different locations, on different days. Every time I saw him, he told me his routine."

She sighed. "Fine. Next up was Joyce, the woman at the corner store up on the highway."

"There's a corner store on the highway?"

"Attached to the truck stop." She smacked his hand. "Seriously, do you not live in this town?"

"That truck stop isn't in this town."

"True. Anyway, Joyce is a lot like me."

"Nosey, prone to getting into trouble, and delinquent in her duties?" His smile softened his words but he hurried on to make sure she knew he was kidding. "Beautiful, sexy, and a great cook, too?"

Another smack. "Be serious. She's also grandmother, and has a son and a daughter. And she was in banking, so we have a lot in common."

"She's quite a bit older, though, isn't she?"

"I thought you said you didn't know her."

"Never said that. Besides, you and I get along so famously, I like to keep track of women like you in case, you know. . . "

"In case what?"

"Nothing." Uh-oh. He was treading on thin ice here. In August, no less. "Continue."

"She and her husband retired to Bear Cove to be near their grands. She said she hasn't seen James, either. Or talked to him."

"And the third person?"

"You're rushing me."

He settled back in his chair, his coffee cooling on the table in front of him. He clamped his lips together and made a zipping motion across his mouth.

She drew a breath. "Okay, so Joyce had nothing new to add. Next up was Harold, at the gas station. In town. Same story. Nothing."

Mike unzipped his lips. "May I ask a question?"

"Go ahead."

"What's Harold's story?"

She leaned in again, clasping her hands together. "Glad you asked. He's in high school. Saving money for college. Wanted to hedge his bets, so he enlisted in the Navy, too. If he gets into a college first, he won't get called up. But if he can't get enough to go to college, he'll use his GI benefits later on."

"What does he want to study?"

"I don't know. I didn't ask, and he didn't say."

"Hmmm. Interesting. Something strange here."

Her brow pulled down and she tipped her head to one side. "How so?"

"You not cross-examining him until he 'fesses up."

She studied him for several heartbeats before a smile tickled her lips. Her very kissable lips, by the way. "You're teasing me."

"Yes, I am."

"But now that you mention it, there was something a little strange about my conversations with them."

He groaned. "Can't you simply say you had a delightful time pestering these poor clerks and leave it at that?"

"First of all, I didn't pester. They seemed happy to talk about themselves. And they all love James." She drummed the table with her close-cut nails. "Which is what's kinda strange."

"What could be weird about that? James can be most likeable."

"It wasn't that. It's just that it was like they all got together and rehearsed what to say if anybody asked about James."

"How so?"

"All three said the same thing."

"And that's strange because?"

"I specifically asked Shannon if James called. She said—and I quote—'I haven't seen James since he bought his ticket.' I didn't think much of it at the time. But then Joyce and Harold said the same." She peered at him. "Doesn't it seem funny to you that three unrelated people should use the same phrase to answer my question? People don't tend to over-answer a question."

"Over-answer?" He chuckled. "I think you're over-analyzing this too much."

She leaned forward and touched his arm. "Seriously, Mike. I asked if James called, and they all said they hadn't seen him."

"You think they're lying?"

"Maybe. But why would they?" She sat back and rested her clasped hands in her lap. "Unless he asked them to say that if somebody came asking questions."

Mike picked up his own half-full mug and her now-empty one and carried them to the sink to rinse. "I think you're reading too much into this. I'm sure there's an easy explanation."

"Such as?"

"Well, you assume these three are unrelated. But they could be family. Or friends. It's a small town. Maybe they eat lunch together." He turned to face her. "Forget it. Now back to work."

She came up behind him and wrapped her arms around his waist, her fingers flicking as though she handled the cups. "Is that all you think about?"

He turned within her embrace and pulled her close. "No, it's not all I think about. And it's definitely not even what I think about most."

She planted her hands against his chest and pushed. "Mike Turnquist, you are incorrigible."

He waggled his eyebrows. "Yes, I am."

$ $ $

Half an hour later, Carly fluffed her hair. Just another of the benefits of working from home was the opportunity to take a break with the love of her life.

She giggled. If asked what she did with her time, she definitely wouldn't include *that* in her list of activities.

But now they had work to do. *Real* work, as Mike would insist. Off to the hospital to take another poke through their billing records and bank accounts. She paused to flip an errant lock of hair from her eyes while compiling a mental to-do list: chat up the employees in the billing department. Check on when the last internal audit was completed. Get bank statements to verify billings against payments.

She snapped her fingers. Oh, yes. Check for long-term outstanding receivables. Sometimes an indication something was amiss telegraphed itself in unpaid billings from astute insurers who noted the double or triple charge for the same service. Most often, these requests for payment for ignored because the insurer assumed the invoice and the statement were the same invoice number.

Satisfied she had a day's work ahead of her—if not more—she headed toward the front door and snatched up her purse which still lay on the sofa. "Hey, Mike, I'm ready."

"Coming."

His muffled reply from their shared office at the other end of the house reminded her of how he might have missed her notification earlier, which, as if on cue, caused another flight of thought. Had anybody called on delinquent accounts? Or, for that matter, did the reported discrepancies even exist in the hospital's accounting system? If somebody fraudulently produced these billings, perhaps they were generated from a separate laptop or PC. Which made more sense. Less likely a keen receivable clerk would call or send the account for collection.

She sighed. The numerous and sundry methods folks worked fraud on others never ceased to amaze her. And a separate accounting system—like a double set of books in the old days—would sure explain why no red flags were raised prior to now.

Mike joined her and they headed for the car. Once safely buckled inside, he backed down the driveway.

Which reminded her of the other mystery on her plate—James. After narrowly missing both her and the mailbox post, he'd simply disappeared into thin air.

Except, he couldn't, could he? Not really. People weren't ghosts or mirages or vapors on the wind. They existed, even if they weren't where they should be.

No, James was very real.

Somewhere.

She simply had to find him.

Once in the accounting department, she kissed Mike and he headed down the hall for another stint in the IT room, whistling a happy tune. She smiled at his retreating back, his shoulders still straight and strong, his waist still narrow—although perhaps a teensy bit padded—these many years later. She shook her head. Life seemed so unfair. He could decide he needed to lose weight by decreasing his milk and sugar intake and poof!

The pounds fell away. Her, she could eat like a bird and still look like a Thanksgiving turkey—stuffed.

She sighed and wove her way through the cubicle maze to the workspace assigned to her. Unlocking the large bottom drawer of the desk, she extracted the stack of files left over from Saturday. Now she had a new direction: comparing receivable reports against the notes from the disgruntled patient with the credit card billing. Although Ted Wilson made it clear he believed somebody hacked into the hospital's computer system, Mike still hadn't found any evidence.

Which made sense if a non-network computer was used to produce the billings.

Chatter across the room caught her attention. Now was the time to talk to the other clerks and see what they knew, before they got busy with projects and phone calls and work. She rose and followed the sounds to the far end of the room where three women occupied stations in a cul-de-sac, their backs to each other as they faced their computers.

She scanned the nameplates atop the fabric-covered walls. SARAH, AR. MILLIE, AP. CONNIE, ACCTG. SUP.

She waited until they finished talking then nodded to each in turn. "Good morning, ladies. I won't keep you but a minute. I have a couple of questions."

Millie smiled up at her. "Can I go first? I have a conference call with the hospital payables supervisor in about ten minutes?"

Her voice rose as though asking Carly if this was true.

*Such an annoying habit.*

"Sure." She looked to Connie for confirmation. The older woman, all business in her grey, two-piece suit, nodded. "When did you have your last internal audit?"

Connie peered at the ceiling. "About eight weeks ago."

"Nothing unusual?"

"No." Connie glared at her. "I run a tight ship here. We always have perfect audits."

"What about an annual external audit?"

"The hospital sends a team in right after our fiscal year ends. In December. So they were here the middle of January or so."

"Everything good?"

"Of course."

Okay. If the audits hadn't turned anything up, she'd try another route. "Have you noticed any unauthorized people here in the department within the last six months?"

Millie thought a moment then her mouth turned down. "Don't think so. You guys?"

A mumbled *no* from Millie and a quick shake of the head from Connie made the response unanimous.

"How about unfamiliar authorized people?"

Millie's brow pulled down. "Like who?"

"Oh, maybe a new network technician. Or a maintenance worker you didn't know but assumed he was authorized?"

Millie leaned forward. "There was the AC guy a couple months ago." She leaned back in her chair, one leg bouncing. "He didn't seem to know what he was doing. And he sure didn't fix anything."

Connie shook her head. "I've seen him around the hospital since." She snorted. "The only thing he seems to know is how to wear his pants down so low you can see his underwear."

"How about a replacement for any of you?"

Sarah, her two-inch nails emblazoned with black enamel and little sparkles, straightened. "There was a guy who took over for me." She turned to the other two. "I was out for six weeks on maternity leave. Remember?"

"Oh, yeah." Connie pointed to a framed photo on Sarah's desk. "June and half of July, wasn't it?"

*Right in the time frame we're looking at.*

Carly's heart beat a little faster. Maybe now she'd get some answers. "Who was he?"

Connie shrugged. "Don't know. Sent here from head office. Knew his stuff. In fact, he was pretty sharp." She turned to Millie. "Remember his name?"

"Jordan?" A quick shake of her head. "No, that's not right. Porter? No, that was his last name. Something beginning with a G. Greg. Gary."

Connie snapped her fingers. "Gordon Porter. Right. He showed up the day Sarah started her leave. We were told head office denied our request for coverage, and then there he was." Her eyes narrowed. "Right."

Carly stepped closer. "What is it?"

"I just remembered. He had a problem with his paperwork. Said it went to the wrong hospital. Site number transposed or something. So he never got paid while he was here."

"You're right?" Millie twirled her chair. "Said he was down to eating Ramen noodles? Like it was a joke?"

Now they were on to something. "Can you describe him?"

Connie lifted one shoulder and let it drop. "Ordinary. Nothing much to remember him by, except he was good at what he did."

No, if this guy was their perpetrator, he was *very* good.

But Carly was better.

$ $ $

A warm breeze blew in through the windows as Carly drove down the highway a few hours later. After spending the morning with her head buried in files followed by a quick lunch with Mike, she needed a break.

Following a Girl Scout salute and three promises to be careful, along with a vow to not be gone long, she headed out to look for James. Once on the highway, the light traffic meant she could settle into the right-hand lane and set her speed control, letting those more anxious zoom on past.

As she drove, she pondered where James could be. If she was wrong and the older man was simply holed up somewhere enjoying his winnings, she'd feel a first-class fool.

But if he wasn't. . .

She shivered. If he wasn't, he could be in real trouble.

Maybe Mike was right, and James had car problems with his land yacht, hunkering down in a tiny hamlet waiting for parts that were almost as old as she. If so, he had to be staying somewhere. Unfortunately, there weren't many of the old-fashioned roadside motels left along the interstate. She exited at the off-ramps where she noted the occasional auto-court-style establishments, always a u-shaped structure of rooms opening to the parking lot, but nobody remembered her neighbor.

When she reached the Portland city limits, she contemplated visiting the possible places he might have stayed, but there were so many—advertising such high prices—that even with his hundreds of thousands of dollars, she doubted he'd deign to stay in any of them.

Instead, she headed home again. About twenty miles outside the city, an off-ramp accessible only from that side of the highway beckoned her—or perhaps it was the flashing neon sign advertising free coffee with fill-up. After indicating her intention to exit by turning on her signal, she disengaged the cruise control and eased off the highway, then pulled into the small gas station-restaurant combination and parked.

Easing herself out of the car, her muscles protesting, she glanced around. Looked like a quiet place today. No other vehicles around. Too far from anywhere for pedestrian traffic. Maybe this would work in her favor.

And if not, free coffee was a fine consolation prize.

She headed inside, pausing to allow her eyes from the sunshine outside. The convenience store, crowded with shelves taller than her own five foot five, reminded her of the junk drawer in her kitchen—filled to the rafters with every conceivable product a person might think they needed or wanted. Cigarettes, snacks, and cold sodas near the cash register. In a cooler on the far wall, beer and milk. Brats and wieners rotating on one of those heaters that always made the item look so good, skin blistering just so, golden brown and tasty.

Behind a counter, a lanky man with a protruding Adam's apple waited, a magazine in hand as he rested one hip on a tall stool. He gave her the ubiquitous Down East greeting—a brisk sideways nod and a click of the tongue—then went back to his article. She snagged a soda from the cooler and a bag of corn chips from the rack then set the items on the counter. Beneath a sheet of Plexiglas, the ten or so lottery tickets the station carried decorated the counter.

He rang up her snacks. "That'll be three dollars and a quarter."

She gulped. Highway robbery. Then she stifled a grin at her inadvertent joke. Wonder how many times he'd heard that one? Never mind. She was here to find out if he knew anything about James.

She handed him the correct amount. "Friend of mine stopped here couple of days ago. Said you had the coldest soda this side of the city."

"Coldest beer, maybe." He stared at her, his pale blue eyes darting back and forth as though he couldn't quite focus on her. "Don't get a lot of traffic out here."

She checked the nametag embroidered over his shirt pocket. "Seems strange, Bill, being on the highway and all."

"Ayuh. But the city growed up practically all 'round us. Used to be it ended ten miles thataway." He gestured toward Portland. "When I bought this place, twenty years ago, fifty miles was a good day's drive. Folks would stop here to fill up their tank and their cooler. Mostly campers, fishermen."

"Not so much now?"

"Nah. Folks rush on past, getting where they're going. Twenty miles is nothin'."

"So you'd remember him, maybe?"

He chewed on his bottom lip. "Let me see." His baby blues peered at her. "Older guy? Older car?"

Carly's heart quickened. This was the first sighting she knew of since James left the lottery commission Thursday morning. "That's right."

"Ayuh. Recall him. Stopped for ten dollars' worth of gas. Paid with a brand new bill. I joked and asked if he had a printin' press at home. He laughed and said he kinda did." He stretched his chin forward, reminding Carly of an old bandy rooster her grandfather once owned. "He in some kinda trouble?"

"No. Nothing like that. I'm his neighbor, and I hadn't seen him for a few days, and just—"

Bill straightened. "Hmm. Mayhaps he mentioned you. Nosey accountant lady, I think he said, lived on one side of him. And a pokey widow-woman on the other." He leaned closer again. "Which one is you?"

She chuckled. "Guess."

He stared at her a long minute then shook his head. "Nah. I'd lose either way."

Smart man. Not enough to foresee the changes coming to the city or the overtaking by the suburbs of his patch of ground, but people smart. "Which way did he head after leaving here?"

"Away from the city. Seemed to be heading home. Made a comment about talking to some folks about a trip to Hawaii." He chuckled. "Figured he was a-talkin' through his hat."

"Anything else you recall?"

"Nope."

"Was he alone?"

"Ayuh."

"Not worried?"

"Dunno about that. Seemed to have somethin' on his mind. Kept an eye on his car, I recollect that. Stood straight. Looked fine to me." He lifted one shoulder and let it drop. "Then again, he did mention having a long day. Early start is what I think he said. So maybe he found a mo-tel down the road." Another car pulled into the gas pumps and he tossed her a smile. "You're my good luck charm today. Don't often get two folks here at the same time."

She picked up her cola and chips and headed for the door. "Thanks for the information."

"No problem."

After getting into her car and buckling the seatbelt, Carly twisted off the cap of her soda and took a deep drink before starting the car and pulling onto the highway.

Next stop—whatever town came next.

And hopefully she'd find James there having the time of his life before heading to the Big Island for the vacation of a lifetime.

And if she didn't—well, she'd cross that bridge when she came to it.

# Chapter 9

The highway sign indicated the next town was two miles up the road. Although why James might choose this particular Podunk town to hole up in, she had no clue. Then again, he'd had an exciting day last Thursday. Learned he won the lottery the night before. Likely didn't sleep much. Headed out early for a two-hour drive to the big city. Visited both the lottery commission and the bank. Then headed home.

Phew! She hadn't done half that, and she was tired simply thinking about it.

Not to mention James was at least twenty years her senior.

The off-ramp came into view, and she eased her foot off the accelerator. A brand-name gas station occupied the corner where the ramp and the road leading into town intersected, so she pulled in there. After stopping the car and turning off the engine, she surveyed the area. A motel just down the road. A garage—that might be a place to check. After this place and the motel.

Judging by the line of customers in the convenience store, this business had an advantage over the previous place where Bill invested his time and money. Maybe because it was further out of the city, or perhaps because a town lay just down the road. She stepped into place at the end of the queue and waited her turn. Most seemed to be paying for fuel, adding a pack of cigarettes or a candy bar as an afterthought. Smart marketing. Maybe she should go back and suggest Bill offer a free snack with a fill-up.

She chuckled to herself. Even complimentary chocolate likely wouldn't increase his trade.

"Next." The efficient cashier with blue-lined eyes and crimson lips nodded at her. "Which pump?"

"Oh, I'm not here for gas." Carly leaned across the counter. "I wanted to ask about my friend."

The woman, identified by her nametag as Winnie, looked past her then met her gaze again, a tiny smile tickling her lips. "Invisible friend?"

Carly straightened, her cheeks heating. "Um, no. He might have stopped here last Thursday?"

Winnie sighed and rolled her eyes while the man behind Carly grunted. "We have a lot of people in and out of here every day. I likely wouldn't remember him if he was here this morning."

"Old guy but stands straight. Might have mentioned Hawaii?"

"Nope. Sorry." Again, Winnie looked over Carly's shoulder. "Which pump?"

Carly slid to one side. The line behind her was longer than the one she originally joined. Winnie was right. Lots of people. And the woman was right about another thing, too. James wasn't particularly noticeable. Unlikely he'd mentioned winning the lottery or having a suitcase full of money in his car.

Like he said, he might have been born at night, but it wasn't last night.

She exited the store and decided on her next step. She could drive up to the garage that was on the same side of the street. Or she could drive over to the motel, which meant a right turn then a left. Or she could simply wait for a break in traffic and jog over there. Leave the car here for now.

Seemed the expedient thing to do. She'd sat enough for one day. Walking a couple hundred yards would do her some good. She could boast to Mike she actually fit in a walk. Wouldn't he be proud of her?

Three minutes later, she stood in the lobby of the dingy and tired-looking motel. Or perhaps it *was* a mote, as the sign said. Like a dust mote, perhaps? The L burnt out of the neon sign outside seemed appropriate. Along with the marquis boasting of color TV and a telephone in every room.

She eyed the bell on the counter and the sign indicating she should ring for help. Always distrustful of the volume and tone—not wanting to sound too demanding or awaken the dead—she tapped on the plunger. Her efforts netted her little more than a thunk so soft she doubted a cat would hear it. She tried again with a little more effort, this time eliciting a strident ring.

Just what she hoped to avoid.

She stepped back from the counter and waited. Maybe whoever answered might think someone else rang the bell and not be irritated with her.

She could only hope.

The man who emerged from a back room could have been Bill's twin. Or at least, a close relative. Which seemed fitting. Both choosing businesses that weren't exactly in the best of locations. Hadn't they listened to their real estate agent? Or taken one of those courses offered by the Small Business Administration? Location, location, location. The three most important keys to running a successful business.

Bill's double—Joe from the sign on the counter that proclaimed him as both proprietor and manager—nodded in her direction. "What can I do you for?"

"I'm looking for my friend."

He peered at her over eyeglasses perched on the end of his nose. "We don't run that kind of place."

For the second time today, her cheeks burned. "No. He's not that kind of friend. He's actually a neighbor, a widower, and he went to Portland on Thursday, and nobody has seen him since."

He peered at her. "So you're out here looking for him out of the goodness of your heart?"

"Yes, I am, as a matter of fact. Taking time off work because I'm concerned about him."

"Nice. Don't see much of that these days. Like the Good Samaritan."

She had no idea why he'd compare her to a hospital chain, unless he knew—wait a minute. Wasn't there a Bible story about some guy who helped another man? "He was in Portland on Thursday. I know that's a few days ago, and a lot of people have come and gone through here—"

"You talking 'bout this place?" He chuckled. "We might look like a going concern, but that's only because my hair is going and I'm concerned about paying my bills."

He ran his fingers through his thinning hair as if to emphasize his point. He was right. There was a lot going.

"Older man named James Norwood." At least, she had no reason to think he wouldn't use his real name. "Likely by himself."

Joe pulled out a thin folder, licked his index finger, and flipped back about two pages before tapping the sheet. "I remember him. James Norwood. From Bean Cove?" He squinted at the page. "Nope. Bear Cove." He looked up. "My writing is atrocious."

"So he stayed here?" Her heart upped its pace, and she took a couple of deep breaths. No point shortening her life just because she was closer to finding James than she had been in the past three days. "How many nights?"

"Paid for the one. Charged him ten bucks extra because there was two of them."

"Two?"

"Him and a younger fellow. Booked a two-bed double room."

"Do you know that man's name?"

"Nope. Not required. He showed his driver's license, paid in cash, paid the security deposit, too."

Joe shifted his feet and looked away.

*He's hiding something.*

She thought over what he said but nothing jumped out as suspicious or duplicitous. "Can I see his room?"

"Been cleaned, and I had a couple in there last night. Cleaned again, ready to go."

"If you don't mind?"

Joe lifted a shoulder and let it drop. "Whatever." He led the way out of the office and to the last unit on the end of the U-shaped building. He unlocked the door and stood to one side to allow her entry. "Lock it when you're done."

She entered a small room crammed with two double beds, a television bolted to a dresser, and a bathroom so small she'd have to come outside to change her mind. A pervasive mustiness lingered, even after the recent cleaning, and the closed curtains added to the overall sense of gloom and doom.

She crossed the room—all twenty feet or so of it—and yanked open the drapes, letting the afternoon sun in. Outdated chenille bedspreads—the majority of the tufts missing—cigarette burns on the green shag carpet, yellowing stains on the ceiling, and the typical landscape painting hanging crookedly over the bed lent the place a definite has-been air.

She shuddered. She wouldn't stay here for all the tea in China.

So why would James? He had enough money to buy the entire

establishment. He could have stayed anywhere. The most expensive hotel in Portland. Or his own bed, for that matter.

And who was this younger man? How did James know him? And why were they travelling together?

Unwilling to touch any of the surfaces, she used a pen from the desk to pull open drawers. Nothing there except the Gideon Bible in the nightstand, an outdated telephone book, and the television guide.

She glanced around the room. Nothing. Not even a remote.

The TV was too old for one, apparently.

Or somebody stole it.

She stopped at the threshold of the bathroom and peeked inside. Nothing. Then through the crack at the hinges. Nothing hanging on the back of the door, either. Drawers and hooks were the two places most folks left stuff in motels. At least, in her experience. She always had Mike do a double-check before turning in their key.

Unable to avoid the inevitable, she got down on her hands and knees beside the bed. Lots of folks lost stuff under beds in motels. An errant earring. A single sock. One time, in a higher-end hotel, she'd found a pair of balled-up underwear behind a recliner when she went to plug in her laptop.

Never could tell what she might find.

Holding her breath against dust bunnies, she lifted the bed skirt and peered under. Lots of dust. A button. And—what was that?

She stretched over to pick up the item—paper—then hesitated. If this were evidence, she'd want to preserve any fingerprints on the wrapper. She glanced around the room then crossed to the ice bucket on the desk. Inside, the small plastic bag designed to hold ice. She slipped it over her hand like a glove.

Perfect.

She returned to the bed and picked up the wrapper then sat back on her feet and studied it. A wrapper. The kind that holds a bundle of money. Under the bed.

Of course, just because she found it in the room James recently occupied didn't mean he dropped it here. Anybody could have gone to the bank and withdrawn a large sum. Maybe somebody buying a car. Or a house.

It could even have been left here by a bank robber.

She turned the wrapper over. First Bank of Portland. Where the lottery commission held its account. Where James cashed his check.

With the date of the lottery drawing stamped there along with the initials of the teller who compiled the packet.

Too much of a coincidence, surely.

James not only rented this room, he rented it with somebody else.

And they opened at least one bundle of money here.

Maybe more.

Once again, reason to be concerned for her friend.

She eyed the phone on the bedside table. No, better to use her own phone. Fingerprints could still exist on the keypad that would identify James' associate or at least confirm if he made a call.

She pulled up Chief Donovan in her speed dial and hit the CALL button. While waiting for him to answer, she studied the room again. Was something out of order? She didn't think so. The room was all the signage outside and the lobby area itself promised—color TV, phone, and mid-seventies grunge.

"This is Donovan."

"Chief, it's Carly Turnquist."

A small groan met her ears, and she could almost see his eyes rolling. "What now?"

"I'm in this little town along the highway."

"If you're in jail, I'm not putting in a good word for you."

The man could be so exasperating. "But Chief—"

"Not doing it. Any words I have for you won't get you out of a pickle. Nosey. Tiresome. Troublesome. Irritating. Those are the good words. You don't want to hear the bad ones."

She needed to talk fast. "I've got a lead on James Norwood. He stayed at this hotel. In the very room I'm sitting in now."

"Great. I'll get a brass plaque and we can put it on the door. JAMES NORWOOD SLEPT HERE. Happy now?"

"No. I need you to come and see what else I found."

"Besides dust bunnies and mold?"

She blinked. "You've been here already?"

He chuckled. "No. But most motels along the highway are all the same."

"I found a bill wrapper from the bank where James cashed his check."

"Could have been there for years. Under the bed, was it?"

Doubly exasperating. Like he could read her mind or something. "Yes."

His chair squeaked as he changed positions. "Like I said, could have been there—"

"It's dated last Wednesday."

Another moan. "Why do you do that to me?"

What was he talking about? "Do what?"

"Mete out the information a bit here, a bit there. If you'd told me that up front, I might have saved all this yakkity-yak stuff."

"So you'll come and investigate?"

"No."

"No?"

"It's out of my jurisdiction." A pencil tapped on his desk. "Here's what I will do. I'll call in the local chief and ask him to assist in our search for James." A long pause. "Our unofficial search, mind you. I'm still expecting him to turn up, and I'm going to look like a horse's patootie."

"How soon can he get here?"

A long drawn-put sigh filled her ear this time. "I don't know. I haven't called him yet. I don't know how busy he is. You are likely to be on the bottom of his list."

That didn't sound like a good place to be. "Look, Chief, the sooner we find James, the sooner you'll have me out of your hair."

"Oh, Carly, you don't know how good that sounds. Promise?"

She gritted her teeth to bite back the sarcastic response dying to escape her lips. Instead, she waited. Most people didn't like silence and usually rushed in to fill the void.

The chief didn't disappoint. "Okay. I'll call him as soon as we hang up. I'll ask him for a personal favor, which means now I'll owe him one. And I'll tell him you have important business back here and could he please handle this soon. How's that?"

"Sounds great. I knew you'd come through for me. I'll wait for him in the lobby."

"Fine. Good-bye."

She returned her phone to her purse and tucked the wrapper inside its makeshift plastic evidence bag next to it. No point in it because of an over-zealous housekeeper.

Not likely that would happen here, but better safe than sorry.

So many clichés ran through her mind as she exited the room and headed for the lobby. She hoped James turned up sooner than later—although four days was already way later than she liked.

And that he was safe and sound.

Hale and hearty.

Full of vim and vigor.

But once she sat in the lopsided plastic orange chair as she waited for the officer, hope faded like the late afternoon sun over the trees. Long shadows left smudges of dark in the dirt parking lot, reminding her of fingers clawing to get out of a grave.

She shivered.

She needed to stop reading so many mysteries.

$ $ $

"Mrs. Turnquist?"

A shadow enveloped Carly's feet, and she stood from the chair where she dozed in the motel lobby, flashing back to seventh grade when she spent a good part of the year sitting outside the principal's office.

A tall man filled the doorway, the crown of his Stetson-style police hat nearly touching the top of the frame. Two fingers touched the brim. "Chief Walter Webb from Marshalltown PD, ma'am."

She extended her hand in greeting. "Carly, please."

He shook her hand then pulled a notebook and pen from his chest pocket. "Chief Donovan says you have evidence that a neighbor of yours might have run into trouble in our little burg?"

"I don't know for certain."

He gestured to the row of plastic chairs. "Let's sit and you can fill me in."

Encouraged that maybe now something would be done to find James, Carly sat and pulled the wrapper from her pocket. "I tried to be careful not to get my fingerprints all over this."

Webb produced a plastic bag from another pocket and she slid the paper in. Then he held it up to the light, eyes narrowed, before nodding and tucking the evidence into the same pocket where he retrieved his notebook. "I'll just make a note of the date and the bank." He scribbled some words then looked up. "And give me your contact information in case I have more questions."

She did, waiting again while he wrote in the book. "So you see, Chief—"

He held up an index finger and she paused. "I better talk to the manager first, please." He stood and crossed to the front desk then rang the bell.

Joe emerged. "Hi, Walt. What can I do for you today?"

"Just here to ask a few questions."

"How's the wife?"

Webb shifted his stance, shoulders relaxing. "Fine as peach fuzz, Joe. Going fishing soon?"

"Next week. Want to come with?"

The two men continued chatting about their fishing plans while Carly waited, thinking about all the things needing doing at home. She gritted her teeth.

*Uh-oh. Sounds like the good old boys network.*

After a few minutes, the two men ran out of mutual topics of interest. Webb cleared his throat softly and tapped his notebook with the pen. "Lady here is worried about her friend."

"Ayuh. Told me."

"You know anything?"

Joe tipped his head in her direction. "Like I told her. Old guy checked in. Had a younger man with him. Paid a cash deposit and room rent."

Webb wrote something down, and Carly longed to see whether he was actually taking notes or simply doodling nonsense to placate her. What she wouldn't give to peek over his shoulder. Maybe he wouldn't mind—she stood, but sat immediately when the lawman tossed her a look that screamed SIT. She sat, rehashing Joe's words around her head.

And then she remembered what she couldn't recall last time. She itched to interrupt, but the officer's broad shoulders--and big gun-- reminded her to wait her turn.

Webb shifted his weight to his other foot. "Did you see them leave?"

"Around three."

"In the morning?"

"Ayuh."

She straightened. He hadn't mentioned that when she talked to him. Then again, to give him some credit, she hadn't asked that question. Still.

Webb sighed. "And?"

"Looked to me like the old man had too much to drink. The young fella had his arm around him, propping him up." Joe leaned across the counter. "You've seen lots of that, right?"

"Sure have. Anything else?"

"Nope."

Carly couldn't stand being ignored one more minute. She stood again and in three steps crossed the small lobby. "Did either of them come in to collect the deposit?"

Joe's shoulders slumped and his gaze darted between the chief and her.

*Aha. Caught him.*

When he didn't answer, she persisted. "Well, did they?"

He met and held her gaze, his chin jutted out. Gone was the good-old-boy attitude. "Nope."

"So did you send the deposit back to James?"

Several more darted glances then he stepped away and retrieved a sheet of paper from a file.

*Interesting that he knew right where to find that.*

He set the page on the counter. "Can't hardly read the old man's writing." He tapped the paper. "See. Like I said. Looked like he was drunk."

Carly checked the page. Joe was right. A bunch of chicken scratches filled the lines for address information. "I can take the check for him. I'll wait while you make it out."

"My bookkeeper isn't in today. Leave me your phone number and I'll call you when the check is ready."

She snorted. "How about I write his address in here so you can read it?"

Chief Webb picked up the sheet. "How about you let me investigate so we can all get on with our day?"

She took a half-step back. "Fine. Carry on."

Webb tucked his notebook in his pocket. "Thanks for your help, Joe. And don't forget me next week when you head out to the lake." He turned to face her. "And thanks for your help, Carrie."

"Carly." She ground her teeth together. If this kept up, she'd need dental work. "Is that it?"

His brow drew down. "Let's see. Got your contact info. Got the wrapper."

"And you have a fishing date."

He smiled. "Yep. Not a total loss."

Maybe not for him.

But her friend James was still just as missing as before the lawman showed up.

In the Money

Chapter 10

Undeterred by Chief Webb's lack of interest in her neighbor's disappearance, Carly headed back down the highway toward home. While others might say that if the majority believes a thing, it must be right, Carly disagreed.

At least in this case.

Law enforcement's opinion of how much she stuck her nose into affairs that didn't concern her mattered little. James was still missing, and somebody knew where he was.

She reviewed the matter in her mind as she drove, keeping her eyes on the road around her. On this August Monday morning, traffic away from the city was light, so there wasn't much to track. She set the cruise control to a notch below the posted speed limit and settled into the right-hand lane—the number two lane, as she knew from studying police reports.

Fact number one: James left in a hurry Thursday morning. Destination: confirmed by his later actions—the lottery commission then the bank. After that: unknown.

Fact number two: he talked to a purported financial advisor the day before. Identity: unconfirmed. Note to self: she needed to get into his house and look for clues. Surely he'd have written down the number or name somewhere.

Fact number three: he bought gas at the station along the highway and stayed at that motel, so he made it at least this far. Could Joe have done him in? After all, the only information they had originated from the last person to see him—at least, until this point. Maybe the younger man was a fabrication intended to throw the search—and her—off the trail. Should she have stuck around and searched the place? Joe's story that the room had already been rented out didn't ring quite true with her. Seemed like a place like that wouldn't have much turnover. And the fact that the one room she wanted to see was likely contaminated from an evidential point of view struck her as more than a coincidence.

Fact number four: James' car was also missing. No sightings by highway patrol since Chief Donovan put out the notice. Although there were many old cars on the road in the area, none like that one. A land yacht if ever there was one.

So where to look next? She could spend the rest of her life stopping and talking to folks along the highways in Maine alone. And the more time that passed between last week and when she made contact with anybody who might have seen something, the less likelihood of their remembering. Or remembering correctly.

Goosebumps ran up her arms. If James was sick or injured, he could die before she found him. Carrying all that cash made him a target for every pickpocket, petty thief, and master criminal for hundreds of miles around. The lottery commission likely wouldn't sit on the news of a single winner. Instead, they'd choose to exploit how the old man, a widower from a tiny town, came in and wanted his money in cash. She could see it now, his face blazoned in newspapers and on television. Speculation about his luck. Other lottery ticket-purchasers trying to reproduce his success.

She chuckled as she rubbed her arms, one at a time. His wedding date: 4-11-53. The number of years he and Sadie were married: 42. The street number of their house: 26. Nothing magical. Nothing fantastical. Simply chance.

She returned to the case at hand. If James was hiding, his car might stick out like a sore thumb. And if somebody snatched him, they might leave his car somewhere out of sight. Or hide it in plain sight. Where cars are always parked. Where it wouldn't be noticed right away.

An airport? A shopping center? Apartment complex? Since even small towns had ordinances against leaving a car parked on a public street for too many days without moving, unlikely they'd leave the car there. And unless they rented a unit in a complex and didn't need the spot for their own vehicle, not there, either.

A large billboard announced the next town—Flatirons—and reminded her of several outlet shopping malls at the same exit. Might be a good place to check. Assuming Joe was telling the truth, and that the younger man with James was up to no good, he'd want to make a move before much more time passed.

Flatirons might be the place.

She signaled her intent to exit and clicked down on the cruise control to slow. Signs at the intersection indicated the town lay to the right, outlet shopping to the left. She'd try the town first.

She made the turn, thankful the speed limit along here was low enough she could scan the businesses. A string of new and used car dealerships dotted the main road, most filled with shiny compacts and the taller SUV's. James' car would stick out like an elephant at a tea party.

She cruised the drag, ignoring a couple of horn blasts from drivers behind who screeched out into the number one lane—the one closest to oncoming traffic—while she continued her search.

They might think her a doddering old woman or someone with nowhere better to be, but she was on a mission.

As she neared the opposite end of town and the number of dealerships and used car lots thinned, she looked for a place to make a u-turn and head in the opposite direction, when she spotted several rows of older-looking cars just off the main street. Turning at the light, she pulled into the lot. If she didn't find anything here, it would make as good a place to turn around as any.

She scanned the lot of mostly older makes and models. The perfect place to hide an old car. And sure enough, tucked between the end of a mobile home marked OFFICE and a dumpster overflowing with bald tires and dented car parts, a car identical to James' peeked out of a corner.

An overweight man clad in pants two sizes too small and three inches short stuck his head out of the office door. He tossed her a Queen-wave then headed her way, taking the steps one at a time, gripping the handrail like a lifeline.

She groaned, much preferring to look around the car on her own. Still, it couldn't be helped. She pasted on a smile and pointed. "I want to see that car over there."

The man huffed and puffed across the ten-foot expanse then extended his hand. "Name's Brad. Of Brad's Bargain Beauties." He gestured with his other hand to the sign over the trailer. "Every customer a satisfied customer."

She shook his limp-fish hand, releasing it after a single pump. "I'm not here to buy."

He blinked a couple of times before swiping at the sweat running down his forehead with the back of his hand. "They all say that."

"People come to a used car lot and say they don't intend to buy?"

"Right. Strange, huh?"

*Not really. They probably don't want to feel responsible for killing the sales guy by asking for the keys.*

"No, seriously. But I am looking for a car."

He grinned. "Well, we got cars. Take this little beauty over here for example." He waved his hand toward a rusted-out Volkswagen bug. "Original chrome and interior. Only three hundred thou' on the odometer. Hard to believe, right?"

She stared. The original paint was gone, worn down to primer. And beyond that, where the bare metal poked through. The rear bumper might have the original chrome on the iconic rounded part, but the front one was missing. And the original interior clung to the seats in shreds. She shook her head. "I know what car I want. I'm not here to buy. I'm looking for that car over there. The land yacht trying to hide behind the dumpster."

Brad's gaze followed her directions. "Don't know anything about that car. Never saw it before."

"It could have been here since last Friday. It belongs to my friend."

Brad held his hands up chest high, palms facing her. "Like I said, don't know nothing about it."

She led the way, Brad shuffling along behind. When she reached the car, she checked to make sure it was the right one. The plates were missing, but hanging from the rearview mirror was the faded Pink Panther toy.

This was definitely the right car.

She turned to the still-sweating—although likely now for a completely different reason—salesman. "Are you certain this car isn't in your inventory?"

He sighed. "Look, lady, I already told you. Besides, if it was, I'd have it out on the lot. It's probably the best car I got."

She rolled her eyes. If looks didn't count but road worthiness was his criteria, he was likely right. She gestured to the office. "Do you have a phone?"

He spread his hands wide. "Do I look like a telephone booth?"

She crossed her arms. "Do I look like I'm here for my health? I need to call the police."

He stepped back, shaking his head as he did. "If that car is stolen, I don't know—"

"Yeah, I know. Nothing." She headed for the trailer. After all, any self-respecting used car salesman would have a phone. She climbed the steps, having outdistanced him by almost twenty feet. He couldn't have stopped her if he wanted.

Inside, she spotted an old-fashioned rotary phone on the desk. She lifted the handset and dialed then introduced herself. "I need an officer to respond to Brad's Bargain Beauties. Yes, the car lot. There is a vehicle here that belongs to a reported missing person." She gave the details, including Chief Donovan's name—great, he'd be thrilled if they checked in with him. "Thanks, I'll wait here."

By this time, Brad appeared at the top of the steps and leaned heavily against the wall before gathering breath enough to make it over to his desk. He flopped into his chair, the springs protesting loud and clear.

Carly perched in the metal-framed, fabric-covered stacking chair on the opposite side of the desk and surveyed the office. Dingy grey carpet. Dark 70s-style paneling. Faded hotel-style landscapes. A girlie calendar next to a cracked mirror.

About what she'd expect from a guy like Brad.

Thankfully, tires crunched on the gravel lot in less than three minutes, and she scurried to the door, hoping it wasn't just another car turning around or a potential customer. A patrol car.

She hustled down the steps before he had a chance to change his mind, and he pulled to a stop beside her.

"Hi, Officer. I called in the suspicious vehicle." She indicated the car's location. "Over there."

The uniformed man exited and put on his regulation cap, then reached in for a pry bar. "I'll call in the VIN to make sure it's the right car."

She groaned. Another delay. James might be injured inside the trunk, bleeding perhaps. Time was of the essence. "It's the right car, Officer. I recognize the Pink Panther in the front."

He smiled. "Still, we have to be certain."

She followed him across the lot. "Could we pop the trunk first? In case he's in there, hurt or kidnapped or something? If he isn't, then you can run the vehicle identification number. Brad says he doesn't know where the car came from."

Brad appeared at her elbow, all smiles and sweat. "That's right, Officer Stravinski. Innocent as a newborn babe."

The patrolman nodded. "As always, Brad. As always." He studied the car. "No plates so no quick ID there."

"Likely what the person trying to hide the car thought, too."

He peered at her. "Watch a lot of crime TV?"

She drew herself up to her full height—still a good six inches shorter than this young whippersnapper. "I do. Plus I've taken several criminal justice courses over the years. I may not be a LEO, but my line of work calls for me to be on top of what's happening in the criminal world."

Stravinski's gaze dropped. "My apologies, ma'am." He hefted the tool in his hands. "Let's take a look." As they neared the car, the officer slowed, nostrils flaring. "Don't like that."

She didn't notice anything apart from her neighbor's car. "What?"

"The smell."

She paused and breathed deep. Oil. Antifreeze. Old metal. Mice—perhaps in the upholstery of the old cars? And—he was right. Something else. Something old.

Something dead.

Her corn chips and coffee rose in her throat, a sour, acidic taste.

This wasn't good.

Stravinski inserted the pry bar under the lip of the trunk and twisted. The metal—although old and the paint dull—groaned, but the lid didn't pop. The officer tried again, putting his weight into it this time.

The trunk opened, and Carly stepped forward.

James!

Gagged and bound.

"Quick, get him out." She reached past the officer, who put out a hand to stop her. "He needs medical attention."

Stravinski turned her away from the car, both hands on her shoulders. "I'm sorry, ma'am. It's too late."

She peered past him, tears blurring her vision. "No, it can't be. It's my neighbor. We need to get him—" She looked up at the officer. "You mean, we're too late?" She whirled away, fists pounding her thighs. "I knew it. I should have found him sooner."

"It wouldn't have helped."

She faced him again. "What do you mean? If I'd come looking for him on Friday, instead of waiting until now, I'd have found him—"

"Just as dead as he is now. You see, he was shot. Through the temple."

In the Money

Chapter 11

The ride home to Bear Cove seemed an eternity, but still not quite long enough for Carly. She sat in the back seat of the police cruiser, zoning in and out of her whereabouts like a moth around a flame. Wanting to remember every detail—any detail—that could lead to finding who committed such a horrific act of violence against her friend. But at the same time, wishing she could forget the frozen look of surprise on his face. The trickle of blood down his cheek. The blue, swollen hands bound behind his back.

Everything else—the smell, the injustice, the unfeeling way his body seemed crammed into the trunk—all of it faded when she recalled the details.

She closed her eyes and leaned her head against the cool glass of the window, glad she agreed to the offer of a drive home. With these terrible images flashing across her eyes like an old kaleidoscope projector, she doubted she'd have managed to get herself more than a few miles down the road before succumbing to her grief. She and Mike could go back tomorrow—or the next day or next week, for all she cared—to retrieve her car.

In the light of her friend's demise, she couldn't think of a single reason why she needed the vehicle anytime soon.

She had no place to go.

At first, the officer tried to strike up a conversation with her, but she couldn't form the words, and he soon gave up. Police chatter emitted from the handset clipped near his shoulder, and after a couple of glances in the rearview mirror, he turned down the volume so that all she now heard was a background series of voices speaking in police jargon. Codes, addresses, SitReps—situation reports. Once or twice James' name was mentioned, but the balance of the message she purposely blocked out.

She knew enough about his death to last her a lifetime.

When the car slowed at the intersection of Main Street and Old Tom's Hill, she straightened and rubbed her eyes, then scrubbed her face with her hands as though she could remove the connection with death from her. At the next turn, onto Jamaica, she ran fingers through her hair. She must look a sight.

And when Mike appeared at the door when they pulled into the driveway, she groaned. Then moaned. Chief Webb—inept at so much— likely called and let him know she was headed home. The fact he met her at the door indicated his level of concern. Which usually meant trouble.

But not this time.

She thanked the officer and rushed from the car, straight into his outstretched arms, reveling in the warmth and security of his love for her.

And then came the tears. Her knees gave way beneath her, and Mike hooked an arm under hers and led her to the living room, where she collapsed onto the sofa. He sat beside her, holding her, patting her back, and murmuring that things would be okay. That they would find out who did this. That he was sorry she had to go through it.

All the things she needed to hear.

When the shivering started, he pulled an afghan over the two of them, and she snuggled closer, her face buried in his chest, leaving wet stains of tears, saliva, and mucous on his shirt.

He didn't care, and neither did she.

Once spent, she rested there, wishing she didn't ever have to leave this safe place. Mike rested his chin on her head and waited with her. At some point, she'd have to sit up and deal with the situation, her emotions, and his concerns.

Just not yet.

That time came soon enough. About an hour later, she straightened and leaned against the back of the sofa, the afghan they shared tucked around them.

If only she could keep the world at bay so easily.

She drew a deep breath and exhaled slowly. "Wow, what a day."

He stroked her cheek with the back of his hand. "You're still pale. Want some tea? Something to eat?"

Even this many hours later, the sour taste of her corn chip snack rose in the back of her throat. "Nothing to eat. Tea sounds good."

He pushed the covering from his knees and stood. "What kind?"

"Surprise me."

As he headed for the kitchen, she relaxed again, enjoying this brief interlude of someone else looking after her. Of course, it wouldn't last. It couldn't. She often joked that if she had no stress or worry in her life, she'd be a cat. That was her paraphrase of a one-liner she once heard where man was used instead of cat.

She managed a wry chuckle. If she asked Mike, he'd insist his life was full of stress and worry, most of it caused by her. He always said she was a full-time job.

Well, right now she felt not an ounce of guilt at being under his ministrations.

And she suspected he didn't mind, either.

When he headed her way with two steaming mugs, she scooted over on the sofa and accepted hers. "Thanks." She inhaled the scent of cinnamon, licorice, and ginger. "Hmm. I love this tea."

"You looked a little green. Thought maybe your tummy was upset."

"A little." She sipped, savoring the hot liquid before swallowing. "My entire being was upset, which translated to my stomach, I guess."

"That's to be expected." He patted her leg. "You're still pale."

"I'll be okay in a bit." She closed her eyes then opened them and set her cup on the table at her elbow. "Maybe a little nap."

"Sounds like a plan." Mike tucked the blanket around her shoulders. "I'm going to call Denise and see if she can come over for a few hours."

"Don't bother her. She's busy with kids, I'm sure."

"She'll tell me if she can't make it. You rest."

Her eyelids weighed so heavy she could only nod.

Yes, it was nice to have somebody else be the adult occasionally.

$ $ $

When Denise let herself into her father's house, the first thing that struck her as out of place was her stepmother asleep on the sofa. While the sun was still up. Almost unheard-of, at least in her experience.

She couldn't recall the last time Carly slept during the daytime.

Even when she visited at Denise's house and played with the kids all day, she still had enough energy to make it through until sundown.

Her father came out of the kitchen, a dishtowel in hand, and she crossed the room to hug him.

"So glad you called, Dad." She glanced back at Carly. "She looks so peaceful now. Not much color in her cheeks, though."

He held her at arm's length. "I'm worried about her. She talks a big talk, but underneath, she's tender."

"Don't let her hear you saying that about her."

"Don't let me hear you saying what?" Denise turned as Carly struggled against the covering that pinned her to the cushions. "How long have I been asleep?"

Denise's father perched on the edge of the sofa. "A couple of hours. Long enough for Denise to get here." He rubbed her shoulder. "I have dinner ready if you want to eat. Homemade mac and cheese."

Carly's eyes widened. "You made dinner?"

"I can cook, you know. And I used your recipe." He waggled his eyebrows. "Browned the edges, just the way you like."

Denise giggled at the interaction between her father and stepmother—well, actually more like a second mother to her. Although she and her brother Tom were already out of the house when Carly entered her father's life, she'd been there through several hard times, including Tom's break-up, make-up, and subsequent marriage to his wife, the birth of Denise's own kids, and then the death of her father's brother and adoption of her cousin Bradley.

A convoluted family tree, to say the least.

But one firmly rooted in love.

When Carly stood and headed for the kitchen, Denise held out her arms for them to link together with her in the middle. "You guys are more fun than a concert." This brought a laugh from Carly, which was her intention. "Let's eat and we can talk later."

Her father's cooking had improved leaps and bounds from when she was a kid, which she always loved reminding him of. "When Dad cooked, it was usually something he called Fridge Soup. He'd empty all the leftovers in a big pot, add a couple cans of vegetable soup, some water, and that was supper. One night, it was so bad, he tossed in a bunch of spices. It was still so nasty, even he couldn't eat it. We made hot dogs instead."

Carly laughed, as she always did, at the story, and her cheeks colored a mite, vanquishing the pale cheeks and dark circles under her eyes. Then she sobered again, the smile leaking away like water through a sieve. But she continued eating, another good sign.

Once dinner was over and they relaxed over cups of decaf coffee, Denise broached the subject of the elephant in the room. "Tough day, huh?"

Carly nodded. "One of the worst."

Denise sipped her coffee. "Want to talk about it?"

Her stepmother toyed with her knife. "I guess somewhere deep down, I knew it was a possibility he might be dead. But I always thought it would be natural causes. Or a car accident." She shuddered. "Never murder."

Her father covered Carly's hand with his own. "We never think violence will touch our lives."

Carly's mouth lifted in a half-smile, half-sneer. "You'd think I'd be immune to all that, given how much true crime I read and the television shows I watch."

Denise reached across the table and covered Carly's other hand, noting the slight tremble. "We tend to distance ourselves from the truth of what we're watching because we know it happened in the past, to somebody else."

Carly withdrew her hands and clasped them in her lap. "Guess so."

Denise refilled their cups. "Well, I've got a couple more hours for us to spend some girl time." She met her father's eyes. "You, bury yourself in your office. I'm sure you have emails to send or programs to program. We gals have plans."

Carly's shoulders slumped. "Sorry to be a fuddy-duddy and spoil your plans. I can't even think about going anywhere."

"We're not going out. But I do have plans."

Mike stood and headed out of the kitchen, pausing in the doorway. "I know when I'm not wanted."

Denise chuckled. "Since my plans include a cucumber facial, bright red nail polish, and candles with soft music, you likely want to skedaddle as far as possible."

Mike nodded. "If you need me, I'm in my office."

His rapidly retreating footsteps communicated his lack of interest in being part of their spa night.

Denise stood and held out a hand toward Carly. "Come on."

"Where?"

"We'll use my old bedroom. I brought all my spa stuff. I'm thinking about going into the home party business, and I need the practice."

"But—"

"No buts. Doctor's orders." She winked. "If I'd asked a doctor, I'm sure he'd agree with me. And Don said you needed something to take your mind off today."

Carly chuckled but stood. "Don is a dentist."

Denise shook her head. "Don't let him hear you saying that. He's still a doctor."

"Okay, fine. But I don't know about bright red polish."

"On your toes only. Brighten up your tootsies when you wear sandals."

"Maybe I need Mike to keep me safe from this crazy party woman who's invaded my house."

Despite her words, they were soon ensconced in Denise's old bedroom, their feet soaking in pans of warm water and a few drops of dish liquid that advertised would do wonders for their hands.

Denise wiggled her toes. "That feels good."

"Suppose you've been run off your feet with the kids."

"They asked me to tell you they're praying for you."

Carly stilled a moment. "Tell them thanks from me."

"I know you're still trying to figure out where you stand with all that."

"If by 'all that' you mean God and stuff, you're right. Most of the time I don't even try to think about it."

"You and about ninety percent of the world."

"And what about you?"

Denise's mouth filled with cotton wool at the question. "Me? God is about all I do think about."

"Seriously? How is that even possible? You're a busy wife, mother, daughter, aunt, friend. How do you have time?"

"That's just it. Whatever I'm doing, I'm talking to Him much like I'm talking to you now. Not always audibly, of course. And He gives me insight into how to accomplish a task faster and easier. How to pray for somebody. How to answer their questions. How to respond to my kids. How to treat my husband. How I can rearrange my schedule so I can help a friend."

"And He talks to you?"

"In many ways. Would you like to know more?"

$ $ $

Would she? Carly wasn't certain how to answer that question.

On the one hand, she didn't need anything else on her to-do list.

On the other hand, she didn't know how to get past James' murder without some help.

Couldn't hurt to listen.

Could it?

Safely ensconced in Denise's childhood bedroom—the one Carly longed to turn into a library for the boxes of books stacked in the attic— she decided to shut the world out.

At least, for the time being.

Denise unfolded a lap blanket from her case and fluffed it in the air. A cloud of dust hung in the air, shining like diamond particles in the beams from the lamps.

Denise laughed and waved off the motes. "Goodness. I can see you don't use this room very often."

"Nope. Unless I need a place to set visitors' coats—which isn't very often."

"My mom used to do the same thing."

"Mine, too." Carly quirked her chin toward the mass of jars and bottles Denise pulled from the case. "What's all that stuff?"

Her daughter-in-love held up a tube. "This is the cucumber facial." She dug around in a pocket inside the lid of the suitcase, pulling out a black velvet sack. "And this is a mini-ped in a bag. Cuticle cream. Nail file. Clippers. Base coat. Polish. And top coat."

"My goodness." Carly reached for this treasure. "All in this little thing?" She pulled the strings and dumped the contents onto the bed.

"Yep. It's all here."

"Convenient for travel or simply for keeping everything you need in one place."

Carly chuckled. "Consider me a customer. I don't fuss much with makeup unless we're going somewhere special, but I like this."

Denise opened the facial tube. "Sit in the chair and lean your head back. I'll smear the cream on your face. Then we can sit for fifteen minutes while it does its magic."

"If this is guaranteed to make me look younger, I'll sit here for an hour and come out looking like a teenager."

They both laughed until a knock at the door interrupted them. "Everything okay in there?"

"Yes, Dad." Denise rolled her eyes. "We'll let you know if we need help."

Carly held her breath as his footsteps receded down the hallway then shook her head. "He wouldn't understand, would he?"

"About our need to smear stuff on our faces and paint our nails? No, I guess he wouldn't."

Carly settled into the chair and leaned her head back. "Go ahead. Make me beautiful."

Denise stood behind the chair and gently smoothed cool cream on her face. "You're already beautiful."

"Right. Wrinkles and dry patches and freckles and all."

Practiced fingers massages the tight areas beneath Carly's eyes and around her temples. "What's on the outside fades. Like paint on a house. The paint isn't what makes the house beautiful. It's the people who live inside."

Oh, that felt good. She could lie here all day if somebody would do this. "Maybe. But when the paint peels and cracks, no matter how nice the house or the people are, neighbors are going to complain."

Denise patted Carly's cheek. "You don't take compliments easily, do you?"

"Always figure it's better to say what others are thinking. Sounds better coming from me. Especially when it's about *me*."

This elicited another pat. "All done. Relax, and I'll get some of this on me. Then we can chat."

Carly relaxed, her eyes closed, breathing in the smooth tones of cucumber and apple. A heady but calming combination. In the background, soft instrumental music from a player on the desk. And on top of all these sensory delights, warm vanilla from a candle beside the bed.

"Dad told me about finding your friend."

So much for calming. "It was tough. I didn't expect it, I guess."

"We never do. A couple of years ago I went to check on an elderly neighbor I hadn't seen for a few days. Found her in bed. Looked like she was sleeping. But she wasn't."

"Dying in our sleep is something we all aspire to."

"But few achieve."

Carly shifted in the chair. "Your dad would say I poke my nose in where it's not wanted. But this was one time I simply couldn't leave it alone. I knew something happened to him. I just hoped he was in hospital or we'd find him in his car." Her wry chuckle held no mirth. "Funny how wishing he was hurt or sick is better than the reality."

"Ever seen a body before?"

Carly lifted one shoulder and let it fall, even though she wasn't certain Denise could see her from this angle. Or if she even had her eyes open. Didn't matter. The movement scratched an itch between her shoulder blades. "A few. Some natural deaths. That reporter a while back. In the park?"

"Oh, yeah. I remember hearing about that."

"But I didn't really know him. Not like James." Carly's voice cracked, and she bit her bottom lip. If she started crying now, she might never stop. "It just seems so unfair."

"I know. Life can be like that. I was just reading the other day in the Bible about a young man whose brothers sold him into slavery just because they were jealous of him."

"Seems extreme."

"Well, some of the brothers wanted to kill him. This was a compromise of sorts."

"Do you think somebody was jealous of James? I never thought of that as a motive."

"I don't know. But it's just an example that life isn't always fair. Which is why I'm so glad God is the one who controls everything."

"Then why didn't God keep James from getting killed? Seems if He was really that powerful, He could have stopped it. He could have warned James. He could have told me. He could have—" Carly wasn't certain what else God could have done. If He wanted to. If He really could. "I mean—"

"I know what you mean. I've asked those questions, too."

Carly twisted in her chair to face Denise. "But you still believe? In spite of the fact things don't always turn out the way you want?"

"I do." Denise opened one eye and peered at her. "Do you ever ask

Dad for something and he says no?"

"Sure. Sometimes it's not convenient. Sometimes he thinks it's a bad idea."

"Do you doubt he loves you when he says no?"

"Of course not. Usually he has a really good—" She smiled. "I get it."

"God isn't a vending machine. Or a genie in a bottle. Sometimes you aren't ready. Sometimes somebody else isn't."

"So why do you think James is dead?"

Denise's mouth lifted in a half smile. "You ask tough questions. I don't know the answer to that." She stood and switched out the CD in the player on the desk. This one was rain, steady but gentle, matching the rhythm of Carly's heart. "But I do know that God sees all and knows all."

Carly held up a hand. "Please don't tell me He won't give me anything I can't handle. Because maybe if I wasn't so strong, James would still be alive."

"You aren't responsible for his death. Somebody bad killed him. Probably for something as temporary as money." She laid a hand on Carly's shoulder. "Can I pray for you?"

A single tear dribbled its way down the side of Carly's face. "I guess it won't hurt."

Denise laid her other hand on Carly's other shoulder and squeezed, massaging taut muscles. Carly breathed deep as her daughter-in-love whispered to the God she believed could move mountains.

And not for the first time, Carly wished she believed in something—or Someone—bigger than herself. Not because she was weak.

But because she was so tired of feeling the world resting on her shoulders.

Chapter 12

Dreams of James in the back of his car, fighting his attacker but losing, filled Carly's night, and when she awoke on Tuesday morning, the last thing she wanted was more of the same.

She should have turned off her alarm before going to sleep the previous night.

Seemed the only thing worth reporting was the discovery of her friend's body, as the news, which normally ended at three minutes past the hour, continued on for almost twenty minutes as the three radio personalities told and re-told the story from several vantage points. Brad from Brad's Bargain Beauties was the primary source—no surprise there. He mentioned the name of his car lot every time he spoke. As if finding a body would make customers flock in.

She wrinkled her nose as she stretched. Despite what others thought of her, death was not a magnet for her attention.

Then Officer Stravinski gave his two-cents' worth, as well as some guy labeled as the mayor of Flatirons but whose name she didn't catch. Like he had anything to add, apart from his shock at the gall of violence to rear its ugly head in their quaint but upscale city.

His words, not hers.

She sighed and pushed aside the blankets. No point staying in bed any longer. She had things to do.

And top on her list was getting a look at James' house. Now she wasn't simply the nosey neighbor intent on snooping.

Now she was the trained investigator.

Okay, not the kind most folks would think of in a murder enquiry.

But she was trained.

That, coupled with her bloodhound-like nose for trouble, should stand her in good stead.

She reached for the extension phone on the bedside table then hesitated. Now that local police knew about James' death, would his house be off-limits until they completed their search? She padded to the window, her bare feet enjoying the cool of the laminate flooring. She peeked out. No sign of any police cars on the street or in the driveway next door. No crime scene vehicles or command station motorhomes from the state patrol. Bear Cove was much too small to boast more than a couple of officers on their force. In fact, when the department received a grant a couple of years ago to purchase a police car for the second officer so they didn't have to share any longer, that was news.

She returned to the phone and dialed Chief Donovan, who, luckily for her, was in.

He didn't agree with her, it seemed, judging by the huge sigh that almost came out sounding like a groan when he answered.

Then again, they rarely walked the same side of the fence at the same time.

But he usually came around in the end.

"Chief, I want permission to take a look inside James' house."

"Fine with me."

"Now wait. Hear me out. I know he was talking to—what?" Carly pulled the receiver from her ear and stared at it. What was going on? Had an alien invaded the chief's body? She pressed the handset against her ear again. "I'm not sure you heard me correctly. I said I want to get into James' house."

Another sigh. "I heard you. I said fine. Now can I get back to work?"

"Wait. No warning that I need to share whatever I find? No reminder that I'm a civilian with no formal law enforcement training and no authority?"

"Nope. Just leave the place the way you found it."

"Can I at least dump the trash so it doesn't smell the place up?"

"Fine with me. You can do the dishes too, if you like. Empty the fridge and the vegetable bin. Take whatever food is there home with you. He doesn't have any family. I already checked with the State and there's no will on file. If you find something, let me know. Or if there's insurance policies, that sort of thing."

"Isn't that something you should be doing?"

"I will. It's on my list. But if you're going over there to nose around, why do double work? You're his neighbor. He gave you a key."

Well, not exactly true. But she knew where to get one.

No point mentioning that little detail right now.

"Okay, Chief. Anything that's not been released to the media?"

"We held back the lottery win, but that probably will leak through later today. And no, before you ask, we haven't tracked down either the money or the killer. Or how he or she got away."

"Yeah, I've been thinking about that, too. No cars stolen from the lot?"

Donovan chuckled. "Are you kidding me? I heard through the grapevine that Brad didn't even notice a car that sat on his lot for several days. He likely wouldn't know if one of his clunkers was missing without an audit." He paused. "Hmm, maybe Stravinski could threaten to call his bank to reconcile his inventory. That might get some answers from the man sooner rather than later."

Carly had taken enough courses about criminal psychology to believe it unlikely the killer was a woman. Or if the murder was pre-meditated, he'd have a car stashed in the area. Then he could calmly walk away from the crime scene, get into his own vehicle, and drive off into the proverbial sunset, and nobody would be the wiser.

Chief Donovan's chair squeaked. "You know what? On second thought, maybe I should go with you."

She bit back a groan, wishing she'd kept her big mouth shut. "Don't trust me?"

"Let's just say, protecting my a—"

"Can you meet me in twenty minutes? I'll have the key."

At least, she hoped so.

$ $ $

Mike sighed. No doubt this was simply another fishing trip on Carly's part.

And somehow she managed to rope him into it.

He waited for her on the front step of James' house while she went next door to Mavis the postmistress for the key. He leaned against the wrought-iron railing, arms crossed over his chest, and tapped his toe.

She was taking a long time.

Likely got to chatting. Had coffee. Maybe a cookie. Mavis was well-known for her home baking. And if they got on the subject of the murder—Mike shuddered.

He could be standing here all day.

His mind cast back to the mountain of work waiting on his desk. Seemed like despite the time already invested into the project that allowed him to close the firewall the hacker poked through, he still had more to do. And standing around here waiting for Carly wasn't getting the job done.

He turned to head down the steps. She and the chief could poke around James' house all they liked. When he reached the bottom, however, he stopped. Carly came skipping across the grass—okay, not exactly skipping because she avoided anything remotely related to exercise—walking across the grass toward him, a key held high like an Olympian torch. And the chief pulled into the driveway, exited the car, and strode toward him.

He sighed, feeling like a rabbit caught between two hungry wolves.

He did an about-face and followed Carly up the steps, with the chief close behind.

Yep. Trapped.

Inside, the house was dim and cold, despite the warmer temperatures outside already and the fact the curtains were open in the living room and dining room. And why shouldn't they be? James left in the morning, fully expecting to return that evening before nightfall.

A shiver ran up his spine. He sidled in the foyer next to Carly. This was one of the last places he wanted to be. Then an aroma caught his attention. Carly was right. The garbage needed emptying. "While you guys do your stuff, I'll take care of the trash. And I'll check the fridge and kitchen for anything else that might go bad."

Carly stepped up on her toes and planted a kiss on his cheek. "Thank you."

He smiled, her gesture warming him from the inside out.

As much as he didn't always agree with what she did, in this case, she was right on the money.

He headed for the kitchen. Grabbing the trash container under the sink, dumping the half container of milk into the sink and washing it down, then tossing in a couple of potatoes with more eyes than a dragonfly and an onion with sprouts long enough to reach to China. Out through the kitchen and into the garage, where James stored his trashcans.

Right into the middle of Carly and Chief Donovan having one of their famous discussions.

He tossed the bag into the container then pressed the garage door opener and wheeled out the receptacle as they argued about which one should search which side of the garage.

After closing the door again, he faced them. "Am I the only mature adult here?"

Carly stopped mid-sentence and turned to face him. "No. You and I make two."

The chief snorted. "Can you talk some sense into her?"

Mike chuckled. "Dangerous territory." He pulled Carly close under his arm. "I say since she's in the minority, let her choose."

She patted his back. "Good idea." She pointed to the corner of the garage near the kitchen door. "Chief, you said maybe he was going fishing, but I told you I saw his tackle and pole through the garage door window."

The chief pushed his hat back on his head. "And I believed you. And, need I remind you, I alerted the other departments up and down the coast because of what you told me."

Mike glanced around the garage. "I don't see anything else around here that might give us some clues as to who James was meeting."

Carly headed back into the house. "Right. I suspect that information is in the house." When she reached the door, she turned. "How about I look through his mail and his desk? I'll get the recent stuff from the mailbox. Chief, you check his bedroom. Mike, the living room and bathroom. Meet in the living room when we're done?"

Mike raised his brows. "He might keep important information in the john?"

"No. But if there are prescriptions in the medicine cabinet, that tells us he wasn't planning on staying away long. So whoever he was meeting was likely somewhere between Portland and here."

Mike nodded. "Unless he had a traveling set of prescriptions."

"True."

He smiled. She rarely agreed with him when it came to sleuthing. He made a mental note to self: mark this on the calendar as a gold-star day.

He saluted her. "Aye-aye, Captain."

Carly headed for the front door, the chief down the hall toward the bedroom, and Mike decided to check out the single bathroom on the main floor. The original harvest gold fixtures remained, along with the same flooring from when the house was built in the seventies. He opened the mirrored door of the medicine cabinets. Three prescription bottles lined the top shelf. He peered into each then checked the date on the label. Seemed as though the count was correct. Not like James emptied a large number into another container to take with.

A toothbrush and paste, a comb with a couple of missing teeth, nail clippers, and a battery-operated mini-trimmer. He looked under the sink. Cleaners. Extra toilet tissue. Nothing of interest here.

In the combination shower and tub, a back brush, soap, shampoo. Towels hung on racks. A bathrobe on the back of the door. No clothes hamper—likely in the bedroom.

He headed toward the living room. The sounds of drawers opening and closing met him. Chief Donovan searching the bedroom. He passed another open door. Made up as a guest room, judging by the tidily-made bed. Unlikely anything of interest in there.

The next room was set up as a sort of office and catch-all. Carly sat at a desk sorting through envelopes. She waved to him with a flyer from the megastore up by the highway. "Find anything?"

"Nope. Report to follow."

She laughed. "Should be a short one in that case."

He waved and continued toward the living room. Same worn furniture as was present the week before. Walls bare except for a couple of cheap prints and a picture of a young couple in formal attire. He stepped closer. James and Sadie on their wedding day. He solemn, she timid.

Apart from that, no other photos, confirming what James told them: he had no family. No relatives.

Nobody to miss him.

Except two nosey neighbors.

$ $ $

Carly stacked the mail and tucked it into a drawer. Hopefully, James' trustee would look after the bills.

But who would alert his friends who didn't live locally that he'd passed? And when Christmas rolled around and folks didn't get a card? Or a missed birthday? She hadn't found an address book, but that might be something his wife kept up. Maybe he didn't have all that many friends, or he stayed in touch through the phone.

Seemed sad for nobody to miss him.

She sure would. As much as he sometimes grated on her nerves during the lottery drawings, he was a kind old man with a neat sense of humor. And a nice garden. Boy, would she love to have his green thumb. Why hadn't she asked more questions when she had the chance?

For the same reason as always—she didn't know it would be her last opportunity.

That was the mysterious thing about death, wasn't it? Creeping up like a fog in the night until suddenly the person was gone from sight. She recalled something Denise said one time: we needn't fear death when we know where we're going.

Easy for her to say. Denise and her husband—even little Margie—were so sure they knew the answers.

Not her. Sure, all this talk about a God who loves everybody sounded nice, but there were simply some people that shouldn't be true for, weren't there? Like those who abused their children. Stole. Scammed the elderly.

Killed James.

She swallowed hard. Especially that person. Because this particular victim wasn't simply another face in an obituary or a news story. He was somebody she knew. Her neighbor.

Her friend.

And if anybody deserved not to go to heaven, it was that person.

She made a mental note to ask Denise about exceptions to her God of love next time she spoke to her.

Because there had to be exceptions, didn't there?

She stood and walked toward the living room. Mike and the chief were already there, chatting comfortably about what? She slowed as she neared them. Football. She groaned. She should have known. Not that Mike was much of a fan. More of a follower, really. Kept up with statistics but didn't spend a lot of time watching the games. Preferred to get the best sixty seconds on the news, he said, a statement he used when referring to any and all sports.

When it sounded like they were done, she entered the room, holding her hands in front of her, palms up. "Nothing interesting in the office.

How about you?"

Mike shook his head. "Prescription bottles look like they have the right amount in them given the date it was filled, so I don't think he planned to be away for long. Nothing out here except what you see. And, I guess, what you don't see."

The chief's brow lowered. "Huh?"

"No family pictures. If anybody visited him here, they'd notice that. Which means nobody would miss him for a while." He glanced at Carly. "Except of course—"

"A nosey neighbor." Carly jabbed her thumb in her chest. "Not that it saved him."

That saddened her. If she'd insisted on going with him. . . if she'd insisted on knowing where he was going. . . who he was meeting. . .

Seemed the chief was reading her mind today. "He'd still be dead, Carly. I think this was planned, and anybody who got in the way would be just as dead. Including you."

She shivered. His words rang true. But that didn't assuage her guilt. "I just wish—"

Chief Donovan leaned forward, elbows on his knees. "Don't you want my report?"

Time to move on. "Sure." She gestured for him to continue. "Find anything earth-shattering?"

"Nope. Course, I don't know him so I can't tell if any clothes are gone. I found three matching suitcases, all different sizes, so I don't think he packed a bag, unless it was a small overnight one."

"His toothbrush and comb were still in the bathroom."

Carly nodded. "If not for his prescriptions, I'd say he could have a travel kit already packed. But I concur. I don't think he planned to be away long." She surveyed the room. "The answer has to be in this house somewhere." She clapped a palm against her forehead. "Did either of you check the kitchen?" When both shook their heads, she stood. "Come on then. Let's get to it. He spent a lot of time in there."

Once there, she directed Mike to check the pantry and utility closet and sent the chief to go through the kitchen cabinets. The junk drawer, a calendar from the pharmacy, and the telephone book on the counter she reserved for herself.

Fifteen minutes later, she turned from searching through a lifetime's collection of twist-ties, pens, and elastic bands. She leaned against the counter, crossed her arms over her chest, and surveyed the kitchen.

Mike backed out of the pantry, a shriveled potato pinched between two fingers, his nose wrinkled. "Yuck. Missed this one earlier." He dropped it into the grocery sack Carly retrieved from under the sink. "Remind me to make sure it gets to the trash outside."

The chief straightened from his investigation of the bottom row of cabinets. "Nothing down here but pots, pans, cookie sheets. Stuff women love to collect. Can't see the old guy used them much in recent times."

She nodded. "I didn't find anything, either. But I want to check the phone."

She crossed the kitchen and lifted the handset then dialed *69 to find out who called him last. Her heart quickened. This might be the breakthrough they needed.

She listened to the computer-generated voice then hung up. "I was the last one to call him. Whoever he was talking to when I came over on Thursday, James must have initiated the call. Even though he told me the financial advisor called him."

"He would, wouldn't he? If he wanted to avoid your questions." Chief Donovan pulled out his cell phone and dialed. "Going to request his phone records." He waited a few seconds then identified himself and the purpose of his call. "Right. It was last Thursday. And the name on the account is James Norwood. Right. Twenty-six Jamaica Street, Bear Cove. Sure, I'll wait." He tapped a toe and mouthed the word *Muzak* to Carly. "Hope they won't be too—yes, still here. Oh? Well, that's not good. And the day before, too? Have you identified the cause? I see. Thank you."

Uh-oh. This didn't sound good. Did she really want to hear what he learned?

The chief's shoulders slumped. "Seems they can't give much information about phone calls anymore because all local calls are routed through a single exchange, so they don't keep track of them like they used to when individual exchanges handled calls. For long distance calls, those records are stored. But they had a glitch on those two days. All the local office call records are lost. They aren't sure of the cause. Hacking is suspected. They're investigating."

No records of any long distance calls made on the day of the lottery and the next day.

Which meant two things.

The likelihood of two different hackers operating in Bear Cove was likely a million to one. Whoever broke into the hospital network probably also hacked the phone company.

And whoever that was, their call would have gone through as long distance.

## Chapter 13

Right after a quick lunch at home, Mike settled into his less-than-comfortable borrowed chair in the IT room at the hospital, bound and determined to figure out how the hacker got in to the mainframe system. And down the hall in the finance department, Carly was likely poring over accounting records.

At least, that's where he'd left her not ten minutes ago.

He sighed, turned on his computer screen, and booted up the terminal. Then again, there was no telling with her.

He wriggled his behind around a couple of times, settling into the lumpy stuffing of the chair, then keyed in the password—correction, passwords—required to access the system. He studied his notes from his previous day's work to refresh his mind as to where he left off, then plowed in.

An hour later, he sat back in his chair, hands clasped behind his neck as he considered his findings. Suspecting the criminal hacked in through a deficient security firewall, he'd started there, discovering a back door in the programming language leading to a dead end. Which didn't make much sense. Why bother breaking into the system and not doing any damage?

He straightened and tried again.

Beginning this time with the login module, he worked back to find—another dead end. And not simply in the hypothetical sense. The coding led nowhere.

Not satisfied to think another programmer would purposely insert code that did nothing, he repeated the steps and ended up in the same place. Another thread of code presented itself, and he followed that, too. Same thing.

He gritted his teeth. This made no sense. Was the hacker taunting him? Showing he could manipulate the system with impunity? Preparing for something worse? Or letting them know—what? So far, he'd found nothing damaging. No Trojan Horse. No metavirus. No spyware. No ransomware.

He clicked some more keys, finding another back door. Leading to the same dead end. Then another tangent of code, leading to—yep, same place.

So what was this person doing? Infiltrating multiple modules, adding code, going nowhere. And why?

He sat back again and closed his eyes, creating the pathways in his mind. Like tunnels in a rabbit warren, leading away from—from the central point. And like rabbit trails, meant to misdirect and confuse.

The answer wasn't where the code led.

The answer was where it started.

At the firewall.

Heart racing with the excitement of the chase, he sat forward and continued searching.

He had him now.

He went back to the firewall and checked code he'd previously dismissed because it was identified as programmer notes. Identified with a different header so as not to be an active part of the module, designers often left themselves notes not easily visible to users looking at the code itself.

Yep, there it was. Dated just over two months prior.

And while the person's name wasn't there, their user code was.

GP243

$ $ $

"GP243?" Carly blinked a couple of times at her husband, whose wild eyes communicated his excitement about his discovery. "And how does that help us?"

He pulled over a chair from the next cubicle and sat, one hand held up, palm facing her, like he was taking an oath or something. "I know. Hear me out."

She sat back and nodded. "Shoot."

"Most of the time, users include their initials in their identifier."

"So, maybe our guy's—or gal's—first name begins with G?"

"Right." He leaned forward, elbows on his knees. "Last name starts with P."

She drew her brow down as she thought. "But, if this person was a hacker, wouldn't that be dumb?"

"Not if he—or she—was a legitimate employee who went rogue."

She saw a thread of logic in her husband's theory. "Right. Maybe the user name was assigned by the hospital?"

"Yeah. And if so, he—can we just assume the hacker is a man, for ease of pronoun use?"

She smiled. "Sure. Most bad guys are—well—guys, aren't they?"

"Most hackers are male, but that likely has more to do with the demographics of computer science programs than that females are less prone to breaking the law."

"Okay. So if the hospital assigned his user ID, then the hospital knows who he is. Easy peasey." She picked up the receiver and dialed the number to Human Resources in Portland. "Becky Powers, please." A series of clicks assured her the call was being transferred. "Hi, Becky. Carly Turnquist here. Can you help me identify an employee if I give you their computer user ID?"

"Should be able to. What is it?"

"GP243."

Tapping on a keyboard confirmed Becky was looking up the information. "Hmm. That's strange."

"What is?" Carly's heart sank like a rock to her toes. Whenever anybody used that term, the reason was rarely good. "Can't find it?"

"Nope. It's not recognized by the system. You sure you have it right?"

Carly covered the mouthpiece with a hand. "She says it's not found."

He shrugged. "Doesn't surprise me. This guy is good. He had me in a maze of dead ends."

"Thanks, Becky. I'll let you know if I need anything else." She disconnected the call. "So how can this be?"

"He could've created a fake profile on the system once he had access with his authentic ID. Which he could then delete once he was done. Or maybe. . . "

"Maybe what?"

"Maybe one of those dead ends wasn't as dead as I thought. He could have programmed a fail-safe so if somebody wandered down enough rabbit trails, it would trigger a wiping of the ID." He snapped his fingers. "Let me go back and look. I'll call if can I figure it out."

When he stood to leave, she cleared her throat softly and pointed to her cheek. "Forget something?"

He smiled and planted a kiss on her mouth instead. "Never. Just testing you."

She giggled. "I'll search the employment records available through the financial side and see what I can turn up."

Twenty minutes later, Carly had a list with a grand total of two names: Gail Prouse, the hospital's chief financial officer, and Gerard Payne, an IT associate. That is, assuming the hacker was an employee. In reality, it could be anybody with relatively unrestricted access to the mainframe or the system. She sighed.

That list could be as long as her arm.

Time for a coffee break.

She stood and wound her way through the rat warren layout of the room to where the other three ladies worked. She tapped on Connie's wall. "Hi, ladies. Ready for a break? I'll buy you a coffee."

Millie pushed away from her desk. "Not in the break room?"

Sarah chewed on a nail. "Can we go to the cafeteria? They have a French vanilla mocha I could kill for just now."

Carly smiled. "Absolutely. Connie, coming with?"

The woman glanced at the other two and back to a stack of folders on her desk then gave a single brisk nod. "Why not? This will still be here when I get back."

Carly followed the other three down the hall and into the elevator, which stopped at the next floor. A man in a white lab coat entered, and the ladies fell silent.

Carly smiled. Funny about unspoken elevator etiquette.

They waited for the man to exit then followed him to the right and into the cafeteria. Sunlight streamed into the large, open area through floor-to-ceiling windows. Sarah headed for the machine that would pump out her choice of sugar and coffee, while Carly and the other two went for the pure stuff.

True to her word, Carly paid for their beverages, as well as some kind of sweet pastry Sarah chose, and then the four sat at a table near the windows.

After settling down and giving them a minute to taste their java, Carly leaned in and lowered her voice. "Do either of you know Gail Prouse?"

Millie set her cup down. "Sure?"

"Very well?"

"No?"

Carly gritted her teeth. Where did that particular affectation of making every response sound like a question begin? She'd have to look it up. Perhaps Millie was insecure? Unsure of herself? She tried a different tack. "She seems like she has a lot of responsibility."

Sarah washed down a bite of pastry with her mocha. "A powerful woman in a man's world. Plus there's her mother."

Ah, something new. "Her mother?"

Connie tossed Sarah a frown. "No gossiping."

Carly sat back. "Not looking for gossip. But I figure we'll be working together while we figure out what's going on with the finances, so I'd like to know more about her."

Connie toyed with her cup. "Her mother is in a very expensive nursing home in Portland. She has Alzheimer's. Needs someone with her all the time." She shook her head. "I don't know how she can afford it. Her father owned a small shoe store in Penobscot, but that closed years ago and all they had was their social security. And I once heard Gail say she'd never stick her mother in one of those old folks homes paid for by the government."

Carly shuddered. She'd heard stories about those places. "And her father?"

"Died about a year after the store closed. But he had cancer, and it took everything they had."

So Gail might struggle trying to provide for her mother. Nursing homes weren't cheap. Maybe she needed to request the woman's bank records. Do a credit check on her. See how much debt she had.

Carly exhaled. "Do you know Gerard Payne?"

Sarah chuckled. "Are these your suspects?"

Carly shook her head. "Just wondering. Mike is working with him on the programming side. He seems very capable."

"Oh, he's that, all right." Sarah chewed on her finely-manicured nail again. "We dated a couple of times before I met my husband."

"Is he nice?"

Sarah lifted one shoulder then let it drop. "Nice enough, I guess. But he has his problems, too."

Connie shifted in her seat. "We all have our own problems, girl."

Sarah jutted out her chin. "Don't we, though? Like, I haven't had a full night's sleep in almost a year. All the time I was pregnant, insomnia like crazy. And now with the baby. . . " She sighed. "But Gerard's problems are bigger. Like gambling bigger."

Carly leaned in. This might be what she was looking for. "He gambles?"

"On everything. Horses. Sports. Whether it will rain or not. He'll gamble on what day of the week it is. Lottery tickets everywhere. Bookies calling for payment. Threatening to send Guido the knee-breaker if he doesn't pay up."

Carly chuckled. "You are so melodramatic."

Sarah's face sobered. "Seriously."

Connie checked her watch. "Time to head back, ladies." She stood, taking her cup with her. "Thanks for the coffee, Carly. I'm going for a refill. Meet you at the elevator."

Carly lingered at the table with Sarah while Millie headed for the restroom. "He actually owes money?"

"It was like a roller coaster with him. He'd win big, lose big. Win small, lose big. Unfortunately, the losses were always more than the wins. And I don't think he was telling me the truth, either."

"Is that why you stopped dating him?"

Her cheeks colored. "No. He asked me for money once, and I said no. He never called again." She sighed. "I'm glad. I was too close, too flattered by his attentions." She glanced around. "I think he's gone through just about every single woman of marriageable age in the hospital. And maybe some who weren't."

"You mean married?"

"And older ones, too."

"Connie?"

"Not sure. Maybe. But you didn't hear it from me."

Carly stood and trailed behind Sarah toward the elevator. If Connie, a married woman almost her own age, had a fling with Gerard—or was still having one—that would explain her reticence to talk about him.

Once back at her own workstation, she called Chief Donovan and shared her information. "So, do you think we might be able to get a warrant for the financial records of either of them?"

He sighed. "I can ask the judge, but I doubt it. Not enough evidence to go prying into the personal lives of two upstanding citizens."

"But both need more money than they have. And both have access to the computer system."

"Have you talked to either of them?"

"No, but Gail Prouse followed Mike and me around the hallways the first day we arrived."

"I'd probably do the same thing. You and Mike can look sketchy."

She harrumphed. "And Gerard owes the mob money."

Another sigh and a squeak of the chief's office chair. "He might owe money, but you do you have proof he owes it to the mob?"

"But—"

"Despite information from the rumor mill to the contrary. I know. But all you have is the word of a former lover. Not enough. And she might have motivation to smear his name. Did you ever think of that?"

No, she hadn't. Not that she thought Sarah was vindictive like that. The woman seemed perfectly nice. Normal. Happy in her marriage. Despite not getting enough sleep. Then again, could post-partum depression cause a woman to look for ways to harm an old boyfriend? She'd have to look that up.

"Okay, Chief. Thanks for nothing."

He chuckled. "Carly, I appreciate your over-active imagination. And I know you've helped law enforcement a time or two in the past, but—"

Now it was her turn to interrupt. "A time or two? I'll have you know—wait a minute. Are you laughing at me?"

"Never. As I say to my cat all the time, I'm not laughing at you. I'm laughing with you."

Carly said good-bye and disconnected the call.

Laughing with her indeed.

So why did his words ring so insincere?

$ $ $

Dinner over, Denise stood from the table. "How about us gals clean up tonight, Dad?"

Carly chuckled. "Nothing special about that."

He pouted, brow wrinkled almost down to his eyebrows. "Hey, not fair. I do the dishes lots of night."

Carly gathered the empty plates into a stack. "True, you do." She waggled her fingers toward him. "Off you go. I want to spend some time with my favorite girls. You can see them before they head home in a few hours."

Denise nodded. "Maybe you'd like to find a movie the four of us can watch in half an hour or so."

Margie, her nine-year-old and big sister to Toby, danced in place. "Oh, Grampaw, can you find a princess movie?"

He smiled. "I think I can do that."

Waiting until he left the kitchen, Denise then assigned her mother-in-love and her daughter to their tasks. "Carly, if you dry, I'll wash."

"Fine with me."

"And Margie, can you carefully clear the table? Put the water jug back in the fridge. And bring the dishes to the sink. I'll rinse them, and you can put them in the dishwasher."

"Yes, Mommy."

Denise ran water into the dishpan, wishing she knew where to start. When her father called and asked her to come back and talk to Carly again, the only thing she could do was pray. Margie, her wiser-than-a-wizard munchkin, begged to come, too. Which also meant Toby came with.

Although not certain how the child might help, she acquiesced.

Out of the mouths of babes.

As the suds developed, she had an idea. She rinsed the first plate then set it on the counter over the dishwasher before dropping the cutlery into the hot water. "Do you ever notice how sometimes a problem can be like dish suds?"

Carly leaned against the counter. "Huh?"

"The more I agitate the water, the more suds I have."

"True."

Denise washed a serving dish and set it in the rack. "But it's all air, really, isn't it?"

Carly blew a huddle of bubbles off the plate. "True."

"Kind of like most things I worry about. Nothing but air."

Carly nodded. "I read somewhere that eighty percent of what we worry about never happens." She put the dish into the counter then waited for the next one, dish towel at the ready. "Mike called, didn't he?"

"He's so worried about you."

"I don't know why. I'm not in any danger."

Denise lifted her mouth in a half-smile. "This time. And perhaps it would be better to add 'yet' to that statement. At least, that's what Dad is thinking."

"Well, I think he's overreacting."

A clean pot in the rack this time. "A man has been killed."

Carly's shoulders slumped. "I know. An old man who wouldn't have hurt a flea."

Margie stepped between them, hands on her hips. "Fleas are bad. They make our puppy itch."

Carly bent over to the little girl's eye level. "Yes, fleas are bad."

"Daddy says we have to get rid of fleas."

"That's true."

"So maybe your friend should hurt *them*."

Denise laid a hand on her daughter's shoulder. "It's just an expression, Sweetie. A way of Grammaw saying her friend wouldn't hurt anybody."

"Oh." Margie returned to her task of loading the dishwasher. "Then why didn't she just say that?"

Carly laughed. "Good point."

"Carly, I'm not trying to say the things you're concerned about are just air, but it does seem the more time you spend on this investigation, the more worried Dad is. It's one thing to deal with a white collar crime like fraud, but quite another when it comes to murder. Killers will often kill again to save their skins. I don't want to see you backed into a corner."

Carly reached over and opened a bottle of olive oil sitting next to the stove then poured a couple of drops into the dishpan. The bubbles burst and the soap clung to the sides of the pan. "Just call me Super Olive Oil."

"What are you doing?" Denise batted at the suds. "Now the dishes will be greasy."

"Just a demonstration of how my worries can vanish with a simple solution. I just need to figure out who GP is."

Denise pursed her lips. "You think your friend's murder and the embezzlement are connected, don't you?"

"I do. Bear Cove is too small a town to have both a murderer and a hacker living here."

"Except you don't know that either of them do live here. Face it, the killer could have met up with James anywhere between here and Portland. Or almost anywhere in the US, actually. Might have been a chance meeting. James boasting about his winnings. Somebody who works at the lottery commission. Or the bank. A customer who saw him walk out with the money. A motel clerk."

Carly shook her head. "I don't think so. I Before he cashed his check, he talked to somebody. And I think James called him. Now, I can't prove it, but I suspect it's somebody with a long distance number."

"Why would you think that?"

"Because the local telephone exchange was hacked into the day of the drawing and the day after. Which means there are no long distance records for that time. Another huge coincidence. Or so someone wants us to think."

"So it wouldn't have to be somebody living nearby."

"You have a point. Except for coincidence number one: a hacker and a killer in town at the same time. I think it's one and the same person." She folded her arms over her chest. "Used to be if a person moved, they had to get a local number. Now they can take their old number with them. Makes my job more difficult. But I'm going to find out who is behind all this. That's my plan."

Margie tugged on her mother's pants leg. "What about God's plan, Mommy? You always tell me we need to ask Him first."

"You're right. Maybe we should."

She glanced at her father's wife, the woman she dearly loved like she'd loved her own birth mother. A lump formed in her throat. Carly needed to know God. To know His plans for her life. But how to get that across to this strong and self-sufficient woman, who, she suspected, secretly thought religion served only as a crutch? Perhaps another analogy?

She tossed a quick prayer heavenward then turned back to the dishes. First a spatula and then a wooden mixing spoon into the rack, then several more plates and a glass for the dishwasher. Then she paused again. "Sometimes, plans can be important. Like when I'm washing dishes, I like to do the glasses first so they come out sparkling clean. Then I do the pots and pans."

"Why not the least dirty items next? Make sure they don't get greasy?"

"Because the plates and stuff are going in the dishwasher anyway.

They'll get taken care of in there."

Carly flapped the dishtowel. "Kind of like the eighty percent of worries, huh? They get taken care of without much effort. Just let it happen."

"Right. Or not, as the case may be." She set the frying pan into the sudsy water. "But if there isn't enough soap left for the greasy stuff, I can always add more. Kind of like prayer. If I don't know the answer, I can ask."

Carly sighed. "I guess I don't like admitting I don't know the answer." She pushed back a stray lock of hair from her forehead. "I should be old enough by now that I don't need help."

Denise dried her hands and laid one on Carly's arm. "We're never so old we don't need help."

"Well, seems we get to a point where we're so old we always need help."

"Now you're talking about physical limitations. Do you really think your friend needed help with the lottery every week?"

"He did sometimes get the numbers mixed up."

"Did he ever go out and spend his winnings before he collected?"

"No, but he called up half the town one time and said he won the big prize."

Denise shrugged. "So he was a little embarrassed?"

"Now that you mention it, not really. Just treated it like it was a joke on him."

"So no harm?"

"Guess not."

"I think he liked spending time with you. Probably got lonely."

Carly's eyes glistened. "He always had a pot of coffee on and a package of store bought cookies." She slumped. "I miss him."

"God misses you every bit as much as you miss James."

Her mother-in-love straightened and turned back to the sink. A couple of sniffs, then she quirked her chin toward the sink. "Let's get these done. At this rate, your dad will fall asleep before the movie even starts."

Denise nodded. She'd touched a tender spot with that conversation.

Maybe that's all the room God needed to make a move on Carly.

She could only pray.

In the Money

## Chapter 14

Carly cast a glance into the rearview mirror as she navigated her car out of Bear Cove and onto the highway leading to Portland. She loved when she had a hunch. And right now, she had one the size of Texas.

After waving Denise and Margie on their way, and making certain Mike was snoozing on the sofa, she grabbed the two photographs of the employees whose initials were GP and headed out. Forty minutes later, she pulled into the gravel parking lot of the motel where James spent his last night.

When she entered the lobby, however, no clerk was in sight. She tapped the buzzer labeled RING FOR ASSISTANCE and waited. Within a few minutes, shuffling noises from the area behind the front desk met her ears, and sure enough, Joe emerged, a dishtowel in one hand and a mug in the other. He gestured toward a clipboard with a registration form attached. "Fill it out. I'll be right back."

"Not looking for a room." She pulled the two pictures from her pocket. "I was here yesterday asking about a friend."

He gave her the once-over. "And I told you we aren't that kind of motel."

She narrowed her eyes. "And I told you he was missing. Older guy?"

"Right. Still missing?"

"No." The word caught in her throat. Still hard to believe he was truly dead. "I found him." She set the two pictures on the countertop. "Recognize either of these people?"

He didn't take his eyes off her. "Nope."

"Please look at them." Tears welled, blurring her vision. "It's important."

"Not to me it ain't." He set the towel and mug on the counter beside the photos. "Look, lady. I don't know what your story is. Or the old guy's, either. But it's got nothin' to do with me."

She clenched her fists, fingernails biting into her palms. If he didn't stop with his attitude, she would—what would she do? What could she do? She bit her bottom lip. She would not cry in front of this man.

She wouldn't.

James was dead. Nothing she did—nothing she learned—would change that.

She looked up and met his gaze. "I know you're busy. I know a lot of people come in here, impose on your time and kindness."

He snorted. "You don't know the half of it."

"But my friend is dead. And I know you had nothing to do with that, but you are one of the last people he probably talked to. Can you help me?"

His eyes skimmed the pictures. "Don't know the woman. That's for sure."

Which meant Gail was off the hook. Unless she and Gerard Payne were working together. "So you're positive he was with a man?"

"Yep. Younger'n him. They looked like they could be related, you know? And the old guy came in, did all the talking. Wanted a room with two beds. Paid for the room with a brand new fifty while the other fella waited outside in that land yacht they drove in."

"Did James—the older man—seem worried? Afraid?"

A quick shake of his head denied her question. "Seemed okay. Like I said. Nothing special. Nothing out of the ordinary. Just two guys traveling down the highway together."

"James didn't suggest he picked up a hitch-hiker, did he?"

"Nope." He glanced at the photo of Gerard Payne. "Looked a little like this guy. But then again, maybe not. Can't tell his height here."

"About six feet, I think."

Joe stuck out his bottom lip. "Could be him. Might not be, too. Like I said, I only got a brief look at him. Definitely not a woman." He leaned closer. "I heard a rumor about a lottery winner in the area."

"Where did you hear that?"

He shrugged. "Don't know. Was it the old guy?"

"Why would you think that?"

"Dunno. Paid with a fifty, like I said. And when he opened his wallet,

I saw a stack more in there. Didn't peg the old guy for being rich. Old car, cheap motel and all."

"Did James say anything about the lottery?"

Joe's brow lifted. "Was it him? Won the Big One?" He slapped the counter, the sound sharp in the otherwise near-silence. "Whoohee. Met me a lottery winner."

"Do you recall who told you about the winner?"

His eyes narrowed, and he tapped a forefinger against his chin. "Lemme see. Was it Brian from across the way? Nope. Haven't seen him in more'n a week. Maybe Cassie down to the supermarket. Or Jolene. She's one of the state troopers. Cute as a button." He shook his head. "Don't rightly remember. Could have been anybody. Likely ever'body knows about it. Folks like to buy the tickets, you know. Been on the list to get a license for a couple'a years now. But until the corner store lets theirs go, I gotta wait. Only one retailer in every so close, you know."

She didn't, but it's not like lotteries were her thing. "Sounds like it was common knowledge in these parts?"

Another shrug. "Guess so. Like ever'where, I s'pose."

Yes, getting rich without working for it seemed a widespread fantasy.

"But you're sure it wasn't James who said something?"

"Pos-i-tiv-ly. And not the fella with him, neither. Like I said, never talked to him."

Carly recalled their earlier conversation and the man's change in demeanor when she asked about James. Something about paying for the room. Now, what was it? She waited, letting the silence build. In her experience, folks didn't like quiet gaps in conversation. Often, they'd rush to fill in the space, many times revealing something they hadn't intended.

Her thinking paid off.

"Yep, paid for the room, extra for the two of them, security deposit." Joe stopped, the words barely past his lips. His cheeks and neck turned red, and the tips of his ears looked like someoneset fire to them. "What I mean is—"

Aha, that's what she recalled. "What you mean is, you took his security deposit and didn't return it."

Joe sniffed. "Didn't see him check out, now did I?"

"What did you do with it?"

A glance toward a desk behind him. "Do with what?"

Carly studied him. Nostrils flaring. Pupils dilated. Stiff posture. Typical fight or flight stance. Or, more likely in his case, freeze or flight. "The security deposit. Two fifties, right?"

He crossed his arms over his chest and smirked. "If you know so much, you tell me."

She peered at him a moment, letting him stew in his own juices. Breathed in deep. Made a pretense of looking around the area, then came back to the desk. "Center drawer."

His eyes widened and his shoulders slumped. He dropped his head. "Not my fault he left and didn't collect it."

"You could have mailed it to him."

"Like I said, couldn't read my own writing."

"Ah, so you do remember our conversation then?"

"It's coming back to me. Slow like."

Yes, slow like.

Like his business.

Like his life.

Like his mind.

Small and slow.

She turned and left. James didn't need the money now.

And this guy was already living in a kind of hell.

Not much worse she could do to him.

$ $ $

That same day, Mike glanced at his watch for about the tenth time in as many minutes. The afternoon dragged on, and still no word from Carly. Around the table in a small boardroom sat some of the best minds in fraud and investigation, but between the three of them, they were no closer to solving this problem than when they started—he checked his watch again—ninety-six minutes ago.

He sighed and tapped the table, garnering the attention of John Backman of the FBI and Bob Powell, the insurance investigator. "Guys, I feel like this is a huge waste of time. For all of us."

John, sitting ramrod straight—did the man never slump?—gave a single shake of his head. "Negative. We've learned a lot already."

Bob Powell—who always slouched, giving Mike the impression of a bear woken early from hibernation—groaned. Or was that a growl? "I'm with you, Mike."

Silver dotted the G-man's hair, but taut muscles stretched his tailored shirt across broad shoulders and a narrow waist. "Believe me, guys. I've investigated dozens—maybe hundreds—of these cases. We always get them. Because they always make a mistake."

Bob's brow pulled down. "Really? Like how?"

For the first time, John's stance relaxed into an at-ease posture. At least, he looked relaxed. Not a worry line in sight. "It's in the code. Somewhere. They always leave something of themselves there. Just to prove they did it. It's like a code of honor."

Made sense to Mike. Then again, he wasn't a criminal. Or some high school hacker with too much time on his hands. Or a girl to impress.

Speaking of which, where was Carly? She said she was going back to the motel clerk to show him a picture of a couple of her suspects. Though why she couldn't leave that for the police chief was beyond him.

No. Back up there. He knew exactly why she had to do this on her own.

She was nosey.

Sure, she might say the chief is busy. Not that interested in finding the killer of an old man who probably only had a few years left.

Truth was, she didn't trust Donovan. Or anybody else, for that matter, when it came to poking her nose in where it didn't belong. He exhaled. Good thing she wasn't a cat, or she might have used up all her lives by now.

He pulled his attention back to the conversation—and the matter—at hand. "Well, we know the hacker left a user code. GP 243."

Bob sat back in his chair, hands clasped behind his head. "Sure. But we don't know if that's a code. Or a real user ID. Or if he—or she—is taunting us."

"Most likely a he." John tapped on his cell phone. "The only woman arrested last year for cybersecurity targeted a specific company and one of their employees because he made derogatory comments that women weren't smart enough to commit high-tech crimes."

Time to rein in the discussion. "Regardless of the gender, what else can we do?"

John pulled a stack of files toward him and flipped through several. "We have checked login records against activity. Verified computer protocols against code and firewall security. I have a document examiner looking at the three strings of code we identified to see if there's more than one perp at work."

Bob exhaled, shadows under his eyes. "Speak English."

"Perpetrator."

Another reminder of his wife's absence. If she was here, she'd know exactly what language the FBI guy spoke. And she'd likely join in, too. "Do you think this person is working alone?"

"I hope so. Although sometimes teams are easier to catch." John closed the final file. "What's been your experience, Bob?"

"Much the same as yours. Teams always have a weak link. Singles are tougher to crack."

John nodded. "But singles sometimes have to subcontract work out to somebody else. And employees are never as loyal as family."

Mike chuckled. "You're making this sound like the mob."

The agent pursed his lips and stared out the window. "Could be. They are branching out into more lucrative—and potentially safer—ventures these days. Bootlegging is gone, of course. Contraband cigarettes are still huge. Prostitution is legalized in so many places that just a few of the older families still run girls. Most pimps now are independents who run a stable of six or less. Drugs are harder to make a profit at when states talk about legalizing the stuff. But stolen identities—that's the new big thing."

Wow, he hadn't known all that. Sitting with these two for just a couple of hours was like taking a university course in criminal justice. Carly would really kick herself for missing this. "So where do we look next?"

"Bob, what can the insurance company offer in the way of resources?"

"Not much more than me, I'm afraid."

Mike leaned forward and gathered his scanty notes. "Well, I for one am glad you're here. You have a lot of experience with fraud investigations. Sometimes it seems like you get inside the hacker's head."

Bob laughed, although his eyes peered warily at Mike as though judging the veracity of his words. Not exactly friendly or outgoing, he seemed more of a loner than a team player. But he did have lots of current know-how. Not necessarily the details and statistics John brought to the team, but useful nonetheless. Mike decided to keep an eye on him. There was something. . .

155

In the Money

He shook himself mentally. Probably just Carly wearing off on him. She didn't like the guy, but that didn't mean he was either suspicious or unlikeable. There were many folks Carly didn't get along with that Mike had no problem with at all.

Sometimes his wife just took a disliking to somebody for no reason.

Then again, sometimes she was right on the nail.

The real trouble was figuring out which was which.

Time to get back to work. He stood, notes in hand. "Thanks for the information and insight. Maybe we should get together at the end of each day. Compare notes. Make sure everybody is kept in the loop."

John nodded. "Sounds like a plan."

Bob remained in his chair. "Sure."

Funny, he didn't sound convinced.

Best to find out now. "If end of day isn't convenient, maybe first thing in the morning?"

Bob's mouth turned down. "Nah, end of day. You keeners probably want to get to work before noon. And I like to sleep late. Not to mention, this isn't my only case. I might get called away in the middle of the night for a suspicious fire or something."

Made Mike appreciate his choice of career even more. While clients might think their project urgent, Mike rarely did. No responding to frantic phone calls at two in the morning. Kind of like the difference between an orthopedic and plastic surgeon—no emergencies.

He headed back to the IT room and his computer console. Writing a program may not raise alarm bells, but hackers did.

And this was one case he would solve sooner rather than later.

$ $ $

Something wasn't adding up.

Carly paused in her pacing in her mini-cubicle and chuckled. No pun intended.

Not adding up.

That was a good one.

She'd tell Mike about her funny-ism at dinner.

But for now, she had work to do.

Something one of the people she talked to today didn't ring true.

But what?

She hitched a leg up on the corner of the desk and reviewed her day.

Went to James' house. Talked to the chief. Nope, not that. Talked to the girls here in Accounting. No. The motel clerk. While the guy was definitely a sleaze and a crook, that wasn't it.

Okay, so maybe not today. Yesterday? She rubbed her forehead. Think. Think. She'd slept since then, making anything prior to about six hours ago seem like a lifetime. Was she getting older? Or merely tired? She straightened. Tonight she'd go to bed early. Get a good night's sleep. Wake tomorrow chipper as a—she snapped her fingers. That was it.

Something said by one of the clerks where James bought his tickets. All three of them with the same response: I haven't seen James.

She thought it strange at the time. Stilted. Curious.

But with a dozen ideas and half a dozen suspects floating through her head, not important enough to delve into.

That was then.

This was now.

She headed for the car. She was on a mission.

First stop—Shannon at the grocery store. The girl buzzed about behind the Customer Service counter, providing cigarettes, money orders, and lottery tickets like a vending machine on a caffeine high. After about ten minutes, though, a brief lull.

"Shannon, I needed to ask you a couple more questions."

"Sure. I saw on the news they found his body."

A lump the size of Alaska threatened to cut off her breath, so Carly tossed her a half-smile. "Yes."

It was all she could manage right now.

Wasn't it supposed to get easier as time went on?

Instead, the James-sized hole in her heart expanded with every mention of his name.

Maybe Denise was right. Maybe she needed God—or something—to help her through this.

And then what? Back to working things out on her own again?

Why did that evoke a sense of homesickness in her?

She shook off the feeling. No time for that.

Shannon chewed on a wad of gum. "Like, wow."

Yeah. Like wow. "You told me you hadn't seen James since you sold him the ticket."

"Right."

"Did you talk to him?"

Shannon peered at her. "I said I didn't see him. I don't lie."

Carly leaned on the counter separating them, hands clasped in front of her. "I believe you. But you talked to him, didn't you?"

Another long wait, reminding Carly of a deer-caught-in-the-headlight look, before the clerk gave a tiny nod. "He told me not to tell anybody."

The girl's response was so low Carly wasn't certain she heard correctly. "He didn't want anybody to know? Or a particular somebody?"

Shannon drew a deep breath and exhaled. "He said the town was full of busybodies, poking into a man's business." A nervous giggle. "I didn't know what he meant. I mean, I love our town. The way folks look out for you. Call if you're sick. Ask you to babysit their kids. You know?"

Carly nodded. Bear Cove residents had many fine qualities. But she understood how James might want to keep his lottery winnings a secret. Long-lost relatives coming out of the woodwork. Gifts suddenly turning into loans, now due for repayment. Sob stories of sick grandmas and ailing dogs, designed to garner the most sympathy—and cash—possible.

Not to mention the out-and-out scams and fraudulent schemes designed to relieve a person of their money.

Carly lowered her voice. "Did you?"

Shannon stepped back, eyes wide. "Did I what?"

Carly resisted the urge to roll her own orbits. Were kids these days really that obtuse? "Did you tell anybody?"

"No. He said not to, so I didn't. I never mentioned it until you came and talked to me. I mean, it was obvious you already knew, so it wasn't like I was breaking my promise or anything."

Satisfied the girl told the truth, Carly headed for her next stop: the corner store.

But here, too, she got a similar story from Joyce, as well as a lecture on corporate ethics that included reminding Carly she was a former banker, entrusted with many details and secrets, and never had she even been gossiped about divulging information.

In short, she didn't break her promise, either.

Which left Harold, or some unidentified fourth person.

As she headed back into town, she sincerely hoped Harold had a big mouth. Because if he didn't, where would she turn next?

Two minutes into the conversation with the high schooler, however, she hit pay dirt.

Not that he actually came right out and confessed to telling somebody else about James' winnings. But the way his shoulders slumped and his feet shuffled told her the story. Refusing to meet her gaze, he mumbled his way through her questions, pausing right before every lie.

Carly smiled. The truth is always easy, even when it might get a person into trouble. But a lie? First the brain has to recall the last lie to see how that fit into the new one. Kind of like doing a liar's jigsaw puzzle. Cutting a little off this piece, trimming a little on that one, gluing a big bit onto that in order to make it fit.

Finally, she'd had enough. "Harold, let's cut to the chase."

He raised his head then slumped again. "Yes, ma'am."

"I know you told somebody that James won the lottery."

"You do?"

"Yes. Who was it?"

"A friend. Sort of."

"A sort of friend?"

"Yeah. More like a customer, I guess. But a friendly customer."

"Who?"

He sighed and fiddled with something in his pants pocket. Car keys, by the sound of it. "Can't say."

"You don't know this person's name?"

"I do."

She pursed her lips. Would screaming at him get her anywhere? She doubted it. He looked about as downtrodden as a pancake. Probably used to folks losing their temper with him. "Man or woman?"

"Can't say. Swore to not say."

"You swore to James you wouldn't tell anybody, didn't you? When he called to share his exciting news?"

"Yep. This was different."

Her mind cast back to the conversation with the motel owner. Not much difference between these two. In fact, if she learned they were related, she wouldn't have been surprised. "I know it was a man."

He peered at her. "Then why'd you ask if you already knew?"

He likely didn't realize he'd just given her a new piece of information. She smiled. "Just testing you. So why not tell me his name?"

Harold glanced over her shoulder. "Got a customer. Gotta go."

"Please, it's important."

He shook his head as he walked past her. "Not as important as my college tuition that's a-waiting for me when I'm ready."

She laid a hand on his forearm. "He paid you?"

"Yep. A lot of money." He gestured to the inside of the gas station. "More'n I could ever hope to earn in this place."

He left her standing there, his words hanging in the air.

Somebody wanted to know about James winning that lottery.

Enough to pay a lot of money.

But were they willing to go even further and pay the ultimate price? Murder?

In the Money

## Chapter 15

The next day, about an hour into her search, Carly discovered a duplicate invoice. Dated six months prior, both for less than two hundred dollars. The original, sent to the state medical insurer. The duplicate, dated two weeks later, remitted to the same department. This one with a slight difference in the amount and a different patient name.

She checked hospital records against both names. The first, an elderly man who'd fallen and broken his hip, triggering the stay and the charge for the prescription painkillers.

The second patient—she typed his name into the database—didn't exist. Strange. She checked the invoice again. Nope, she spelled it the same as on the invoice. Perhaps the patient ID? Ah, success.

Except—this patient only had the one prescription. No treatment notes. No admission. No ER records. Nothing.

As if he wasn't real.

Which, of course, he wasn't.

And which opened another whole can of worms.

Medications were controlled by the prescription, which triggered the issuance of the drug, the creation of the invoice, adjusted original inventory, and eventually resulted in a computer-generated order when supplies ran low.

In order for inventory records to agree with physical product, the pills had to be removed from the pharmacy.

She dialed the pharmacy and asked for the head pharmacist. When he answered, she introduced herself and went straight to her reason for calling. "I'm looking into some billing irregularities, and I wanted to follow up about a prescription issued in February."

Tapping of keys filled her ear. "Give me one second while I access the archives." More tapping. "Okay. What's the scrip number?" Carly read the digits from the original invoice while the pharmacist typed them in. "Okay. I see it here. Oxycodone, 50 milligrams, three to four times daily. Big dose, but not unusual for post-operative pain or chronic pain."

"Do you see any refills?"

"Nope. Is there a problem?"

"Can you check this one for me too?" She read out the duplicate invoice details. "Is that in your records, too?"

"Sure is. What's going on?"

"Have you had any discrepancies in your inventory? Particularly for this drug, but for any?"

A long pause before he cleared his throat softly. "Well, as you can imagine, there's always a margin of error, particularly in high volume drugs like this one. I don't recall anything that stands out. Let me check. Hold on." She waited as he tapped on the keys. "So, we do an inventory every month. The February inventory shows we were two short on Oxy. Nothing out of the ordinary."

Which meant that the second, duplicate prescription was taken from inventory.

Which meant—the hacker began with stealing drugs.

And then graduated to money at a later point.

That was the only conclusion she could come to at this point, since the hospital was listed as the remitter of both invoices. So payment came to the hospital, which was none the wiser because its drug inventory wasn't out of whack.

Not ready to jump to a bigger conclusion at this point, Carly decided to delay revealing the extent of the problem until she knew more. "Thanks. I'm going to do some more digging. Will it be okay to call if I have more questions?"

"Absolutely. And I'd prefer if you didn't talk to anybody else about this until we know what's going on, okay?"

"Same for you?"

"Absolutely."

She disconnected the call. Duplicate invoices was one thing.

Stolen drugs was another.

She returned to the financial records and worked her way forward, focusing on the smaller invoices. A week after the first fake invoice, two more totaling just under a thousand dollars this time. Similar method, using an original invoice as the template, changing the patient name and ID. She checked this account as well. Yep, just the single charge with no other services or care provider notes. And apart from the drug charges, the other services were now items that didn't affect inventory or payment for the service providers. Generic charges such as x-rays, CT scans, and MRIs.

By the time she got to the end of the month, she'd identified over fifty fake invoices totaling more than ten thousand dollars. Each one a greater value than the last. Each one creating a new patient account with nothing else in it but the single drug or service.

She sat back in her chair. The thefts started in February, slowly at first then increasing in frequency and amount. Like he—or she—was testing the waters before making the big leap. The question she wanted the answer for was when did the hacker make the leap to charging real clients for fake charges, because that was ultimately how the hospital learned they even had a problem.

She stretched her hands high above her head, did a couple of shoulder swivels, then settled into position as she scrolled through records. The first week of March, more invoices with fake patients. But by the tenth of the month, the first duplicate invoice issued that was almost identical to the real one.

And then she noticed what she'd missed before. The remitter. A similar but slightly different name. Instead of Down East Health Group, the remitter name was Down East Hospital Group. The account number was also different, as was the mailing address.

She went back to the previous invoices.

Yep. The same remitter.

Time for another call.

She punched in the numbers for the state medical aid office and asked for the accounts payable supervisor. Once again she went through introductions and a brief explanation without giving enough information to raise alarms.

At least, she hoped so.

"I was wondering specifically about two invoices from February."

The woman on the other end of the call who definitely hailed from the South chuckled. "I know we're slow sometimes, but I don't think I have anything outstanding that far back."

"No, it's not outstanding. But I have a question about it."

"Sure thing. I can pull them both up at the same time. The wonder of computers."

"Yeah. It's a love-hate thing, though, isn't it?"

"You better believe it, Honey. Boss thinks because we got computers, we should be able to do twice the work with half the people." She tsk-tsked. "Life just doesn't work that way."

"Sure doesn't."

"Okay, here they are. Oh, right, I recollect these. We had to create a new payables account for the second one. I called the folks on the other end of that one to make sure it was legit. Answered with the hospital name and got transferred to the department." A pause. "And the strangest thing. They had a man doing payables. First time I ever encountered that."

Carly's heart picked up its pace a mite. She drew a couple of deep breaths. No point in using up all her heartbeats before her time. One reason why she didn't like—and didn't promote the use of—exercise for a longer life. No, siree. Why cut life short by spending heartbeats on an activity that just made her sweat? "Progress, I guess."

"I guess. Anyway, he said the hospital had a charitable branch that sometimes helped folks pay for their medical costs, and the charity issued this invoice. So we added them to our payables database and paid the invoice. We've had a number of invoices handled by the same charity since." Keys tapping. "Quite a few, actually."

"Could you send me a list of those?"

"Sure thing. Looking into them, are you? Hope they didn't get themselves into trouble."

"Me, too."

Carly hung up, and within minutes, she received an email containing a listing of invoices, which she then used to locate the originals. Sure enough, the value of invoiced services increased in amount, focusing on non-inventory and non-provider services, until about six weeks prior.

That's when each duplicate invoice notated a credit card payment by the patient.

Which was why the patient with minor surgery complained.

The hacker escalated their illegal activity from drugs to fraud to credit card theft.

No wonder the FBI was involved.

The amounts on the list in front of her exceeded half a million dollars.

Big money in anybody's book.

$ $ $

Later that evening, Carly collapsed onto the sofa and turned on the television. A glance at the clock confirmed two things: working overtime was no fun. And the ten o'clock news would start in about ten—nine—eight—

"Good evening, and welcome to the latest in news, weather, and sports."

Carly grunted. Not like they were offering anything all the other stations weren't. And, in her experience, weather always came last, forcing viewers to sit through all the sports first. Another grunt. Sports. Just another way to shorten a person's life, in her opinion. And why folks wasted time going to games or watching them on television was beyond her.

First of all, the outcome of a game didn't change the lives of most of the people who invested time and money in them.

And secondly, they should do something useful with their time and money, and do as she did: see the best ninety seconds of the game during the news.

Mike wandered down the hall, stretching and yawning. His long fingers almost brushed the ceiling. "News on?"

She nodded, numb and mute from her exertions today, then managed enough energy to shift a few inches to her right as he sank down next to her.

"Our top story tonight is an update on the Down East Health Group financial scandal."

Mike sighed. "They make it sound like the hospital is to blame."

She nodded. "And we don't even know for sure it's an employee."

The news anchor, a different perky blonde—*do they shoot them out of a mold on demand?*—continued. "Calls to the hospital this evening have not been returned."

Mike groaned. "Did they consider the possibility the administrative offices could be closed?"

"They do it on purpose, I'm sure. To make it sound more mysterious."

He turned to look at her. "I agree."

His easy acquiescence surprised her. She peered up at him. "I should mark this on the calendar."

He pulled her close and planted a kiss on her forehead, his lips warm and soft against her skin. "Come on. I agree with you lots."

She chuckled. "Let's listen." She clicked on the remote to raise the volume a notch or two. "I want to see if they mention us."

"I certainly hope they don't."

"Why not? It could be good for business."

"Only if we solve the problem. Otherwise, we'll forever be known as—" Another groan. "Oh, no."

She turned her attention back to the television. "What?" She watched a moment. "Oh, that's my picture. Not a very flattering one, either." She squinted at the set. "I think that one came from a news conference I did a year or so ago, outside, on a windy day. I really needed a haircut. And do they spend all their time waiting for folks to close their eyes before they take a picture?"

Mike pulled the controller from her hand and turned on closed captioning. "If you're going to talk your way through yet another program, I want to at least read the abbreviated version."

She jutted out her bottom lip in protest, but focused on the news.

"The hospital group has called in a local forensic accountant, Carly Turnquist, to investigate. She has been involved in many crimes in the state over the years, and according to Police Chief Donovan from Bear Cove, in several other states as well."

Now it was Carly's turn to groan. "They need a new writer. They're making me sound like the criminal. I've solved many crimes that the police were totally lost in."

Mike patted her arm. "I know the truth."

"Right. But not exactly good advertising, is it?"

He shushed her with a kiss.

"A confidential source has told us that the number of patients whose credit cards have been compromised increases every day. Apparently, this problem began some six months ago, and the hospital just this past week began looking into complaints."

Carly sighed. "Now they're making it sound like the hospital ignored all those people, when they didn't contact the hospital until now."

"To date, more than a dozen patients' credit and health information has been impacted, with more expected. We'll keep you updated as we learn more. Now on to our next story."

Mike clicked off the set. "What she really means is they'll dig up more lies and innuendoes and report that as fact."

"I wanted to share what I found today."

He stood and reached out a hand to her, which she accepted. He then pulled her to her feet. "Great. But let's get something to eat. I'm starved."

He nuzzled her neck, his arms secure around her like a warm blanket. She pressed in closer, trying—but failing miserably—to imagine what her life might be like without him. No wonder James was so lonely ever since his wife passed.

They stood that way for several minutes until she stepped away. "I have homemade beef soup in the freezer from the last batch I made."

"Sounds good. Maybe a grilled cheese sandwich, too."

Once their makeshift dinner was ready and they sat, Carly turned the conversation back to the hospital. "I went back through records today and found where the fraud began. In February." She took a bite of ooey-gooey sandwich, savoring the crunchy toast and melted cheddar goodness before washing it down with hot tea. "Small amounts at first, like they were trying out the system."

Mike spooned in soup, dipping his sandwich in the bowl. "Pretty common for thieves to do that."

"Always creating a fake patient ID with just that invoice on it." She set her sandwich down. "In the beginning, seemed like their focus was on opiates. Oxycodone, that kind of thing."

His brow pulled down. "So you think they're dealing drugs?"

"At first. And there must have been someone in the hospital, because the inventory was always spot on, according to the head pharmacist."

"Ah, so they use the billing system as an inventory control, too?"

"Right. But after about six weeks, they switched to billing for services. Always for things that wouldn't affect payroll, like a special charge nurse. And wouldn't affect provider payments, like a doctor visit."

"Maybe they decided to move up."

"Or maybe they almost got caught doing the drug thing." She smacked her forehead with the back of her hand. "I should have asked the pharmacist if there was an instance where a prescription was questioned. Or the person picking up the prescription seemed dodgy."

"You can call and ask that tomorrow. Then what happened?"

She filled him in on the rest of her discoveries. "It was like they wanted to get as much money as possible in as short a period of time as possible."

Mike nodded, his lips pursed. "Sounds like a description of pretty much every crook out there."

"They even set up a fake payee. The lady at the state medicare office said she talked to them to make certain the first invoice was correct, and the man assured her it was."

"So now we know it was a man. No more pronoun confusion."

She chuckled. Mike could find humor in a donut hole. "I went through the list she provided me. The double billing stopped just last week. Or at least, no more invoices have been received."

"Maybe they're just not in yet? Or maybe they thought they were found out so they started double billing somebody else?"

She shook her head. "I think they've moved on."

"To what?"

"To a better deal."

"Like what?"

"Not what. Who." A lump formed in her throat, and it wasn't a bite of underchewed beef. "Maybe the same person who hacked the hospital billing system also killed James."

Mike sat back, his plate and bowl empty. "That's a pretty big jump to make."

She itemized her thoughts with a jab of a forefinger on the table. "Well, let's think about it. Point one, they start double billing in February, increasing the frequency and amount until by the middle of May, they're sending two invoices a day, Monday through Friday."

Mike frowned. "That's a lot of invoices."

"And a lot of money. Point two, they move from drugs, which requires street knowledge as well as an understanding of the hospital billing system, to services, much more difficult to detect since x-rays and CT scans aren't inventoried."

"We aren't dealing with a fool here, that's for sure."

"Point three, they move on around the middle of April to double billing credit cards of patients for these same services."

"Getting bolder?"

"I think so. You'd be surprised how many people don't check every charge on their credit card statement. If it looks right, they pay it. Millions of dollars of bogus charges every month here in the US alone."

"Unbelievable. We check every penny."

She nodded. "And call the company when it's wrong." Another jab. "Point—" She paused. "What number am I on?"

"Doesn't matter." He covered her hand with his own. "Carry on."

"So this escalates until last week. When James wins the lottery. Then it stops. Not a single duplicate invoice issued since the Wednesday night drawing."

"So you think James called this person, told him he'd won, and they decided to hook a bigger fish?"

"I do."

"So who did he call?"

"I talked to the three clerks where he bought his three tickets each week. I know he talked to them. Two swear they never told a soul, but Harold at the gas station here in town was cagey. Admitted he told someone, but wouldn't say anything more."

"Maybe the police need to have a chat with him."

"Maybe. But breaking your promise to an old man isn't exactly a crime."

"No, but conspiracy to commit murder is."

"I don't think Harold knew what our hacker planned. Although—"

"Although what?"

"He did let slip that this person paid him for the information."

"A reasonable person might question why there was any value in knowing that James won."

She nodded. "True. But this is a high school kid we're talking about. Not exactly the brightest bulb in the box, if you get my drift."

His mouth lifted in a smile. "So now what?"

"Now I have to think."

Mike moaned. "Oh, no."

"What?"

"Those are dangerous words. Means you've got an idea and you're going to run with it."

"You know me too well."

"Yes I do."

"And that's why you love me."

He reached across the table. "I do love you. But I don't always like the predicaments you get yourself into."

"Why Mike." She batted her eyelashes at him. "How much trouble can I get into? We're investigating a white-collar computer crime. Safe as a walk in the park."

He shuddered. "Don't say that."

"Why not?"

"The last time you walked in the park you found a body. Remember?"

"But that was completely different."

"Dead is dead. And don't forget the time you were almost killed here in our home. And what about our New Mexico trip? And the mob hit in Arizona?"

"Oh, you're being so melodramatic."

Still, maybe he was right.

Sometimes being one of the good guys in the white hats was dangerous.

But that wouldn't stop her.

She couldn't stand the thought of a murderer enjoying his ill-gotten gains for a single minute longer.

She'd get to the bottom of who killed her friend.

No matter what.

# Chapter 16

On Thursday morning, Carly exited the elevator and headed toward her cubicle jungle. The hospital chief financial officer, Gail Prouse, rounded a corner with her arms full of folders, and collided with Carly, sending her backwards a couple of steps, and creating an avalanche of papers.

Carly regained her balance, a sharp retort on the tip of her tongue, but when she saw the woman's predicament, she restrained herself. No point in adding insult to injury, as the saying went.

Even though she wasn't the cause of the latter.

She bent and picked up a sheet of paper. "Hospital budget. Boy, I don't miss those days."

Gail practically snatched the report from her, her face red and lips pinched. "If you don't mind, that's confidential."

Carly chuckled. "Not much. I have access to every financial record on the system." She could hold back no longer, and leaned in close. "Such as your benefits package. And your CV. And that nasty little reprimand in your personnel file."

Gail's face went scarlet, then purple, then faded to a green paleness. "There is no reprimand in my file."

Carly tilted her head to one side. "True."

The CFO stepped back. "Then why say something like that?"

She exhaled. "I don't know why, but we seem to have gotten off on the wrong track here. I think it started when you followed my husband and me that very first day."

"I wasn't following you. I happened to be going that way."

"Uh-huh. Which is why when we turned around, you did too and promptly went the other way. Forget something?"

"Yes. No. I don't remember now."

Carly took a single step forward, her nose almost squarely planted in the taller woman's chest. "Listen, Gail. We're looking into allegations of hacking the hospital's financial records. And your attitude and your behavior has landed you near the top of our list."

She stepped back. Maybe that would make the woman consider just how suspicious she looked.

Gail's nostrils flared as she peered down her nose for a long moment. Finally, her shoulders relaxed, as did the muscles around her eyes and mouth. "I'm sorry. I've been under a lot of stress lately."

Carly nodded. "I know. Your mother. Can't be easy."

The CFO stiffened again. "What do you know about that? My personal life has nothing to do with what's going on."

"But you must see how it looks. We're knee-deep into the finances." Carly decided to try a slightly different approach. "But I'm sure you'd have no reason to steal from the hospital. You like your job, right? And they treat you well."

"Yes."

Carly waited for the woman to expand on her response, but when that didn't happen, she continued. "You can probably help our investigation. Keep an eye out. You know the people who work here better than we do. As we get closer, they're bound to get nervous. Perhaps you could tell me if anybody's been acting suspiciously lately? Taking expensive vacations? Buying a new car? Anything like that?"

Gail studied her, eyes narrowed. "Funny you almost accuse me of stealing, then you mention all these ways somebody else might spend ill-gotten gains. But you didn't mention how a loving son or daughter might steal to provide decent care for an aging parent." She crossed her arms over her chest. "Or do you think a thief wouldn't love their mother? I think you're trying to railroad me by catching me off guard."

"Oh? Why do you need to have your guard up? Have you done anything wrong?"

"I haven't."

"Then you needn't worry about me suspecting you. Besides which, I only have enough time and energy to find the real criminal. This is not one of those weekly police shows where everybody and his neighbor is a suspect."

Well, that wasn't quite true. She and Mike had a list of three or four good candidates. Including Gail Prouse. Because while she'd originally crossed the woman off her murder suspect list due to the motel clerk's allegation that the man with James was a man, that didn't mean the crimes were connected, or that a woman wouldn't serve as an accomplice. After all, the hacker needed somebody on the inside with access to pick up prescriptions, as well as someone who knew how the accounting system worked.

Gail's mouth lifted in a half-smile, half-sneer. "You love digging into people's private lives, don't you?"

"Actually, it gives me little joy, unless they're guilty."

"No, I think you like it. In some dark, evil little corner of your mind." The CFO's bottom lip quivered. "Well, maybe you need to know how it feels. Maybe somebody needs to poke into your secrets." She finished arranging the folders in her arms, then turned to leave, pivoting on her heel to face Carly again. "Better watch your back."

Then she strode down the hallway, her heels clacking on the highly-polished linoleum flooring.

Carly swallowed back a bitter taste. Had she pushed the woman too far?

Or was this simply Gail's attempt to deflect suspicion by trying to turn the tables?

A woman in a high-power position such as chief financial officer of a large hospital conglomerate should have thicker skin than this.

Perhaps Gail hoped to remove her name from the list of suspects by this passive-aggressive response. If so, she was sorely mistaken.

If anything, she'd just moved to second from the top on the list.

$ $ $

Twenty minutes later, following a quick stop at the ladies room and then the coffee bar, Carly dialed Gerard Payne, number one on her list, and introduced herself.

"What can I do for you?"

With no discernible accent, Carly couldn't place his origins, which bugged her. She prided herself on identifying where a person was born or raised within a sentence or two. She sighed. Not the time to ask questions about that. Cut straight to the chase. "You probably know Mike and I are trying to identify the hacker who infiltrated the hospital accounting system."

"Right. I've been telling them for a couple of years now that they needed better cybersecurity, but every time I mentioned it, Ted's eyes glazed over, and Gail muttered something about not enough money in the budget."

"It's a typical response. Everybody hopes it won't happen to them."

"Yeah. Ted said so long as nobody took hospital files home with them, we were safe."

"Well, we hear how information is stolen off laptops that employees took home that get left in unlocked cars while they spend the evening in the bar, and we say how terribly irresponsible of them. What we don't consider is somebody breaking in through the Internet."

"I still don't know how I can help. I don't know anything about hacking. I can't even remember my own passwords, let alone figure out somebody else's."

Carly chuckled. "I hear you. Still, I figured somebody in the IT department might be a good candidate. Sitting around all day, fixing what other folks mess up. Must leave you with time on your hands and an inquiring mind."

"Not me." His chair squeaked, and in the background, a phone rang. "Not devious enough, I guess."

"I suspect we all have some of that deep down." When he didn't reply, she decided to let it go for now. She had other calls to make. Other rocks to turn over. "Well, if I need anything else, is it okay to pick your brain?"

"Sure."

She disconnected the call and went on to the next on her list: Gaming Protocols Inc.

Another GP.

And Gerard Payne's former employer.

And what she learned there confirmed her belief that Gerard wasn't being entirely truthful with her. Seems he had a whole other life he forgot to mention.

Fired for developing video games for his employer and then selling them under a pseudonym. Once GPI discovered what he was doing, they marched him out of the building, without notice, under the watchful eye of two armed security to ensure he didn't take anything with him. Even boxed up his personal belongings later and had them delivered—after they did a thorough manual and electronic search.

But Gerard didn't let go easily. Within three days, he hacked his way into their system using back doors he created while working for them, and programmed a series of time-delayed viruses triggered by specific events. When their accountant did the next month bank reconcile, a Trojan-style virus wiped out the previous month's financial records. A quarterly directors' payment triggered a forty-eight-hour shutdown of the entire system.

And an annual audit report resulted in an email advertising a pornographic site to everybody in the company's contact list—of which there were thousands. The company server crashed partway through the send, so when their hosting company resolved that issue, the email send began from the beginning—and continued to do so every time it was restarted. Hundreds of customers, contractors, and other business contacts called and emailed to complain, creating yet another crash of the company's phone and internet systems.

"So why isn't he in jail?"

The human resource manager sighed. "We couldn't figure out the extent of what he'd done. It seemed that every time we tried to fix the problem, something else happened. So in exchange for him agreeing to remove all the viruses and close all the back doors, the company agreed not to prosecute, and to give him a neutral recommendation."

"But that's—"

"I agree. Immoral. Unfair. So what's he done now?"

"I don't know he's done anything. But he's top of my list of suspects in the case I'm working on. I can't say much about it because the client wants to keep it quiet, but it sounds a lot like what he was up to with you guys."

"I'll let upper management know that when they caved, they set another organization up for the same kind of treatment. But it sounds like he's not doing this out of retribution to your client. At least, not yet."

"Right. He's still working for them. But money has gone missing, and we're pretty sure at least one party involved is on the inside. Which is right where Gerard is sitting."

"Gotcha."

Carly remembered something else she wanted to ask. "Was there any evidence he had a partner in crime when he hacked your system?"

"Nope. That was a lone wolf thing."

"How about when he was writing and selling the gaming stuff?"

"We were never certain." She paused. "At first, he wasn't even a suspect because we didn't think he was smart enough to do this. He always seemed more of a follower. Get my drift?"

"Uh-huh. Lots of people have the skills to be criminals, but not the methodology and the mindset to carry it out."

"Right. And if they try, they get caught right away. But Gerard was doing this for about six months before the company caught on."

"That's about how long it's been happening with my client, too."

"We thought maybe he just got lazy. You know, easy money and all that. Pride. Catch-me-if-you-can mentality."

"It's the downfall of a lot of crooks."

"Yeah. So we were looking into a couple of other programmers, and when they didn't pan out, we kind of fell into Gerard because he was the only one left of the lot. But we always wondered if someone else wasn't the lead. No proof, though."

After assuring the woman she'd likely call back with more questions, Carly hung up, then sat back to ponder what she now knew.

Gail Prouse acted suspicious, but was that really a reason to seriously keep her on the list? Apart from the GP initials, and the fact she needed money to keep her mother in an expensive care facility—which began around the time of the initial drug thefts—what else did she have on the woman?

Nothing much except she didn't like her. And Gail Prouse would never be president of the Carly Turnquist Fan Club, either.

Which made her a suspect. After all, who wouldn't love a quirky forensic accountant like herself?

And Gerard Payne had a track record of doing almost exactly what was happening here. Ill-gotten gains, lots of money, lots of secrecy. The thrill of putting one over on a big corporation. The belief—false as it was—that this was a victimless crime. Lying about not having the knowledge to hack into the system.

No, these two were high on the list of suspects.

Now, to prove how one—or perhaps both of them—infiltrated the hospital system.

Fortunately, Carly knew somebody perfect for that task.

Somebody who wouldn't stop until the truth was known.

Herself.

## Chapter 17

Mike stepped aside to let Carly enter the conference room on Monday morning, then paused to survey the attendees. John Backman, the FBI special agent, sat at the far end, his back to the wall, while Ted Wilson, hospital director, occupied the seat opposite.

*Wonder which one of them thinks he's the head and the other is the foot?*

Gail Prouse, the finance lady, sat between Gerard the IT guy and the insurance fellow, Bob, who was also their neighbor.

The hospital had a talented team of dedicated professionals on their side.

Now he and Carly simply needed to pull their weight and both identify and stop the thief.

Carly slipped into the seat nearest the door, and he sat next to her. The others each had at least a stack of papers in front of them. Backman had several folders, while Bob limited his materials to a single folder. Beside him, Carly laid three binders, while he preferred working with a yellow legal notepad.

Ted Wilson cleared his throat and stood. "Good morning. Thanks for coming. While our regular daily meeting isn't slated until later this afternoon, I've been alerted to several late-breaking developments, and I thought we should pause and go over those before we start our day." He nodded toward Agent Backman and then to Bob Powell. "The FBI and our insurance investigator have been working together diligently, and they have information to share."

Agent Backman stood, his expensive designer suit and tie a little overdressed for the occasion, at least in Mike's opinion. He nodded to each around the table then opened the top file, eyes on the sheet inside. "We've also had the assistance of local law enforcement. I always like to acknowledge their assistance, because sometimes folks get the wrong idea about the FBI. They think we swoop in and take over because local LEO's are inept. Bumbling country hicks. And that's the furthest from the truth."

Bob Powell nodded. "Agreed. Police Chief Donovan has afforded us every assistance and practically seconded his resources to our use."

Keeping his eyes on the papers inside the file folder, John continued. "Right. So, let's get down to it, shall we? We've spent the past few days investigating similar crimes. Calling local agencies up and down the coast. Asking hard questions." Gail raised a hand, and the agent looked up. "Yes?"

"Why are they hard questions? Seems as though everybody involved has the same goal. To catch the bad guy."

"Right. Well, what happens is that when similar crimes are committed, some agencies are under-resourced, so they don't find the perp. Some get close, but they don't have the expertise or know-how. And oftentimes, in some jurisdictions, the attitude is that cybercrime is victimless, so it lands on the bottom of the pile. Once in a while, another bigger crime comes along and resources are diverted, and they never get back to it."

Carly leaned forward, hands clasped in front of her, a tiny smile curving her lips upwards. "So it's not like on TV where a huge team of investigators spends every waking minute solving the crime?"

Another nod from the fed. "Not like TV at all." He flipped over a page. "So let's cut to the chase. How we found this information isn't the important thing. What we found is." He quirked his chin toward the insurance investigator. "Do you want to take over?"

Mike stifled a snort. Of course Bob Powell wanted to take over. The testosterone level in this room was enough to gag a bull moose. Undercurrents of hostility rippled through the men—but why? How could any of these men be in competition—unless it was to be able to claim the win for their team, so to speak?

Seemed they should all be on the same side.

So if they weren't, why not?

Probably because each was concerned the others would lay the blame for the crime on their own doorstep.

Which was illogical, of course. Immunity to cybercrime was practically impossible. As soon as a better firewall was developed, a tougher code to infiltrate was written, or a more complex virus protection was installed, hackers took that as a personal challenge.

Mike sighed. If only they would use their superpowers for good.

Bob Powell nodded and stood, while the FBI agent sat. "Like John said, we spent a lot of time calling other agencies. Asking about similar cases."

Mike sat back in his chair and resisted the urge to roll his eyes. Was the man going to repeat everything the agent just said? Was he being paid by the word?

But no, Bob cut to the chase. "And we got a hit." He opened his folder and spread a series of sheets on the table in front of him. "A hospital, which shall remain nameless because you'd recognize it if I said, had a similar breach of security and invoice fraud perpetrated on it last year."

Carly quirked a brow. "I don't remember hearing about that on the news."

"Didn't make the news." Bob flipped over a sheet. "Instead, they paid a sizeable ransom to an anonymous party to obtain the key to correcting the program." He tapped another page. "But they lost in the area of ten million dollars, including a two million dollar ransom. They wouldn't tell us the exact amount."

"Wow. That's a lot of money." Carly scribbled a note on her folder. "Why just pay up? Why not let the police know so they could find the guy and put him in jail?"

"It's a private hospital with shareholders who wouldn't be happy to know management knew about the breach but didn't do anything about it for a month or so, hoping it would go away. But, of course, it didn't."

John stood again. "Right. And in that thirty days, they perfected their methodology and changed their protocols, making it more difficult to trace them. It was like chasing smoke, the director told me. Their IT guys didn't stand a chance."

Bob's eyes narrowed at the agent, who sat. "As you can imagine, however, words gets around in the medical community. So when a national health insurer experiences a breach of their system with a harmless piece of code, one that makes pirate images appear randomly on their computer screens, along with a ransom note, they also paid millions to buy off the hacker."

Mike sat forward. "So you're saying that in just these two cases that you know of, somewhere in the neighborhood of five to ten million dollars has been stolen and or paid out to these criminals?"

Bob nodded. "Right."

Didn't make sense to him. "So why are they bothering with small stuff like they've been doing? I mean, according to what Carly said, they started at just a few hundred dollars and have only now worked themselves up to thousands."

"Good question. We think it's because although they got away with so much the last two times that we know about, they almost got caught in Chicago. So we think they—and we use the term not necessarily because we think there's more than one person involved—they decided to go a little more slowly so they don't raise attention right away."

John sat back and crossed one ankle over a knee. "And they didn't raise any red flags until they accessed credit cards. If we don't catch them this time, they probably won't make that mistake again. Instead, they'll stick with the fraudulent billings only."

Carly turned over another sheet of paper. "I also discovered they began with drug theft. Creating invoices that triggered prescriptions and then somebody picked up the pills."

Ted Wilson's face turned red. "That's serious business. Are you certain?"

"Yes. I talked to the pharmacy manager. He confirmed the inventory was fine, which meant pills actually left stock."

The director's brow pulled down. "A billing should have to match a prescription."

Carly nodded. "Might be a cross-check system you need to implement. Or enforce."

Wilson scribbled a note. "I'll make certain to look into it."

Carly continued. "I think something may have happened, though. Maybe a prescription was questioned, because that happened only a few times, then the hacker switched to billing for non-inventory and non-provider services, such as scans and x-rays. Nothing that triggered a materials order or impacted payments to contractors or employees."

Mike scratched a couple of notes on his own notepad then stood. "Great. Got enough information for now. Let's meet back here at the end of the day as usual." He nodded to Bob. "Can you give me whatever information you can share about how they accessed the other systems so

I'll know where to start?"

"Sure." Bob peered at him. "Have you signed a confidentiality agreement?"

"Not today I haven't. And isn't that a little like closing the door after the horse is out?" He turned toward the door then paused. "Bob, I'm not asking for the key to Fort Knox. Just your notes about the back doors and firewall protocols he breached."

"Give it to him." John's voice echoed through the room, commanding attention and announcing his authority. "If he wanted to, he could already have run off with every cent this hospital ever hopes to make. Don't be an idiot here, too."

This caught Mike's attention, and he turned to face the agent. "Here, too?"

John's mouth lifted in a sneer. "Bob forgot to mention. He was the investigator on those other two cases. Called in to advise the companies." He tossed a hard look carrying daggers interlaced with accusations and innuendoes toward Bob. "Suggested they take the quiet but expensive way out and pay off."

$ $ $

At a quarter to five that evening, Mike sighed. Hopefully this meeting wouldn't be as tense as this morning's. Why did folks think they needed a spitting contest all the time? He entered the conference room, finding all the same players as earlier today.

A shoulder roll eased some of the aches in his neck and back, but he looked forward to a hot shower, a hot meal, and an evening of vegging out in front of the television, his wife cuddled up beside him.

And speaking of which, here she came, shoulders slumped, eyes bleary, only a tiny hint of a smile decorating her lips.

Add another thing to his to-do list tonight: cheer her up, too.

This time it was his turn to take the lead.

He stood, waiting for all voices to still before beginning. "Thanks to the information provided by Bob and John, I was able to identify not only those protocols the hacker is using in this case, but that led to several other key areas of firewall penetration, which I was able to close. The flow of invoices should be stemmed now, perhaps even dammed altogether."

Ted Wilson clapped a couple of times. "That's great news. Thanks to all on the team."

Mike held up a hand then checked his notes. "That's not the end of the story, however. I was able to trace the computer access to a terminal at a nurse's station in this hospital."

Gail Prouse shook her head. "I find it hard to believe a nurse would be involved."

Carly chuckled. "Anybody can do wrong, no matter how noble their profession."

Gail frowned. "That's not what I meant. I meant I wouldn't think a nurse would have the computer knowledge necessary. They are trained, of course, in college and on the job, but the level of hacking in this case indicates somebody with more than that."

"You're right." Mike squinted at his scribbles. He really should take more time and care with his writing. "I don't think it was a nurse. Or a doctor. Or any healthcare provider. I followed a complicated series of routing and re-routing to a number of terminals, through several servers around the world. I finally lost them in a coffee shop in Nepal."

Bob snorted. "So you think some busboy or barista in Nepal did this?"

"No. I simply said that's where I lost the trail. And then I ran out of time. But I wanted to update you all. Maybe the FBI can look into the server at that coffee shop. See if there are any other cases that passed through there. I'll keep looking. Backtrack and see if maybe that was a rabbit trail and the hacker simply left that dead end to confound us."

John Backman nodded. "I'll get on it tonight. The Nepal field office is awake right now."

Ted's brow pulled down. "There's an FBI field office in Nepal? I thought you guys were domestic only."

John offered a half-smile. "Don't you know spooks are everywhere? We're the guys in the white hats. We never sleep. We always get our man."

Carly stood. "Well, I'm going to get my man home."

Mike smiled. That sounded good to him. Work and hackers and world problems could wait until tomorrow.

His other full-time job awaited him.

Keeping Carly out of trouble.

$ $ $

After dinner—thank heavens for a crock pot—Carly and Mike snuggled on the sofa for an hour or so. But after he fell asleep, his head laid back and his mouth half-open, snoring to beat the band, she decided to go for a walk.

Just a short walk.

Like next door.

Using the key Mavis provided on their first foray into James' house, and which the chief neglected to retrieve, she let herself into the back door. Pausing in the kitchen, she drew several deep breaths until the ache in her chest and the lump in her throat dissipated. Soon another family would purchase this house, and people who never knew her friend would live here. Happily, she hoped. As happily as James and his wife had.

And longer than they had, if she had anything to say about it.

She headed down the hallway toward James' office. Her search of a few days ago hadn't revealed anything, but now that she knew more about the case, maybe she'd see something she missed. She settled into his chair, and a shiver ran down her back. She glanced around the room, checking the corners and resisting the urge to leave. She wasn't intruding. She was assisting the police investigation into his murder.

Another shiver. Were those low-budget movies about souls of people who were killed in a violent manner and able to rest true? Or was she simply letting her overactive imagination run away with her? James' house was cold and empty because he wasn't here. If he had simply taken a vacation, the house would be the same.

Somehow, knowing he'd never come back made a difference. Maybe Denise was right. Death wasn't the end. That was a nice thought. Thinking about James in a better place, where there was no getting old, no sickness, no bad people. Walking along with his beloved Sadie. Sun always shining.

She turned back to the papers in the desk. But really, what was the likelihood of all that being true? Was it simply wishful thinking on behalf of her daughter-in-love and people like her? Still, was it likely that millions of people over the years would all subscribe to the same fallacy? So if God was real, and His plan for human beings was heaven, then where did that leave her?

She spied a small journal and pulled it out of a pigeonhole. James' name inscribed on the cover, along with the current year. Tears pricked at her eyes, blurring her vision. She flipped through the pages. Not just a journal, a calendar, too, in the front, where he apparently made notes about appointments, the weather, and something else. Maybe his weight? Looked like he kept it pretty steady. Apart from some joint pain, he was hale and hearty to the end.

The last time he wrote in the journal was to make a note of the weather on the Thursday he disappeared. And his weight. Up a pound. She turned to the front. Not an active social calendar, by the looks of it. A doctor's appointment every few months. A note about Sadie's birthday and their anniversary. She checked out the months following August. Another doctor's appointment in October. Driver's license renewal in November.

Funny, she'd known him all these years but never knew when his birthday was.

Back to August. Nothing on the day of the lottery drawing, but a notation on the Thursday made her heart race: G 1:30.

G again. The same G as in GP243? Seemed unlikely. Would have to be a really small pool of G's for that to be the case.

Then again, the hacking ceased following the lottery drawing. As if the thief's attention was now diverted in another direction. Was it possible that James knew his killer? After talking to the motel owner and learning about the stranger who wasn't a stranger, she leaned toward believing that the person who James called and the man with him at the motel, were one and the same.

Despite being a huge believer in coincidences, sometimes the situation didn't add up.

And right now, she didn't know whether she was looking for one person, or two.

She groaned.

Numbers were always her friend in the past. They never changed. They always remained the same. Unlike the old accounting joke to the job candidate of "what is one plus one?" and the clever reply of "what do you want it to be?" numbers never let her down.

Until now.

No, not exactly let her down.

But caused a conundrum.

Because there was no doubt that finding two different people just doubled her work load.

# Chapter 18

Friday morning, Carly convinced Mike to work from home for a few hours. A change being as good as a rest, and all that. He took some convincing, but finally agreed, although his lowered brow and piercing dark-chocolate eyes bored into her soul, practically accusing her of trying to pull the wool over on him.

Leaning against her desk, she jutted out her bottom lip. "Michael Turnquist, you make it sound like I'm a schemer or something."

He chuckled, the crinkles around his laughing eyes softening his words as he swiveled in his office chair like a kid at a soda fountain. "As if you haven't thought about it."

"Really. Am I that devious?"

"Nope." He pulled her into a hug. "Just that obvious."

She laughed and wriggled out of his grasp, noting his wagging eyebrows. That particular mannerism usually meant her husband had one thing on his mind, and she didn't need any distractions right now. "You are too smart for me. You're right. I'm going to pop over to Mavis' and see if she knows anything more. Then a quick stop at James' to make sure we got out all the trash, and I'll be back in a flash. I can get some work done here at home, too, then we can go to the hospital and work there for the afternoon. Sound like a plan?"

He nodded as he sat in his chair. "As long as lunch is included. Here, at home. I don't know if I can stomach another soggy cheese sandwich or too-salty bowl of soup from the hospital cafeteria."

She rubbed the back of his neck and shoulders, and he leaned back and sighed. Oh, oh. Better not let him get any ideas. She gave him a quick pat and a peck on his cheek. "Back in two winks."

"And stay out of trouble."

She planted her thumb in the center of her chest and did her best Miss Piggy imitation. "Moi?"

He laughed. "You never get tired of that, do you?"

She headed down the hall. "Because it always makes you laugh."

His baritone chuckle followed her out the door. Life with her husband was never boring. Of course, he often said the same thing about her. Almost accusing—no, there was no almost about it—saying she was a full-time job.

But she was pretty certain he wouldn't have it any other way.

She often thought about his Life Before Carly. BC, as they termed it. Married to his high school sweetheart, Sophia. Raising their children. Establishing his career. Normal, stable, and predictable, but never boring.

Totally unlike her.

As much as she craved adventure, loved solving mysteries, and had a strong sense of justice, she hoped he never regretted marrying her. So unlike sweet Sophia, who died too young of cancer. Leaving him to finish raising their two teenagers.

Then along came Carly. And his life was never the same again.

And neither was hers.

Both recently left single by the death of their spouses—although her story wasn't nearly so idyllic. Nothing to look back on with fondness or longing. No reason she wanted life to be different—married to an alcoholic abuser who hit her regularly. Her face heated as she crossed James' lawn and headed for Mavis, the postmistress, on the other side. Even after all these years, shame filled her at the memories of how she wasn't strong enough or brave enough or something enough to leave—him. She still couldn't bring herself to even think his name.

Thankfully he died in a car accident while drunk before he killed her in a booze-induced rage.

A voice from across the street called her name, and she paused and turned.

Bob Powell.

The unfriendly party host and insurance investigator.

Maybe she could put him off with a smile and a wave.

Snap.

No such luck.

He crossed his lawn and stood on the sidewalk on his side of the street. "Good morning. Gotta love those independent contractors who milk the client for their morning constitutionals."

She stared at him. "Actually, I'm not one of those people. My client can trust my timekeeping."

"Sure, sure." He studied her a moment before continuing. "I just put on a fresh pot of coffee. Got a few minutes to stop by?"

*Oh, so now he wants to make friendly.*

She groaned. If she refused, he might give her a hard time in the investigation. Or badmouth her to her other neighbors. If she accepted, then what? Images from the house party surfaced, and she grappled with her choices. After all, the invitation for coffee was just that—they would never be bosom buddies. But his meanness and creepy behavior at the party unnerved her.

And what about that comment about knowing the contents of her refrigerator? And the brand name? And what kind of cat food she fed Doc?

She hesitated.

Too long, apparently, since he crossed the street and stopped on the sidewalk on her side, looking up at her where she stood on James' lawn. "If you don't have time, completely understand. Just trying to be neighborly."

She glanced at Mavis' house. If she didn't catch the postmistress before she left for work. "Well—"

He backed away. "No worries. I can see you have *other* friends to spend time with. I guess I know where I stand."

She frowned. Was he serious? He sounded like a three-year-old about to throw a temper tantrum because his best friend played with somebody else. And they were anything but besties. "I guess I have a few minutes."

He raised a hand. "No, think nothing of it."

"Maybe Mike and I could have you over for coffee or dinner?"

She snapped her mouth shut. Why had she said that? She didn't want the man anywhere near her house.

Or her fridge.

No telling where else he might snoop in their house.

Or if he'd take that single invitation as *carte blanche* to drop in unannounced any time. Whether they were home or not.

Because one thing was certain: either the man was psychic, or he'd been in their house when they weren't there.

His mouth lifted in a half smile. "Sure, sure. No worries. See you at the hospital."

A shiver ran up her back and down her arms as he headed back to his own house, entered, and shut the door a little more forcefully than necessary.

Like an exclamation point on the end of the sentence.

Carly gritted her teeth as she walked up Mavis' walkway, pansies and coneflowers gaily decorating the beds alongside. If there was a God, surely He'd strike her dead for such thoughts.

She rang the bell and waited, studying a nearby red maple, the sunlight glinting off the leaves, painting more shades of red than any artist could surely conceive. Then again, maybe Denise was right, and God made everything. If so, He sure had some imagination. Could it be?

Mavis answered the door, a smile brightening her face as she stepped aside and beckoned her inside. "Come on in. What a nice surprise. Have a cup of coffee with me before I head out for work?"

"I don't want to hold you up." Carly entered the home, the flip layout of her own, and paused, inhaling the fresh smells of lemon and cinnamon. "Have you been baking already today?"

"Cinnamon buns. Got room for one?"

Carly giggled. "Maybe more than one."

She followed Mavis into the kitchen and sat. The three houses—hers, James', and Mavis'—were so similar she felt instantly at home in all of them, despite the different colors and patterns. She loved the butter-yellow paint in her own kitchen, but Mavis' choice of lime green and tangerine created a beach party effect that always cheered her.

So unlike the tired paint and dull woodwork in James' kitchen, untouched since Sadie's passing, and the dusty plastic plants and faded wallpaper.

She inhaled the warm, buttery scents of recent baking while Mavis filled their coffee cups and set a platter of cinnamon delights on the table. After sliding a warm bun onto a napkin, she sipped her coffee, allowing Mavis time to do the same before broaching the reason for her visit.

While the postmistress intimidated her when they first met years ago, the woman proved helpful for Carly's investigation into numbered companies and mysterious figures. Thinking back to those days often brought a smile to her lips, replacing the quivering knees and dry mouth of the time.

After the appropriate small talk about the coffee blend and deliciousness of the pastry, Carly broached the other reason for her visit. "When was the last time you saw James?"

Mavis set her cup down. "The morning after the lottery." She chuckled. "You know, at first I didn't believe him when he said he won two million dollars. I don't know how many times he swore he won, and when I checked the numbers, he hadn't."

Carly smiled at the memory. "Same here. It's why I started going to his place for the weekly drawing. I think his eyesight was failing."

Mavis nodded. "But he insisted this time. Even suggested he already had buckets of money stashed away where nobody could steal it from him. Which I never believed, of course."

Carly nibbled at her delicacy. "But that morning was different?"

"It was. He insisted he won. Told me to check the numbers if I didn't believe him." Mavis grinned. "This time, he was right. He'd won. And when I saw on the news that only one winning ticket was sold, I was so happy for him. I think if he had to share the prize, that would have crushed him."

"What else did you talk about?"

"He said he was going to take the girl from the grocery store to Hawaii with him. I thought that was funny, but he said she already agreed to go. Seemed strange to me. And I suggested he not claim the prize himself. That he should hire a lawyer or somebody so his face wouldn't be plastered all over the news. But he was so excited. Thought he'd just waltz in and they'd give him the money."

"I know. Mike and I said the same thing. But he wouldn't listen."

Mavis shook her head. "No, James might have appeared mild-mannered, but he sure had a mind of his own. Practically accused me of trying to steal his money."

Carly exhaled. So James' reaction wasn't personal. That was a relief. "He did the same with Mike and me."

"You know how they say that a will brings out the worms. Maybe a lottery ticket is the same."

"Maybe. Did he say anything else?"

In the Money

"Just that there was only one person he could trust." Mavis sipped her coffee then set the cup down. "And judging by the way he didn't want to talk any more, I'm guessing that person isn't me."

"Or me, either. He tore off out of here on Thursday like—like—"

She paused, at a loss for words. Here two of James' neighbors sat, talking about him as if they expected him to walk in the door at any minute.

"Like the devil was on his tail?"

"Yeah, something like that."

"Well, he might have been. James was a strong believer in God, you know, and the devil always tries to get to us."

This was a side of Mavis that Carly knew nothing about. "Us?"

"Christians." Mavis reached across the table and laid a hand on Carly's. "You didn't know that about James or me, did you?" She removed her hand and sat back. "Shame on me. And shame on him."

Carly chuckled. "No worries."

"Oh, yes, dear. Big worries. I want to live my life so differently that people want to know what's unusual about me." She stood and retrieved the coffee carafe, refilling their cups. "James and I talked about that sometimes, you know."

"I didn't." Might be a good time to change the subject. "Any idea who his new friend was?"

Mavis clapped her hand to her neck. "Ooh, whiplash at the abrupt switch." She grinned. "I have a feeling God has been trying to get your attention lately."

Carly lifted one shoulder and let it drop. "I guess any time I think about death, I wonder. And Mike was worried about me, so he called my daughter to come for a visit. Twice. She and her husband—and my granddaughter Margie—all believe in God."

"Honey, the devil believes in God."

"And Jesus, too. They're always telling me we need to let Him into our heart, whatever that means. Making their point with little stories and examples. Suggesting that maybe this is happening or that happened because God was—" She paused. "Like you said, trying to get my attention."

"But you don't believe that?"

"Sometimes I want to. But other times, I—"

"Just want to run along and do things your own way."

Carly shook her head. "Do you always do that?"

"You mean, finish other people's sentences for them?" The postmistress laughed. "Used to drive my husband crazy. Now that he's gone, I have to practice on others." She grinned. "How am I doing?"

"Great. But you're right. I think there might be a God only when I need something. And I have a feeling that's not the way it's supposed to be, is it?"

Mavis leaned on the table. "Would you like it if your kids only came to you when they wanted something and ignored you the rest of the time?"

"Of course not. But He's God, right? He doesn't need me. He doesn't need another person to look out for."

"Would you say that to your second child? 'I don't need more kids. I have enough to look after without you'."

"No, of course not."

Mavis stood and pulled a book from a small shelf near the back door. "Here. Read this. One of the best books I've found that explains what it really means to follow Christ."

Carly accepted the thin volume. *Making the Decision.* She looked up. "Is that what it is? A decision? Seems to me it's giving up a lot of stuff for what?"

Mavis laid a gnarled hand on her shoulder. "Let me tell you something. You don't have to give up anything you don't want to. So don't let that stop you from choosing. Because that's what it all comes down to. We get this time on earth to decide where we want to spend eternity. And then God blesses us with time to share with others." She glanced at the clock over the sink. "Now I have to scoot. Come back anytime."

Carly stood, the book clutched against her chest. Like a lifeline. Is that what it was? Would it change her life—or her—in any way?

Could it?

And if not, what did that say about her?

$ $ $

When Carly neared the back door leading into James' kitchen, she paused, tilting her head. Was that the phone? She jammed the key toward the lock, missing the first two times. When she finally managed to hit the target, she twisted the key and the doorknob at the same time, but the door wouldn't open.

What the—?

She sighed as the jangling continued, released the knob, then gave the deadbolt a final vicious yank before trying the door again. The door swung in and she stepped across the threshold, crossed the kitchen, and grabbed the handset from the charger near the coffeepot.

"Hello?"

She breathed deep through her nose to slow her breathing. No point in sounding like she'd run a marathon.

A soft cough. "I'm sorry. I must have wrong number."

"Who are you trying to reach?"

"James Norwood."

"I'm Carly, his next-door neighbor. And you are?"

"Mr. Norwood's solicitor. Is he available?"

Apparently the attorney didn't watch the news or listen to the radio, since the story of James' win and his subsequent murder. "Sorry. He died."

A sharp intake of breath. "Oh, dear. I saw the news story but didn't catch the name."

"Were you working on something for him?"

"Yes, his new will. He called on me the morning after the lottery drawing. Said he wanted to update his will since his wife's passing and now this added asset to his estate."

"Can you tell me anything about the will? Like who his beneficiaries are?"

"Sorry, no can do."

"Just a hint?"

"Not without a subpoena. Thank you."

Carly replaced the handset and considered her next option. She could sneak into the lawyer's office tonight and peek in the file. However, since she didn't want to spend the next five to ten years in prison, that was off the table. She didn't know any truly bad guys who weren't already incarcerated, so she couldn't turn to a friend for help.

She sighed. Seemed the only choice was to go to the Big Man himself.

Yep.

Police Chief Donovan.

After waiting several minutes for the call to transfer through, she got straight to the point and explained about the phone call. "So you see, Chief, maybe him changing his will propelled his previous beneficiaries to kill him."

"Carly, Carly. Not everybody has murderous family and charities, you know. Maybe you do, but I certainly don't."

"Well, I think you should get a look at his old will. That beneficiary is now a very rich person."

"Only if we find the money."

True. Something else to add to her to-do list. Find the money.

As if the task were as simple as that.

In the Money

## Chapter 19

On Saturday morning, Carly walked down to Main Street a few minutes after ten. She waved to a couple of townsfolk opening their places of business, including Mrs. Olsen at the pharmacy and Mavis at the post office, who waved her over.

"Good morning, Carly. How's the reading going?"

Carly's face heated at the image of the book Mavis gave her the previous day sitting on the end table in her living room, unopened. "Fine. Pacing myself, you know."

Mavis' smile widened, deepening the wrinkles around her eyes. "I know exactly. Took me a while, too. I bet I had that book for two years before I cracked it open."

"Good to hear I'm not the only one." She glanced toward the bank, two doors down. "Better get going."

"Sure. Don't be a stranger. I loved our chat yesterday."

"Me, too."

Yes, indeedy. Despite the fact the conversation turned to one subject she tended to avoid—God—the woman was a treasure. One she wished she'd gotten to know better, sooner.

Carly continued on, past the dress shop, and up the steps of the bank. The white granite structure and fan-shaped Crotch Island lavender-tinged steps gleamed in the morning sun. At the top, she pulled the solid oak door toward her and stepped inside.

Maine oak, well-polished over the hundred or so years the bank stood here, reflected the light, creating a warm and homey feeling. Thirty-foot-high ceilings, still lined with the original punched tin tiles, and the Wharf Quarry polished granite flooring bespoke old money and detailed care.

She crossed the lobby to the bank manager's office and tapped on the door.

Mr. Anderson, his vest stretched taut across his ample girth, looked up from his computer. He tossed her a smile. "Come in, Carly."

She slipped into one of the two wooden chairs and settled her backside into its carved seat, marveling—as she always did—at the comfort despite having no cushion beneath her. "Hi, Mr. Anderson. I'm hoping you can help me."

He sat back and folded his hands together in his lap. "That's what I'm here for."

"I'm a friend of James Norwood."

His brow pulled down. "Sad story, that. I've known James ever since he and Sadie moved to Bear Cove." His gaze reached for the ceiling. "Must be at least twenty-five years."

"Thirty, he said."

He peered at her. "So what do you need?"

Maybe this would be easier than she anticipated. "I don't think James ever made it back to Bear Cove after he collected his winnings, but I thought I'd check anyway and see if he did and made a deposit?"

"Don't know whether he came back, but he sure didn't deposit anything here."

"You're sure?"

A single nod. "He doesn't have an account here. Didn't trust banks. Especially after Sadie passed. I think she kept him on the straight and narrow, but the day after her funeral, he came in, paid off his mortgage, and closed his accounts. Had a sizable amount, too, as I recollect."

Strange. As the only bank in town, Aroostook National carried accounts for most everybody in town, and for some who didn't even live in Bear Cove but liked the personalized service. "You're sure?"

He chuckled. "I love it when people do that. Ask me if I'm sure. Like I would say something I knew to be untrue. Or would speak with certainty on a topic I knew nothing about."

She stood. "Well, thanks for your help."

He held up a hand. "He didn't have an account, but he does—or I guess did—have a safe deposit box."

Her heartbeat quickened. This was great news. But why would a man who didn't trust banks entrust something important enough to keep under lock and key?

Mr. Anderson nodded. "I can read your mind. Asked myself the same question. But if you want to see what's inside, you'll need a subpoena. That's the law." He leaned forward and grinned. "Unless you're his beneficiary and you have a copy of his will and the key?"

"No, nothing like that. Just a friend trying to find his killer."

"Yes. I remember you have a predilection for that kind of thing."

Her face heated for the second time that morning. Mr. Anderson, friendly enough today, wasn't quite so amiable the day his bank was robbed and he denied it ever happening. Said it was a drill.

Sure, which is why the old bank guard fired off his gun after the speeding getaway car.

She headed for the door then paused and turned to face him. "I'll see the chief about getting the necessary documents."

"I'm sure you will."

Thankfully, Police Chief Donovan took no time requesting the subpoena, and within thirty minutes, he led the way into the bank and toward the manager's office, Carly close on his heels.

Mr. Anderson barely glanced at the document then gestured toward a door leading into the vault area. Resisting the urge to push to the head of the line, Carly followed the two men, standing to one side while the manager set the box on the table and opened it.

Pieces of paper of varying sizes and shapes, all covered with numbers, packed tight inside.

Lottery tickets.

Dozens of them.

Chief Donovan emptied the contents on the table and Carly picked through the bits and pieces, each one with numbers scribbled on them. She selected several and studied them. Looked like he thought he'd won. Stars and exclamation points covered the surfaces. Numbers circled. Others crossed out. WINNER, WINNER AGAIN, and HAWAII HERE WE COME scrawled on the front and back of many.

A lump formed in her throat. This was the James she knew and loved. She held up a couple of tickets. "He thought he won."

Mr. Anderson cleared his throat softly. "Again. More than once. Unfortunately. I think his eyesight was failing."

She shook her head. "Some of these go back almost twenty years. His eyes were fine then. I think he was simply addicted to the rush of believing he'd won."

The chief nodded. "Maybe so. Different strokes for different folks."

"There's just one thing, though."

And that one thing was a very big one thing.

"How could he really believe he'd won yet never claim his winnings?"

Chief Donovan gathered the old tickets and sifted them through his fingers, letting them fall to the table again. "You're right. Never thought of it like that."

Mr. Anderson shoved his hands into his vest pockets. "He'd come in and sit here for an hour at a time, just looking at those old tickets."

Carly stacked tickets into a pile then tapped them on the table before returning them to the metal container. "Did you ever talk to him about it?"

The bank manager shook his head. "Only to ask him if he really wanted to renew the box year after year. He was adamant he would keep his treasures safe."

Carly sighed. "Maybe they were mementoes from his time with Sadie?"

He shrugged. "I don't think he started buying tickets until after she passed."

"What triggered that behavior, do you think?"

"Don't know. She had a long, lingering death. Cancer, I think. Just about bankrupted him. But he said he'd have sold his soul if it would have saved her. Desperate, I guess, is how I would describe him. He wanted to mortgage his house to pay for a non-traditional experimental treatment, but because of his age and income, he didn't qualify."

Chief Donovan leaned against the bank of deposit boxes. "Might be why he didn't trust banks."

"Maybe." The bank manager looked at the mess on the table. "Are we done here?"

Donovan nodded. "I think so. Gives me insight into the man, but doesn't point to who might have killed him."

Carly peered into the box. "His will isn't here. Strange. That's one of the documents a person usually keeps safe. I didn't see it at his house, either."

The chief headed for the door. "His attorney probably has it on file."

Likely so.

But why keep old tickets safe, but not think a will should be?
Particularly for a man who didn't trust banks.
What did that say about his thought process?
Or the value he placed on one document over the other?

In the Money

Chapter 20

Feeling at a loss for what to do next, Carly returned to James' house. There had to be something she'd overlooked on previous excursions. But what? He didn't seem like a man with a lot of secrets. Then again, he had a safe deposit box and she hadn't found a key.

After letting herself in through the back door again, she headed down the hallway. Sure, the bedrooms had already been searched, but maybe they'd missed that single, vital piece of information that would lead her to the solution to his murder.

And the theft of the money, of course.

Although, that was likely easier to resolve.

Greed, pure and simple.

She slowed as she neared the last room at the end of the hall, the one James and Sadie shared for so many years. The one where he'd slept alone up until last week. She resisted the urge to knock on the door—somehow simply entering what was usually out-of-bounds for visitors made her squeamish. Like she was totally invading his privacy.

She stood in the middle of the room and turned around slowly, considering every nook and cranny. The dresser? Unlikely. Too common and every day for a special secret. The bedside table? No. The first place a thief—or a sneak—would look. Bathroom? Mike said he already went through there with a fine-toothed comb.

She wound herself around, feeling much like the little ballerina in a jewelry box she owned as a child. The two-inch doll, dressed in pink tulle, twirled around when she opened the lid. She had no necklaces or bracelets worth speaking of, but she'd sit for hours watching the beautiful dancer, wishing such graceful pirouettes, points, and passes upon herself.

She drew a deep breath and exhaled.

*Think, Carly. Where would you hide something you didn't want somebody else to find?*

She lifted the bed skirt and peeked under. Nothing but a dust bunny and a lone sock.

The only place left was the closet.

She slid open the door. Women's clothing hung on the right side, men's on the left. Appeared James didn't have the heart to dispose of his wife's belongings. On the shelf, shoeboxes, a hatbox or two, several blankets encased in clear zippered bags, and three puzzle boxes.

Hmm. That could be something.

But no. Brand new puzzles, still sealed.

She shoved the boxes back on the shelf.

Perhaps the shoeboxes? The labels indicated women's shoes, but she wouldn't believe anything until she confirmed it for herself.

Again, shoes and nothing but. She even removed the footwear and tipped them out on the bed in case he'd stashed anything in the toes. She'd heard that was a safe place to hide valuables. But apparently James and Sadie didn't subscribe to that particular theory.

On to James' side of the closet. A couple of suits, a spinner of ties, four long-sleeve dress shirts, and the rest of the hanging space occupied with blue jeans and flannel shirts—his usual attire. She checked suit pockets—nothing. Pulled aside the clothes to check for hooks holding hidden items behind. Nothing.

On the shelf, three shoeboxes. One labeled steel-toed work boots. Probably a hang-on from his working days. Another marked patent leather loafers. To go with his suits, no doubt. The final box, under the other three, indicated running shoes.

Strange. She hadn't thought James the running type. Or even the exercise kind of guy. He was more likely to go for a walk to the post office. Or spend time working in his garden, or fixing something in his house.

She simply couldn't picture James jogging on a path, running on a track, or even speed-walking down the street.

She pulled down the three boxes and checked inside the top two. Nothing but shoes.

After setting those back on the shelf, she lifted the lid of the third box and peeked in.

And gasped.

Money. Lots of it.

Letting the cover fall back into place, she carried the box to the bed and set it beside her on the faded quilt, likely lovingly made by Sadie. Wedding Ring. Traditional wedding gift for many years. In pale blues, greens, and pinks. A family heirloom, to be sure.

She blinked back tears.

Except no family would claim this beauty.

She removed the lid and set it aside, revealing bundles of bills. Hundreds and fifties.

Thousands of dollars. Maybe hundreds of thousands. She'd never seen so much money in one place.

She stacked the bills according to denomination, then peered inside the box. Down in one corner, a tarnished bit of brass peeked out. She tipped the box from side to side until the item worked its way loose then she picked it up.

A safe deposit box key.

But not stamped with the Aroostook National Bank's name.

No, this one was for another bank, or so said the inscription. PNB. She slipped the key into her pocket then returned the money to the box. Now what to do? Should she put the box back where she found it? Or should she turn it in to Chief Donovan? Or James' attorney?

The house was safe enough. And maybe James mentioned the cash in his will. If so, the beneficiary would receive it in due course.

She slid the box back into place under the other two, checked to make sure nothing looked disturbed, slid the door shut, and headed for the back door, the key practically burning a hole in her pocket.

Funny how a man who didn't trust a bank account would trust not just one safe deposit box, but two.

James was a mystery inside a puzzle wrapped in an enigma.

Or however the saying went.

$ $ $

Monday morning, feeling more refreshed than she had in days, Carly tracked down PNB. Portland National Bank. And surprise—it had only branch. Across the street from the lottery office.

The same one James visited after collecting his check.

Where he cashed same check.

She called Chief Donovan. "Chief, I found another deposit box key in James' house."

He sighed. "I'm not even going to ask how and where you found it."

She decided not to mention the money. "It's for the Portland National Bank across the street from the Lottery Commission."

"But we know he left the bank with the cash from his winnings."

"Doesn't mean he hasn't been there before." Was the man choosing to act obtuse on purpose, or was this his natural method of investigation? "When you talked to the bank, did they mention he had a box with them?"

A long pause, a squeak of the chair, and a soft clearing of the throat filled what would otherwise have been an even more lengthy silence. "Well, here's the thing. . . ."

She gritted her teeth. She wasn't going to like what he'd say next.

"I didn't actually talk to the bank."

She was right. She didn't like it even a teensy bit. "Isn't that standard protocol in an investigation?"

The overworked hinges on the chief's chair protested again. "Normally, yes. I talked to the Lottery Commission, and they called the bank to see if the check was cashed. It was. James called there first thing that morning and said he wanted cash. Then he went to the commission when it opened, and returned to the bank before noon. They had the money ready."

"And you got this from?"

"The gal at the commission."

"But you didn't ask her about whether he was a customer of the bank?"

"Well, to be fair, Carly, even if I had, they'd have said no, most likely. Accounts and safe deposit box departments aren't always connected, particularly in smaller banks. Which this one is."

"What can we do?"

"I'll get the judge to issue a subpoena, fax it to the bank, and get them to open the box just like we did here in Bear Cove. Will that satisfy you?"

She stared into the handset, drew a couple of breaths to cool the heat rising in her face, then swallowed back what she really wanted to say, instead pasting a smile on her face. Wasn't that what sales people did? Smiled into the phone so they exuded an atmosphere of peace and calm?

"This isn't about satisfying me. It's about finding who brutally killed an old man and stole his money. Maybe there's more money missing than his recent winnings. This could be an entire conspiracy."

He chuckled. "And maybe it's where he kept more old, losing lottery tickets. Or his will."

"Possibly. So how long before we know what's inside?"

"I'll get the paperwork going. Call a contact on the Portland PD and ask him to send someone down to the bank. Noon, maybe."

"Okay, I'll wait at home for your call. Mike and I can head over to the hospital this afternoon for our gig there."

After disconnecting, she strolled into the kitchen where Mike was busy at the stove, scrambling eggs and cooking sausage. They enjoyed a hearty breakfast while she filled him in on her morning's adventure.

He shook his head when she finished, right about the same time as she mopped up the last of her eggs with a slice of toast. "I declare, you get more done in a few hours than most people accomplish in an entire day." He swiped at his brow with the back of his hand. "I'm tired just listening to you."

"Well, I told the chief I'd wait here for his call. I have bills to pay, a couple of reports to finish for another client, and hopefully by that time, we'll have heard from him." She stood to clear the table. "What do you want for lunch?"

He grinned. "Hardly finished one meal and already planning the next."

"Okay. You can be in charge of the menu."

He finished his coffee. "No way. I did breakfast."

She laughed as she rinsed dishes and set them in the dishwasher. Doc wound his way around her legs, so she took a few minutes to fill his dish and pat him, scratching behind his ears the way he loved. After throwing a load of laundry in the washer, she went to her desk and immersed herself in the paperwork that multiplied if she didn't deal with it.

Right around the time her rumbling stomach told her the noon hour approached, the landline rang.

She snatched up the handset, her breath coming in short pants. "Hello?"

"Carly, it's Chief Donovan. Got your answers."

Not likely. She had more questions than she could shake a stick at.

"Shoot."

"The box contained more old lottery tickets. Dozens and dozens. Just like the box in town."

She winced. This wasn't what she expected. Or hoped for. Then again, maybe James left town with more than his lottery winnings.

Maybe whatever he secured in that box was now long gone.

"Is that all?"

"Nope. There was cash in there, too. Thousands of dollars. And something else."

"What?"

"Several more deposit box keys. At the same bank. They opened those up, and found more money. All told, almost half a million dollars. In used bills. No bank wrappers."

Unlike the money in the shoebox in his closet. That was all new bills with plain paper bands. "What do you think he was doing?"

A long sigh. "I don't know. I guess I'll have to subpoena his tax returns and see if he claimed this money, because I don't see how he could have saved it on a train engineer's salary."

"I agree." Which was unusual. Maybe she should make a note on her calendar. TODAY I AGREED WITH CHIEF DONOVAN. A fact which would prove that members of the porcine family could take wing. "Could be an inheritance."

"Right. Or life insurance."

"Yes."

She chewed on the end of her pen. Or it could be something else. Life insurance, inheritance, and lottery winnings would be included on his tax returns.

So they should be able to confirm its origin.

Unless it was illegally—or immorally—acquired.

Because that amount was almost exactly the amount embezzled from the community hospital.

Not including the money in the shoebox, of course.

Could James have been in cahoots with the hacker? Mental note to self: check if James had a connection with the hospital.

Or was he an unwilling accomplice?

If he died because of his involvement in the theft from the hospital, they were looking in completely the wrong direction. Perhaps he crossed his cohort. Threatened to tell somebody about the money. Maybe once he won the lottery, he decided to come clean.

This meant that the motive for James' death might now be linked with the hospital hacker. Who had motive, means, and opportunity to kill her friend? Gail Prouse and Gerard Payne, to be sure, if either of them was the hacker. Up until this point, the investigation focused on proving who broke into the hospital's computer system. There had been no connection between James' death and the hacking.

Did the director and the IT guy have an alibi for the time James went missing? She hadn't asked that question before.

And if they did, then who else might it be?

She sighed.

She sure had her work cut out for her.

In the Money

## Chapter 21

Mike held open the door to the conference room to allow Carly to precede him. He wasn't sure what she was up to, but judging by the glint in her eye and the determined look on her face when she hung up from talking the chief about two hours before, she was on to something.

He just hoped she didn't intend going out on a short limb. She could make leaps of conclusion that would embarrass Superman. Unfortunately, sometimes those huge jumps ended up suspending her over a chasm. Still, she always managed to work out the puzzle and solve the mystery.

Not that past success was always a guarantee for the future.

The chief trailed them into the room and chose a chair where he sat with his back to the window. Gail Prouse and Gerard Payne already occupied seats, Gail nervously toying with a pen, while Payne sat with his arms crossed over his chest, leaned back in his chair as though relaxed and unconcerned.

The slight flaring of his nostrils and the pinched lines around his mouth told a different story, however.

Carly sat in one of the two chairs nearest the door, and Mike slid into the other. Chief Donovan agreed they could sit in on the interviews, but warned them this was his investigation. At first, Carly protested—as Mike expected she would—but after Donovan reminded her he needn't allow her in the room at all, she quieted and agreed to remain silent.

Mike stifled a smile.

He'd like to see her not get involved. Just once.

Payne straightened and set his hands on the table, palms down. "Why are we here? I have a lot of work to do, and calling me in here makes me look bad."

Carly snorted, and the chief tossed her a warning look. She sat back in her chair, hands clasped in her lap.

So far, so good.

Chief Donovan nodded to both Gail and Payne. "I appreciate you taking time from your busy day to meet with me."

Gail cast Payne a glance. "I don't see we had much choice."

The chief's mouth turned down for a flash as though commiserating with her. "We—" He coughed. "I have a few more questions. We've just uncovered more information about a crime we thought was previously unrelated, but now appears to be connected, so I need to confirm your alibis again."

Payne shook his head, disgust evident in his drawn brow and narrowed eyes. "We already went through that. There is no evidence I was involved in the hacking. You haven't found any because it doesn't exist."

Gayle nodded. "And the same goes for me."

"Oh, did I not mention it? This is now also a murder enquiry."

Mike bit the inside of his cheek, reminding himself to remain impassive. Payne's jaw muscles worked up and down a couple of times, while Gayle's face lost all color. Interesting how the mention of murder and their possible involvement changed their entire stance.

Was that a sign of guilt?

Or merely fear?

Payne recovered first, shaking his head. "I don't know what you're talking about."

The chief nodded. "No, because I haven't told you who is dead. But it's interesting how you both reacted."

Gail frowned. "We are not in a courtroom. You can't railroad us into pleading guilty so you can close out two cases at once. I. Am. Not. Guilty."

Chief Donovan smiled at her. "Of anything?"

Her mouth opened a couple of times, but no sound came out.

The lawman nodded once. "As I thought. Few of us are entirely innocent." He swiveled his head to address the IT guy. "And what about you?"

Payne shrugged. "I didn't kill anybody. That I'd remember, I'm sure."

Mike winced and glanced at his wife. Her friend died. Would she be able to keep her word in spite of the man's nonchalant attitude? He reached across the foot or so separating them and gripped her hand. She squeezed his fingers. He exhaled. She'd be okay.

Donovan scribbled a note on the paper in front of him. "Let's start with you, Gail. Where were you the evening of a week ago Thursday?"

"That's a fairly specific timeframe for the hacking."

"This is about murder."

The hospital director stared at him. "I said I didn't kill anybody."

"Good. Then where were you?"

Her gaze went to the ceiling. Mike was fairly certain she was about to tell the truth, judging by her body language.

She returned her stare to the chief. "At a team-building exercise with my department heads. All day Thursday from around ten until around five on Friday."

Donovan made another note. "Folks will vouch for you?"

Her eyes narrowed. "Yes."

"Fine. I'll want a list of who was there." He turned to face Payne. "How about you?"

"Last Thursday? Let me see." He closed his eyes then opened them. "Nope. Can't remember." He held out his hands, wrists together. "Guess you'd better arrest me."

"Think again."

The chief's command came out as a growl. The man could be tough when he wanted.

Payne's cheeks colored. "I worked all day. Went home. Had dinner with my wife. Around ten she went into premature labor and I took her to the ER. We were there until noon on Friday."

"That was easy. Why not simply say instead of trying to look like a tough guy?"

"Force of habit, I guess."

Donovan wrote again. "Interesting habit, obstruction of justice." He looked up. "Where did you say you lived before Bear Cove?"

Now the color ran down Payne's neck. "I didn't."

"That will be all. Thank you."

Gail stood. "We're free to leave?"

"Yes."

She harrumphed and exited the room, leaving behind a trail of expensive perfume. Payne followed in her steps, closing the door more forcefully than necessary.

At least in Mike's humble opinion.

When the chief snapped his notebook shut, Carly finally spoke up. "So what do you think?"

"I'll check out their stories, but it seems as though neither could have killed James. But it doesn't mean they aren't in league with the hacker. Or the killer. And I'm sure hoping these two crooks are one and the same."

Mike nodded. "Me, too. Seems a strange coincidence for two mastermind criminals to be operating in this town at the same time."

Carly sighed. "Even though they both have the skills to accomplish the fraud, I agree. Both are looking less likely."

Mike stood and offered her his hand, which she accepted, slipping hers into his like a glove. A comfortable glove, at that. "So what's next?"

The chief rounded the table and opened the door. "We keep looking." He glanced at Carly. "And by that, of course, I mean we the police."

She grinned. "Sure. I knew what you meant. But you have to admit, I've found some leads you didn't know existed."

"Right. Tripling my workload on this case."

Carly exited first, with Mike following in the chief's wake. He clapped the lawman on the shoulder. "That's about par for the course with Carly. I always tell her she's a full-time job."

Carly turned to face them, forcing them to an abrupt halt. "But that's what keeps life interesting, right?"

Both men laughed, and Carly and Mike returned to their respective work assignments.

She was correct, though.

Never a dull day since he married her.

$ $ $

After dinner, Carly left Mike snoozing on the sofa to make a quick trek to Flatirons. The place where James' body was found had to be significant. Otherwise, why not simply kill him in Portland? Or at the motel? The killer would have taken fewer risks by getting rid of the body in a large city. In fact, done correctly, they may never have learned the fate of their friend and neighbor.

She shuddered. The idea of his body being unceremoniously dumped in a landfill or submerged in a lake or buried in the forest horrified her. Thinking of him out there by himself was too much to fathom, even though the James she knew and loved no longer resided within his mortal shell.

Unfortunately, this morbid train of thought did nothing to improve her mood or her reasoning ability. Dark already, thinking about bodies and death and murder sank her even deeper into her thoughts. Which led her to seek a remedy. Nothing came to mind. She turned on the radio, but the scratchy Portland station irritated her already tender nerves. Something akin to a fog settled over her brain, preventing her from thinking through everything she knew.

She gritted her teeth. What she really needed was a stack of index cards and a flat surface to organize her ideas. Swap and rearrange until the story made sense. Like plotting out a book.

Weary of mind and body, she focused on the driving. The sooner she got there, the sooner she'd get home. And if she let herself get too tired, she might succumb to a Maine speed bump—a deer or moose crossing the highway.

Wishing she'd thought to stop for a coffee, she soldiered on, turning on the AC full blast and popping in one of her favorite music CDs. At last she turned off the highway to the small town and headed up the main drag to Brad's Bargain Beauties. Thankfully, the lights were off and the gate closed, corralling the vehicles inside and would-be low-budget car thieves outside.

She parked and got out. The lot looked exactly as it had the day she found James' car. As she suspected, Brad didn't make a lot of sales. Didn't have a lot of turnover. Which was why the car likely sat there for several days before she found it.

She studied the street, noting the various businesses, some still open. An old-fashioned drive in. A newer pharmacy, one of the big brand names. Several other used car lots. A row of red brick-faced businesses, including a flower shop, a bridal dress salon, and a crematorium.

She giggled, wondering if the latter got much walk-in business from the other two.

Probably not.

She turned and looked in the opposite direction. Brad's lot was really near the end of town. A gas station, a garage, some empty storefronts, then a bridge and a sign indicating drivers were leaving town and exhorting them to come back soon.

She sighed. Flatirons was like so many other small towns in Maine.

Population decreasing as subsequent generations left for college and jobs. Mom-and-pop businesses struggling to survive. No plans for the future, always living in the past.

She glanced up at a couple of pigeons on the telephone wire over her head. Stupid birds. Always leaving their droppings everywhere and anywhere. They'd better not—she followed the pole down toward her level.

And spotted it.

That clue she knew was there but didn't know where to look before now.

A NO PARKING sign. On Thursdays. Street sweeping day, apparently.

Note to self: ask Chief Webb to check tickets issued last Thursday in this area.

Maybe this was the break she needed.

Because if somebody followed James here—or parked their car on this street in advance of the murder—they might have gotten a ticket.

She could only hope the meter maids in Flatirons were as diligent as the ones in most cities.

Chapter 22

The next morning, Mike kissed Carly good-bye at the door leading into the hospital finance department, then headed back to the conference room for yet another meeting.

That was definitely one benefit of working for himself—fewer meetings.

Still, this one included only the team directly investigating the hacking side of the breach of cybersecurity. In his experience, fewer attendees meant less time spent away from where the real work was done.

When he entered, John Backman, the federal agent, and Bob Powell, the insurance investigator, were already seated. Backman flipped through a file, while Powell checked something on his phone.

Or played one of those new-fangled games called apps. Mike never saw the point of lugging around a gaming device. His own cell, simple and flip-style, suited him just fine. It made calls. That was about it.

He sat across the table from the other two and set his notes in front of him. "Good morning."

The Fed tossed him a smile. "So who called this meeting?"

Mike raised a hand. "I confess that I did." He opened his file folder. "I think I'm seeing a pattern in some of the coding, but I wanted to pass it by you guys, as experts in the field, before I go to Ted about it."

Powell leaned forward, elbows on the table. "Good idea. Don't want to get ahead of ourselves."

No worries about that. So far, this entire process moved about as fast as maple syrup running uphill on a winter's day. Mike exhaled. Patience. Isn't that what he always told Carly? A smile tickled his lips. No, he always told her she was a full-time job.

One he was happy to be the only applicant for.

Because no matter how much she confounded, surprised, and tested him, he loved her dearly and would have her no other way.

He pulled three sets of sheets from his stack and slid a set across the table to each of the two men. "Take a look at these, and then we'll talk."

The men studied the pages then sat back, Bob Powell the last to finish. He tapped the papers. "So what are we looking at?"

"I compared the code changes from this hospital with the changes in code at the insurance company and the other hospital group."

Powell's face darkened. "And?" He made a show of thrusting his hand out and checking his watch. "Cut to the chase. I don't have all day."

John Backman cleared his throat softly. "We're all busy, but this is the job we've been assigned."

One corner of Powell's mouth lifted in a sneer. "You might be assigned one case at a time, G-man, but not me. I have at least ten other investigations going on demanding my time and attention."

This was going nowhere but downhill. And fast. Mike spread the papers in front of him. "If you look at the introduction to the code change in each case." He pointed to the top lines of the pages before the other men. "Right there. The hacker uses an unconventional format. And it's the same in all three."

John compared the coding. "You're right."

Mike nodded, gratified he scored a point with at least the FBI agent. Powell might be a tougher nut to crack. "I'd never have noticed it if I wasn't looking at them side-by-side."

Powell peered at him. "Okay. So maybe it's not the same guy. Maybe they had the same teacher."

"I considered that, but since it is so unconventional, I thought it unlikely it would be taught in a school setting."

Backman sat back in his chair. "So what made you think to look at all three like this?"

Mike shrugged. "I was getting nowhere with the other methods I used. I couldn't get back through all the protocols and server transfers. This guy is good."

This time a smirk from Powell. "Better than you?"

"I found this, didn't I?" Mike exhaled. Why did some guys think they needed to tear others down to make themselves look good? "Now that we know his signature, so to speak, we can look for other instances where he hacked into other systems."

Backman laced his hands behind his head. "I'll get in touch with victims from other reported instances of cybercrime and have them check the code. Maybe we'll find out where this guy has been."

Powell frowned. "Seems to me that's just opening an entire Pandora's box. The more cases we find, the more difficult to figure out who is doing it."

John shook his head. "Actually, it makes it easier to uncover the perp since the pool of possible suspects diminishes with each instance. The number of people in two places at a specific time is huge. The number of people in ten places at a specific time a crime occurs is very small. Usually only a handful or so."

Mike gathered his papers. "Good. I'll keep looking for other examples of similarities in the code while you do your bit."

Powell muttered something under his breath that Mike didn't quite catch. Something about opening up a can of worms.

Mike smiled as he followed the investigator from the room. One thing about having worms—made it easier to catch a fish.

And with any luck at all, he'd snag a trophy-sized big-mouth bass.

$ $ $

Carly scanned the employee list from the three companies identified as potential victims of the same hacker. Beginning with the other hospital group and starting about eighteen months ago, through the insurance company, and ending with the Down East Health Group, of which Bear Cove Community Hospital was a member, there were hundreds of names on each list.

Apparently healthcare was a huge industry.

And a fluid one, judging by the number of names on two lists. More than a dozen.

But only four with the initials GP on all three lists.

Gail Prouse and Gerard Payne, as well as Gabrielle Purdue and Galeesh Pradati.

Under the Human Resources tab, she typed in James' name. She was fairly certain he'd never worked at the hospital. Perhaps his wife?

Nothing.

Another prompt under the HR page: VOLUNTEERS. Could it be? Yes. He volunteered at the hospital for the past two years, but not in the last month or so. Strange. Had something happened to disillusion him from his service there? Or was something more nefarious going on?

Was he involved with the hacker? Maybe got cold feet? And now lay on a slab in the morgue because of it?

But trying to imagine James as a thief—even unwittingly—was a huge leap of faith she wasn't prepared to take. Like he said, he might have been born at night, but it wasn't last night.

Still, it was an interesting piece of information. One she'd keep to herself for now.

She called Ted Wilson, the hospital director. "Do you have a few minutes?"

"Sure. What can I do for you?"

She gave him a quick recap of her findings. "I have four names on all three lists that could fit the timeframe of all three breaches."

"Can you prove it was one of them?"

She sighed. "No. In fact, Gail Prouse and Gerard Payne, while they haven't been ruled out conclusively, are looking less and less like the hackers."

An exhale. Relief? Frustration? Or just weariness of the entire topic? "I have a board of directors meeting next week, and I want to be able to either give them a name, or assure them we've identified our losses and our insurance will cover it."

"Well, I think that given enough time, Mike and I can identify who's behind this and have sufficient evidence for the police or the FBI to take it from there and convict."

"Have you seen the news lately?"

"I watch the ten o'clock news most nights. Why?"

"Then you know the media got its teeth into this and they won't let go. Their reporting puts us in a bad light. Suggestions have been made that perhaps HIPPA laws have been broken."

"Would you rather catch and stop this criminal, or have the media talk nice about the hospital?"

"I shouldn't have to choose."

Dream on, big boy. In Carly's experience, there was always a choice to make. Sometimes the lesser of two evils. Sometimes between two good alternatives. "No client information was breached."

"I don't know that. The criminal got into our patient and billing systems. He created fake invoices, then deposited checks into a bank account. He stole from us, from patients, and now from our insurer."

"What else is going on, Ted?"

"What do you mean?"

"Last week when you hired us, there was no smoking gun hanging over our heads. Now all of a sudden, when we're getting close to identifying the hacker, you're getting cold feet." She paused. Was Ted involved and now trying to throw them off the trail? "If I didn't know better. . ."

"If you didn't know better what?" A couple of sputters filled the phone. "Are you implying I might be the hacker?" He chuckled. "No worries. I can check email and that's about it."

"So what is it?"

"Bear Cove Hospital is up for accreditation again. The director kindly reminded me yesterday we don't need to look for ways to draw an unfavorable review from the committee."

Carly harrumphed. "I'd think identifying the thief would garner you extra points."

"But it makes them look more closely into our data procedures if they think somebody could break into our system."

Carly understood well of what he spoke. Some of her past assignments included auditing businesses for valuation, and when she discovered even a small anomaly in their accounting practices, she always dug deeper.

Where there's smoke, there's fire. As the old saying went.

She said her good-byes and disconnected the call.

Ted had valid concerns, that was certain.

But to allow a criminal to escape justice—well that wasn't in her.

And it wouldn't be this time.

Not if she could help it.

$ $ $

That afternoon, Carly slid into the last row of seats in the already-packed church, a lump in her throat the size of Texas threatening to cut off her breathing.

James' funeral.

About three rows from the front of the sanctuary, Mavis' well-coiffed head identified where the postmistress sat. Carly studied the oversized photo of James with a woman—Sadie, perhaps?—and the large arrangements of flowers lining the steps leading to the raised platform where an older man sat. She nodded to several others from town that she recognized, then addressed the small pamphlet containing the order of service and the story of her friend's life.

The same photo, this one in miniature to fit the piece, smiled out at her. A happier—and healthier—time for both of them. Sadie's shy smile in contrast to James' expansive expression, his arm around her shoulder, holding her close to his heart.

Carly's eyes misted over as she read about him. A longtime member of his church. Active in visiting shut-ins. And despite his recent diagnosis of kidney failure, he never failed to drive friends who could no longer get around.

She stopped reading. Recent diagnosis. He'd not mentioned a word to her. Not that they were close friends. After all, she went to his home once a week for a few minutes during the lottery drawing. It wasn't as though they were besties or anything.

A portly man stood over her, and she looked up. He gestured to the seat beside her—not nearly enough room—and smiled. She slid over on the wooden bench—pew, wasn't it?—and settled in again.

The man sat and offered his hand. "Peter Drew. James' attorney."

Her breath quickened, and the lump disintegrated at this serendipity. "Carly Turnquist. Neighbor and friend."

"And something to do with investigating crimes, if I'm not mistaken?" His soft chuckle reminded her of Doc's purring. "He said you had one of the best minds for mystery he knew."

Her cheeks heated. She didn't know James thought that of her.

The things a person learned about somebody at their funeral.

She smiled. "He was a good man. He sure didn't deserve to die like that."

Peter leaned a mite closer. "Are you helping the police?"

"Doing what I can."

"We talked recently, didn't we?"

"Yes. You called to tell James that his will was ready."

Peter's smile slipped away. "Yes. Sorry I couldn't help you more. But client confidentiality, and all that."

"So did you also prepare his original will?"

"Yes."

"Can you tell me anything else?"

He quirked his chin toward the paper in her hand. "You know he was in advanced kidney failure?"

She rattled the paper. "Not until I read this."

"Ayuh. Didn't want to go through dialysis. Said he lived a good life. Refused to go on the transplant list. Wanted a younger person to have that chance." He sighed then folded his hands across his belly. "But that's why he wanted to update his will. To get his affairs in order, he said. His estate was minimal. The house. His car. Some savings."

"Who was he changing the will to benefit?"

The attorney glanced around before settling back in his seat. "I guess it's okay to tell you now, since the will has already been read. He wanted to split it between his church and the town library. Like I said, there wouldn't have been much after probate and taxes."

"Who was the previous beneficiary?"

"Still is the beneficiary, of course, since he died before he could sign the new one."

"Right. Who is it?"

"A small faith-based charity that helps people struggling with addictions such as drugs and alcohol. I don't recall the name right now, but if you need to know, call and I'll get you their contact information."

"Thanks."

The older man on the platform stood behind the lectern. "Good afternoon, friends of James. Shall we begin?"

While the man, who identified himself as the pastor, talked about James and his life, Carly sat back to think through this new information from the lawyer. How terrible that James was facing a terrible illness and didn't share that with her or Mike. Had he told Mavis? She'd have to ask, but she doubted the postmistress would hold back that bit of news from her.

And despite the attorney's belief that James had a small estate, Carly knew better. Including the recent lottery winning, the man was worth somewhere in the neighborhood of two million dollars. Or perhaps more.

But who would kill a man with a terminal illness? Maybe somebody who didn't know of the diagnosis.

Perhaps somebody connected to the original beneficiary who knew

James planned to change his will.

Somebody who knew about the most recent lottery win who wanted to get at the money through less-than-legal means?

But what about the rest of the money James had squirreled away? The original beneficiary would get that as part of the estate.

Unless the killer knew about the money and had a way to get to it.

She sighed.

Seemed like there were more scenarios and more unnamed Somebodies than she could shake a stick at.

But she was like a bloodhound when it came to solving mysteries. James was right about that.

She wouldn't give up.

James would get the justice he deserved.

# Chapter 23

Carly compared Mike's list of four suspects with the initials GP to the employment lists provided by the hospital Human Resources department, confirming the four had worked at the three organizations affected during the time of the known fraud.

Hmm. That was interesting. Another name popped off the pages before her.

Ted Wilson, the Down East Health Group director.

Interesting he hadn't mentioned his connection to the other two.

Of course, his initials weren't GP.

Not that the hacker would definitely use their own initials.

Pretty stupid if he did, actually.

Almost as dumb as Wilson hiring her to identify the thief if he was actually the guilty party.

Then again, crooks weren't nearly as smart as they thought they were.

At least in her experience.

So now she had five names. Three, actually, since phone calls about Galeesh Pradati indicated he'd died about a year ago in a car crash. Gabrielle Purdue had married her multimillionaire boss and had no financial reason to hack into the system. Appeared they were off her list.

And Gail Prouse and Gerard Payne had cast iron alibis for when James was killed, so if they were as involved as her theory suggested, they had a partner.

Which left Wilson.

She went back and reviewed the files sent to her by the other hospital group and the insurance company, setting aside several reports, when yet another name leapt off the page.

Bob Powell.

Every report contained his signature and contact information.

For all three investigations.

Interesting.

Time for a phone call.

She dialed Powell's number then introduced herself. He grunted a less-than-welcoming reply, and she plowed on ahead with the reason for her call. "I was going through files from the other two hacking investigations that were similar to the one we're currently working on."

"Uh-huh."

"Noticed your name on the reports from both."

"Really?" A long sigh. "Possibly. I handle a dozen or more cases every month. Can't remember them all."

"You recommended in one instance that the medical insurer pay blackmail to the hacker who infiltrated their system so he'd give them the key to reverse it."

"If I did, it was the cheapest way out of the problem."

"Did your company pay out on that blackmail?"

"Not my department."

She stifled a snort. Not his department indeed. "And the hospital network that didn't even report the loss to the authorities but paid the ransom for the solution, that was your case, too."

"Look, my job is to investigate to make sure the client isn't trying to rip off the insurance company I work for. We insure businesses against losses of many kinds. And sometimes paying a ransom or blackmail—and those are your words. You absolutely won't see that in any report of mine—is a quicker and cheaper resolution to the problem."

"When you were looking into those thefts, did you get anywhere close to identifying the hacker?"

"Not my—"

Now it was her turn to sigh. "I know. Not your department. So you have no clue as to who GP is?"

"You know, just because they use those initials doesn't mean that their name really begins with those letters."

"Right. But if someone was working for a company and adopted a user ID that didn't match their name, wouldn't that raise red flags for somebody in HR?"

"Not necessarily. They might say it's their kid's name. Or where they honeymooned. Or their nickname for their wife. Stuff like that." Tapping of a pencil on the desk filled the phone. "Plus, most systems don't assign the user ID. It's set up through an administrative function. So even the fact that the hacker is using 243 doesn't mean there were several hundred GP's before him. Make sense?"

"Perfectly. So what you're really saying is that GP243 could be as fake as a wig."

"Right. But like a good wig, it can also serve as a red herring and lead an investigator down the wrong path. Like a rabbit trail."

"Gone down plenty of those already. This guy is good. Mike said he's run into plenty of dead ends in the coding, too. Kinda like mazes. I never was good at those."

"Takes a different kind of logic for those."

She sat back in her chair. "Numbers are my friend."

Yes, indeedy. People might change, but numbers never did.

No matter how they were manipulated, they always added up.

Unlike Bob Powell. Tentative, terse, abrupt at the beginning of the phone call when she asked about his cases, but talkative and almost joking by the end, when the subject turned to user ID.

Which told her two things.

He didn't mind talking about tangential issues.

And his cases were the key to her investigation.

$ $ $

Her next call was to Ted Wilson's college, where she talked to the dean and gained some important information.

Then she dialed Ted's number. "I was going through the case files from the other two investigations we've learned about that are similar to what's happening in your hospital group, and there are some things that just pop out to me."

His chair squealed. "Yes?"

"Yeah. The first thing is that you neglected to mention you worked at both of these companies during the time there was an ongoing enquiry into missing money and hacked systems."

"Did I?" A softer squeak. "Golly, I'm sure I mentioned that."

"Not to me you didn't, and I'd think that was a pretty big coincidence, wouldn't you?"

A nervous chuckle. "Well, I've had a few jobs. Always a horizontal move. Looking to improve my situation and find my niche."

Right. Like a weed trying to infiltrate a rock garden. "So tell me about it."

"Look. I'm not a programmer, first of all. Don't know my way much beyond email and spreadsheets. Most of what I do is fundraising for the hospital and attending board of director meetings. That kind of thing. Health administration."

"Well, that's interesting. Before I called you, I spoke with the dean at the University of Illinois, your alma mater."

"Oh?"

Although she couldn't see him, she picked up on the catch in his voice. "And he said you were enrolled in the computer sciences program, but changed your major in your third year."

"All true." A deep sigh. "Truth is, I was flunking out. My parents scrimped and saved to send me to college, and I knew how important it was that I get a degree. So I switched to health administration because I managed to scrape through the two or three computer courses required for that degree."

So maybe he was telling the truth about his techie-ness.

Then again, maybe he wasn't.

But that didn't mean he wasn't involved in James' death in some way. "What were you doing last Thursday?"

"Let me see." Flipping of pages. "Right. I was in a team-building exercise put on by Gail Prouse. All day and all evening, too." A book snapping shut. "Why? Did something happen specifically during that time?"

Yes, but she didn't want to get into another long explanation when obviously he couldn't have done it. Plus, unless he and Gail were in cahoots, they both alibied each other. She swallowed down a lump in her throat. "Just wondering. Thank for your forthrightness."

She disconnected the call and sat back, mentally crossing Ted Wilson off her list of suspects for both the hacking and the murder.

At this rate, she'd soon be down to nobody on either list.

This wasn't how it worked for Sherlock Holmes.

## Chapter 24

Speaking of suspect lists, who was left?

Nobody except Bob Powell. And as much as she didn't like him, that wasn't proof he was either a hacker or a murderer. She needed to find a connection.

Preferably without having to actually talk to him. Rude to the *nth* degree at his housewarming party, smirking and sneering all over the room at their briefing meetings, and practically snarling on their previous telephone call, she'd erase him from her world if given the opportunity.

Not literally, of course. Just the stick-her-fingers-in-her-ears-and-close-her-eyes kind of removal.

Rather than call and ask him more questions he would dodge, attack, or just plain lie about, she decided to go back over his employment records. Being the investigator on three similar hacking cases seemed too good to believe. In reality, with that much experience, he should be able to close out this particular instance in a flash.

Instead, he floundered about like a fish out of water.

She dug his file from beneath the pile on her cubicle desk and sat back, wishing for another cup of coffee to appear magically—or by any means, really—before her. She flipped to the back of the pages inside and worked her way forward through the application he completed for his current position, wading through background checks, letters of recommendation, performance appraisals, and paperwork related to medical insurance, pension, and the like.

After about twenty minutes, her eyes drooped and her head snapped. She straightened, set the file aside, and stretched. Time for a coffee.

After returning with a hot cup of java, she delved into the remainder of the file, pausing at a form regarding life insurance benefits and beneficiaries. The first line asked for full given name. Glen Robert Powell.

GP.

Her heart raced. Was this the break she sought?

Or had she merely jumped to conclusions because she wanted him to be guilty of something?

However, as Bob said, the hacker's use of these initials wasn't conclusive evidence of their name.

Which, if it was him, was something he'd say in an effort to distract her.

Then again, most criminals didn't think they'd ever be caught, so often they let their guard down. The hacker's disdain of law enforcement—particularly as this was likely his third time around the block—might overwhelm his sense of self-preservation.

Her cell phone vibrated on the desk, and she answered the call. "Hi, Chief Webb. How are you?"

"Doing well, thanks. I checked into those parking tickets like you asked."

Her heart rate upped a notch. "And?"

"You had a good hunch. Fourteen citations were issued last Thursday for the block that the car lot occupies."

She made a note on a pad. "Busy day."

"About the norm. Mostly folks from out of town, since residents know about the street sweeping in the area."

"Anybody we know?"

"Actually, yes. Well, maybe."

"Maybe?"

"Just because a vehicle was ticketed doesn't mean the owner parked it there."

"True. It is circumstantial. But it's a good place to start. So who owns the vehicle?"

*Let it be Bob.*

She closed her eyes. Would this be a good time to pray?

Would God even hear such a selfish, vindictive prayer?

She stifled a chuckle. Likely not.

"New England Commercial Insurance."

*Gotcha.*

*Almost.*

One more T to cross.

"Do we know why any other investigator for the same company would be in the area?"

"Nope."

"Any idea who was driving?"

"No, but I did put in a call to the company. Talked to the guy in charge of the car pool. Said the car was checked out to Bob Powell."

"Then I think we need to encourage Bob to do the right thing."

Chief Webb chuckled. "Sure. Like he's going to walk into the local police department and turn himself in."

"Well, if he won't, then we need to figure out a way to convince him to do just that."

This time the lawman laughed, a deep rumbling that started down low and worked its way through the phone. "And how do you propose we do that?"

"Leave it to me. First, can I fax you a picture and have you show it to the manager of the motel out on the highway?"

"Sure. What do you want to know?"

"If this was the man he saw with James."

"Got it."

"Okay. Expect a call from Chief Donovan soon."

"You'll be careful, won't you?"

Now it was her turn to laugh. "Have you been talking to Mike?"

"Not lately. Why?"

"He says I've got a nose like an elephant for a mystery."

"I'm glad you do. Talk to you soon."

She disconnected the call and considered her next step. She needed to confirm one more piece of information first.

Then she could tighten the noose around the smarmy investigator.

$ $ $

Carly made a couple of calls to determine where Bob Powell was at the moment. Apparently he'd taken up residence in the conference room generally used for their briefing meetings. She walked past the half-open door to confirm. Sure enough, sitting like a king at the head of the table, staring out the window that overlooked the parking lot.

He surely wasn't checking for a great view.

Next she walked to the end of the hall to place a phone call to the clerk at the gas station. "Harold, it's Carly Turnquist. I talked to you a few days ago about James."

"The old guy who died?"

The mention of her friend's demise generated an ache in the center of her chest. "Right. Got a question for you."

"Shoot."

She winced at the offhand remark, reminding herself not to assign any blame to the teen for the callousness of his words. He didn't understand. Kids that age thought themselves immortal, and considered anybody with gray hair as old and almost deserving to die. "I want you to think back to when James called and told you about winning the lottery. Do you remember that?"

"Yes."

"You said you told somebody about that conversation."

A silence so long she thought they'd been disconnected. "Harold, I'm not saying that what happened to James was your fault in any way. You won't get in trouble by telling me the truth."

"I said I wouldn't tell anybody that he asked."

She exhaled. "You also told James you'd keep his win to yourself, right?"

"Yeah, but I didn't see any harm in sharing with this guy. After all, he was like my boss."

"The man who hired you?"

"Not to pump gas. Not that boss. The guy who hired me to mow his lawn. I was trying to make extra money."

"That shows some real initiative."

"Whatever. So I didn't see anything wrong. After all, he knew James. Was like a neighbor."

"A neighbor?"

"Sure." Harold sighed. "I guess it's okay to say. It was Mr. Powell. He's a good guy. Pays really well. Gave me a bonus of twenty bucks because I did such a good job. Said I had promise and should have a full scholarship to go to college when I was ready. Said he'd put the money into a bank account for me"

"Was that before or after you told him about James winning the money?"

"After. I was done with the mowing, and we were talking. He was telling me about his job, and looking into arsons and murders, and I just said James better watch out that somebody didn't kill him for his money. Well, once I let the cat out of the bag, I didn't see no harm when he asked what I meant. So I told him."

"Great. Thanks, Harold."

"You're sure I won't get into trouble?"

"You didn't break the law, so no, you won't."

"Great. Thanks, Mrs. T. Talk to you soon."

She hung up and planned her next step, including making a couple of phone calls, one more difficult than the other. The puzzle pieces were coming together, but there was still a hole in the middle of the picture.

She knew the who, the why, and the how.

Now she simply had to—as Chief Webb said—have Bob turn himself in.

$ $ $

Back in the finance department, Carly tapped her toe while waiting for the chief to answer. "Chief Donovan, I need another favor." When the lawman exhaled, Carly stared at her phone. What was it about men? They always seemed to do a lot of sighing whenever she was around. "Can you get hold of Bob Powell's banking records?"

"How quick do you need them? And how far back?"

Wow. "Yesterday. As much as you can get."

"Got the last two years here."

"You think he's guilty, too?"

"Wasn't sure, but since I was asking for backgrounds and financials on your other suspects, figured I'd include him, too. Less explaining for the judge."

"Can you fax them over?" She gave him the number. "I'll wait by the machine."

"On their way."

Carly wove her way through the cubicle maze to the station where the common facsimile machine resided. Until she knew for sure one way or the other, she didn't want to risk somebody else seeing the statements.

The machine soon whirred and beeped before churning out more than twenty pages. When the fax ended, she gathered the pages and turned to leave, but paused when it spit out a single page.

Had the chief missed one?

She picked it up.

A photo of Bob Powell.

The same one she'd faxed to Chief Webb.

With a huge YES scrawled across the surface.

She had him.

Back at her desk, she leafed through the pages from Bob's bank. Sure enough, beginning about six months before—before he even moved to Bear Cove—small amounts were transferred from another account at the same bank. A few hundred dollars at first, increasing in both frequency and amount, corresponding with—she checked her list of fraudulent invoices—almost perfectly with the invoices paid by the insurance company.

She checked the balance at the beginning of the scheme. More than twenty thousand dollars. Likely some of the ill-gotten gains of his other two hacking enterprises. The statement ran up to just two days ago. A sizable deposit of more than a hundred thousand dollars in, and an equally large withdrawal annotated MORTGAGE PAYOUT.

No doubt the ill-gotten gains stolen from James.

The scoundrel was so sure of himself, he was running the money through his personal account.

And paying off his brand new mortgage with it.

She had what she needed.

$ $ $

Carly held her cell phone aloft. Drats! What a time for no signal. Maybe if she moved a few feet this way. Nope. How about now?

Bob Powell appeared in the conference room doorway. "Can I help you?"

She smiled. "No, thanks. Just trying to make a phone call. Sometimes this building seems like a lead box, designed to thwart me at every turn."

He quirked his head toward the window. "Want to try over there?"

"No, thanks. I'll give it another go here."

"Or you could use a landline."

"True. But I don't want anybody listening in, if you know what I mean."

He chuckled, but the mirth didn't make it to his eyes. He peered at her. "You could always go outside the building."

"Too lazy to walk the length of myself, as my mother used to say."

He peered down the hallway. "You've already done that just by walking here from the finance department."

"True again." She pointed with her phone. "I'll go over to that window and try."

Bob nodded and ducked back into the room, shutting the door partway, while she strolled the extra ten feet or so, standing with her back to the glass.

She dialed a now-familiar number. "Hi, Chief Donovan. Carly here. Fine, thanks. Listen, Chief, I've figured out who killed James. Right. Yes, I have the evidence. I'll come to the station in the morning. No, I don't have time right now. Uh-huh. Okay. Nine it is. Thanks." She disconnected then called her husband. "Mike, I just called the chief to let him know I'll bring in the evidence tomorrow." A pause. "No, Mike. I've got to do this. You know I'm right." Another pause. "Well, fine, go visit Denise in Riverview. If you're going to be like that, I'd prefer to be on my own tonight." Three heartbeats. "Whatever. Bye."

She headed down the hallway, pausing at the conference room door and sticking her head in. "Hope I didn't disturb you with my calls. See you in the morning."

"No worries."

The investigator returned to the file before him, and Carly headed home, enjoying the walk and the fresh air. She had a lot of thinking to do, and needed the time.

After all, if she was right, somebody would try to kill her tonight.

In the Money

# Chapter 25

He waited until the lights in the house across the street went out, leaving the windows as dark as eye sockets in a skull, then glanced at the clock. She might be in bed, but he'd wait another twenty minutes or so to make certain she was asleep. Her car sat in the driveway, but Mike's wasn't anywhere to be seen. According to their overheard conversation this afternoon, she and Mike had a tiff on the phone. She told him to go to their daughter's. Said it was fine with her.

And even more fine with him. Overhearing her other call to the local copper was serendipity, to say the least. Meant he had to move his plans up a few days. And her husband's absence meant tonight was the night.

He paced the living room for several minutes. Finally, the timepiece confirmed what his gut already knew: it was time.

He pulled a black ski mask down over his face and eased out his front door. Pausing at the sidewalk, he glanced both ways before crossing, stifling a chuckle. How embarrassing to be run down by a late night driver.

And dressed all in black, to boot.

He trotted in black runners around the side of the house and checked the back door. Unlocked, as usual. Oh yes, he knew all her habits. Locked the front door all the time. Closed but didn't latch the ground floor windows. Never locked the door at the rear of the house.

Senses on high alert, he stepped into the kitchen. Thankfully almost every house on this street bore a similar floor plan. For certain, this one, the old man's, and his own. He hesitated at a thunk! from the living room, then relaxed when a large marmalade cat rounded the corner and sat in the middle of the floor. Her cat. The one that was so finicky she traded out cat food like young boys traded baseball cards.

He reached into his cargo pants pocket and extracted a bag of cat goodies, which he dumped into its food dish. Doc sauntered over, flicked his tail, then dug in, crunching in time with its swishing tail.

He crept around the cat, taking care not to startle the animal or to step on its tail. Checking the floor for cat toys, he tested each board before bringing his weight to bear. No point in failing because of a squeaky step.

Down the hallway toward the large bedroom at the end, and he paused again. He dug into another pocket and pulled out a small bottle and a rag. Wet the cloth with the foul liquid. Opened the door.

Soft snores emanated from the lump beneath the covers. He headed around the bed, yanked back the cover to expose her face, and clamped the damp cloth over her nose and mouth. Her eyes opened wide. She struggled, feet thrashing. Hands scratching at his.

But he held tight.

Her eyes rolled back, closed, and she went limp.

Hefting her to his back using the fireman's lift technique, he returned to the kitchen, her hands and torso dangling over his back, legs in front, right arm and leg in his grip. He reversed the technique and let her inert form slip feet-first to the floor, taking care not to bump her. A bruise would show up in the postmortem, raising questions.

No, this had to look like a suicide.

He smiled. He could see the headline now: DISTRAUGHT WIFE TAKES HER OWN LIFE AFTER ARGUMENT WITH HUSBAND.

Wouldn't be the first time a domestic incident led to a suicide. Particularly so close to the time her dear neighbor friend also died. After he was done here, he'd head to the hospital to erase whatever evidence she thought she had about who hacked into the computer system.

Bob turned on the gas oven then blew out the pilot flame. His nose wrinkled at the odor of the fuel. Then he lifted her body and propped her up on the door, her head in the oven.

He stepped back. Perfect.

Nobody would guess—

The kitchen flooded with light, blinding him. Sending shivers of pain through his head as though shot from a cannon.

Somebody shouted for the gas to be turned off. A sharp click and the rotten egg smell dissipated.

He blinked, covering his eyes with his hands.

Voices shouted at him. Commanding him. Who did they think—

Rough hands grabbed him. Forced him face-first to the floor.

His own arms twisted behind his back. What felt suspiciously like a boot planted into the small of his back.

He turned his head, but all that filled his line of sight were shoes. Boots. Military black, laced up the front. Camouflage khakis.

He grunted at the pressure in his shoulders. Mucous stifled his breathing. Tears blurred his vision.

Or perhaps anger was the cause.

This couldn't happen to him. No. He'd planned carefully—methodically. Everything down to the last detail. He turned his head to the other side. Somebody eased that nosey accountant onto the floor. Had she been in there long enough to do the deed?

He certainly hoped so.

Even if it meant spending the rest of his life in prison for murder—Maine had no death penalty, as every self-respecting criminal knew.

Just so long as she was—what?

*That's not her?*

Strong hands gripped his arms—now handcuffed behind his back—and yanked him to his feet.

Bringing him eye-to-eye—or at least her eyes to his chest—with the woman of his nightmares.

He looked from the still-unconscious form on the floor to her and back again before addressing *that* woman. "I suppose you think you've outwitted me." He lifted his chin to stare down his nose at her. "I assure you. Nobody beats me."

Her mouth lifted in a half smile. "I'm not the one in handcuffs."

He looked over his shoulder at the officers in uniform. "Speaking of which, you can expect several unlawful arrest complaints against you and your department."

A paramedic entered the kitchen and knelt beside the woman prone on the floor, whose eyes fluttered a couple of times before she raised herself on one elbow and moaned. "Last time I go along with another of your harebrained schemes, Chief."

An officer he didn't recognize stepped forward. "Good experience for you, Liza."

"Yeah, well, Chief, you'd better make certain to give a good report to my captain." She groaned and her face twisted. "Ohh, I have a killer of a headache. And why is the room spinning?"

The paramedic checked the woman's eyes with a flashlight. "You'll be fine in a couple of hours. Take it easy for the next day or so. Fatigue, dizziness, and a headache are common residuals."

She looked up at the man she called Chief. "Hear that? I think I need some sick leave time."

The man chuckled. "If we do that, we'll be overwhelmed with volunteers next time."

She rubbed her temple. "No next time for me."

Bob quirked his head toward the woman. "Who is she?"

Carly smiled. "A state patrol officer looking for a promotion for going above and beyond."

A man appeared in the doorway. The husband. "What are you doing here?" Realization dawned, and with it, his heart dropped like a stone to the tips of his toes. He glared at Carly. "You set me up."

She nodded. "We had enough evidence to prove you were the hacker, but not quite enough to conclusively prove you killed James. But once you thought I had the evidence and would turn it over tomorrow, if you took the bait, we had you."

He grunted. "So what was the giveaway?"

"Paying off your brand new mortgage was stupid. As was running it through your checking account. Large deposits raise red flags. Didn't you know?"

She was sharp. "Yeah, which is why the initial deposits were always under the limit."

She nodded. "But the Bank Act of 1970 directs financial institutions to track all large cash deposits."

He dropped his gaze to the floor. Dumb. Dumb. Idiot. He should have known. "Okay. What's your question?"

"Was James in on the hacking scam with you?"

He blinked. "That old guy? No way."

"So the fact he volunteered at the hospital while you were stealing from them is nothing more than a coincidence?"

He shook his head. "Never met the guy until I moved in across the street from him."

"Is that when you targeted him?"

He grinned. Why not answer her questions? Things couldn't get any worse. He might as well play along with this Sherlock-Holmes-wannabe. "Nope. He called the gas boy who called me. I called the old man. Implied I was a financial advisor." He shrugged. "Which I am. Like Robin Hood. Taking from the rich and giving to me." An unfamiliar ache centered in his chest. Fear? Regret? He shoved it aside. "The old man was lonely, and he didn't trust banks. I worked on that. It was easy."

"So why'd you kill him?"

"He wised up before I conned the money from him. Threatened to call the cops. Couldn't have that."

A guy in a uniform—Chief Donovan, he thought the guy's name was—stepped up behind him. "Glenn Robert Powell, you are under arrest for the murder of James Norwood and the thefts from Down East Health Group and two other entities to be named in the indictment and list of charges." The head lawman prodded him in the back. "Let's get going. I'll read you your rights in the car."

He shrugged off the man's touch. "Take your hands off me."

"You've got a holding cell with your name on it at the state patrol office."

He nodded toward the woman he mistook for Carly. "How did you know I wouldn't just shoot you?"

Carly stepped back. "I was fairly certain you'd choose the accidental death or suicide route. Anything else would have opened an entirely new investigation. And I didn't think you'd want any more eyes on you."

He lifted one side of his mouth in a sneer. "Got a feeling it's not the first time somebody tried to off you."

The only good thing about being arrested was he wouldn't have to see her smirking face again anytime soon.

$ $ $

An hour later, Carly pressed in closer to her husband as they watched through the two-way glass of the interview room at the state patrol office. Chief Donovan, Chief Webb, and Special Agent John Backman asked questions of Bob Powell. Chained to the floor by shackles on his hands and feet, their neighbor looked every bit the part of dangerous criminal.

Which, of course, he was.

The FBI agent took the lead. "We're being recorded." He introduced those present for the benefit of anybody listening to the tape later, and included the time, date, and location. "You've been read your Miranda warning and have elected to answer questions, knowing that whatever you say may be used against you in court. Is that correct?"

Bob nodded.

Backman persisted. "You need to speak your answer. The tape can't hear your body language."

Powell leaned closer to the recording machine. "Yes, I understand." He sat back and spread his hands as far as the short chain permitted. "What do you want to know?"

The Fed opened a notebook. "Why don't you start at the beginning?"

Over the next hour, Bob detailed how he started hacking into computer systems to provide himself a job. Cybersecurity was relatively new, and businesses didn't want to spend money hiring employees for something they didn't see as a threat. However, commercial insurers understood the potential losses, and they cast about for qualified investigators to deal with the increasing number of cases.

"New England Commercial Insurance hired me on a six-month contract, contingent on how well I did. We didn't have a single case of cybersecurity fraud for more than four months. So I figured I'd better get busy if I wanted to stay working." He clasped his hands, jingling the chains. "I liked the excitement. It was all new territory. Hardly any case studies on the phenomenon. I was writing the text book, you might say."

"So once word got out that you were good at resolving these claims, suddenly you're in demand?"

"Right. I moonlighted as a private investigator for companies that didn't have commercial fraud insurance. I worked weekends for a couple of high end operating system coders and virus protection companies." He chuckled. "Little did they know that I was embedding modules into their systems that worked behind the scenes, funneling pennies here and nickels there. They never noticed."

Chief Donovan made a note. "Then what?"

"I picked the companies carefully. Never two in a row in the same industry. Caused just enough trouble to make it worth my while, then went in and bailed them out."

Donovan looked up from his scribbling. "So what made you move from hacking to murder?"

"When the kid told me about the old man winning the lottery, I called him. We'd already talked, so he kinda knew me. Said I was a financial advisor. I figured to scam him out of the money. Went with him to collect his winnings. For safety, I told him." He laughed, his shoulders heaving. "It was like fishing in a barrel, except for one thing."

Carly pressed her hands against the glass. The way this monster talked about her friend made her want to wring his neck. Or punch him in the nose. Or something.

Mike reached up and grasped one hand, squeezing it. She smiled over at him. It was like he was reading her mind. She sidled to stand close to him, enjoying the solid feel of him beside her.

This was the only safety she needed.

Or was it?

One of the things her daughter said about a relationship with God was that she always knew God was there for her, with her, protecting her.

Right now, she wouldn't mind knowing He was doing the same, standing on her other side.

Mike and God.

What more could a gal ask for?

"The old man was smarter than I gave him credit for." He swiveled in his seat and stared at the mirror. Carly shrank from his glare. It was almost as though he could see through the glass at her. "Almost as smart as you, nosey accountant lady." He turned back to the lawmen. "He wasn't having any part of giving me the money."

Webb sat back in his chair. "So what did you do?"

Powell related how he lured James to the used car dealer on the pretense of using some of his winnings to buy a new car. Then he killed him, stuffed him in the trunk, took the money, and left in his own car. "How did you know I was there?"

Webb smiled. "Parking ticket."

Powell swore under his breath with a sneer. "It's the little things that get you, isn't it?"

Murder wasn't a little thing in Carly's book.

And the death of her friend was a big thing as far as she was concerned.

The only good to come from this was that Powell would spend the rest of his evil life in prison. Murder, grand theft, attempted murder of a law enforcement officer—hopefully the man wouldn't see civilian life ever again.

Justice wouldn't bring James back, but it would have to do.

## Chapter 26

"Okay, Chief, thanks for filling me in on the rest of the story." Carly hung up the phone and turned back to Mike. From here, life looked so ordinary. So peaceful and organized. Lunch on the table. Doc basking in a sunbeam coming in through the open back door. She returned to her grilled cheese sandwich and tomato soup. "Chief Donovan said their interview went on until almost midnight. He's exhausted today."

"I bet." Mike set his sandwich down. "Anything new?"

"Talk eventually turned to all the money we found in James' house and in the safe deposit boxes. Bob didn't know anything about it. So the chief looked into it more. Apparently there were some winning tickets in the boxes, and when he called the various lottery commissions going back twenty years or so, James collected his winnings. A few hundred here, a couple of thousand there. The biggest win was about ten thousand in 1986, which probably fueled his passion for the pastime."

"It would sure fuel mine." Her husband's mouth tipped up. "You know, I'm really glad we didn't have a real argument."

She covered his hand with hers, James' absence intensified by their discussion. "Me, too. And I'm even more glad that when we disagree, neither of us runs away."

"I tease you about your choice of exercise, but I find I've also perfected a new way to move my muscles."

She was all ears now. "How so?"

"Rolling my eyes. At your antics." He chuckled. "It's easier than arguing, because I know you're going to do what you want, no matter how dangerous."

She brushed off his words. "I was never in any danger this time. That poor Liza took the chance, not me."

"Can you imagine how I felt when Powell said he could have shot you?"

"But he didn't." She patted his hand. "Isn't that what's important?"

"I don't want to lose you."

"And you won't." She sipped her coffee. "But back to James. The consensus is that he saved all that money by living frugally and not trusting banks. Apparently he never had a credit card or a loan. The only time he ever borrowed was to buy the house, and he paid that off in about six years."

"Sounds like he was a wise financial steward." Mike shook his head. "I should have asked him more questions, got to know him better."

She nodded, the ache easing as pleasant memories of him replaced the bad. "He had a green thumb. I could have spent the rest of my life learning about plants and gardening."

Down the hall in their home office, the fax machine beeped.

She stood. "I'll get that. Might be something new on the case."

She retrieved the single page: a job offer for Mike.

When she set it on the table beside him, he skimmed the words then groaned.

Her brow drew down. "What's wrong?"

"Just when I thought we could get back to some normalcy, this comes along."

She snatched up the paper. What could be upsetting her husband? She read the letter then laughed. "This sounds like exactly what we need."

"What? Another mystery?"

She tapped the page. "The word isn't even in their offer. It's a job, Mike. In Colorado. I've always wanted to visit."

"Right. Sounds like the working vacation to New Mexico. Working for me, vacation for you."

"And your point?"

"I worked, and you found a twenty-year-old mystery that needed solving."

She chuckled. "Well, you do what you're good at, and I'll do what I'm good at."

He shook his head. "You're good at being frozen to death. Shot at. Run off the road. Smothered. Gassed. Pushed off a boat. And stuffed into a furnace. Oh, yes, and chloroformed."

"Admit it, Michael Turnquist. I make life interesting." She gestured to the offer. "And this sounds really interesting. Mineral rights. And I'm ready for a vacation."

He rolled his eyes. "I've heard that before. Why is it you can take a vacation from work, but not from solving mysteries?"

She stood, walked around the table, looped her arms over his shoulders and patted his chest, then planted a kiss on the top of his head. "Think about it, Mike. Beautiful Rockies. Breathtaking scenery. High-paying job. They're practically begging you to come. They say price is no barrier. They want *you*." She snuggled him to her chest. "I've got a great book I want to read. One Mavis loaned me. And after all, how much trouble can I get into in Colorado?"

He shook his head. "I know I've heard that somewhere before. And the answer is always the same: more than enough."

She giggled. "Mike, what would you do without me?"

"I'd have a lot more free time, because you are—"

"I know. A full-time job."

In the Money

Leeann Betts writes contemporary suspense, while her real-life persona, Donna Schlachter, pens historical suspense. This is the tenth title in her cozy mystery series. In addition, Leeann has written a devotional for accountants, bookkeepers, and financial folk, *Counting the Days,* and, with her real-life persona Donna Schlachter, has published two books on writing, *Nuggets of Writing Gold* and *More Nuggets of Writing Gold,* a compilation of essays, articles, and exercises on the craft; as well as a contemporary suspense, *In Search of Christmas Past.*

All books are available on Amazon.com in digital and print, and at Smashwords.com in digital format.

Leeann publishes a free quarterly newsletter that includes book reviews and articles on writing and books of interest to readers and writers. You can subscribe at www.LeeannBetts.com or follow Leeann at www.AllBettsAreOff.wordpress.com

Website: www.LeeannBetts.com Receive a free ebook just for signing up for our quarterly newsletter.

Blog: www.AllBettsAreOff.wordpress.com

Facebook: http://bit.ly/1pQSOqV

Twitter: http://bit.ly/1qmqvB6

Books: Amazon http://amzn.to/2dHfgCE and Smashwords: http://bit.ly/2z5ecP8

www.ingramcontent.com/pod-product-compliance
Lightning Source LLC
Chambersburg PA
CBHW051428170626
46809CB00006B/2374